"D[...] [...]elica asked.

"No[...] [...]d in the car with Angie's perfume, Tricia wondered if she'd ever be able to smell anything again.

"Something's definitely burning . . . or maybe smoldering," Angelica insisted. Shading her eyes, she turned her head from right to left and sniffed loudly, her nose wrinkling. Tricia watched as her sister moved a few steps toward the Cookery, where a thin veil of smoke drifted from the painted flap in the door.

"Dial nine-one-one," Tricia ordered, shoving her cell phone into her sister's hands.

She grasped the Cookery's door handle, which yielded to her touch. The smoke was thick, but there was no sign of flames. Tricia took a deep breath and plunged inside. "Doris?" she called, and coughed. "Doris, are you in here?"

Grateful for the security lighting, Tricia searched behind the sales counter. No sign of Doris. But a glance to her right showed that the little Lucite case that less than an hour before had housed Doris's treasured cookbook was no longer perched on top of the shelf. Tricia stumbled over something and fell to her knees. The air was definitely better down here. Righting herself, Tricia pivoted to see what had tripped her. She gasped as she focused on a still form half hidden behind the kitchen island, a knife jutting from its back . . .

Berkley Prime Crime titles by Lorna Barrett

MURDER IS BINDING
BOOKMARKED FOR DEATH

MURDER IS BINDING

Lorna Barrett

BERKLEY PRIME CRIME, NEW YORK

THE BERKLEY PUBLISHING GROUP
Published by the Penguin Group
Penguin Group (USA) Inc.
375 Hudson Street, New York, New York 10014, USA

Penguin Group (Canada), 90 Eglinton Avenue East, Suite 700, Toronto, Ontario M4P 2Y3, Canada
(a division of Pearson Penguin Canada Inc.)
Penguin Books Ltd., 80 Strand, London WC2R 0RL, England
Penguin Group Ireland, 25 St. Stephen's Green, Dublin 2, Ireland (a division of Penguin Books Ltd.)
Penguin Group (Australia), 250 Camberwell Road, Camberwell, Victoria 3124, Australia
(a division of Pearson Australia Group Pty. Ltd.)
Penguin Books India Pvt. Ltd., 11 Community Centre, Panchsheel Park, New Delhi—110 017, India
Penguin Group (NZ), 67 Apollo Drive, Rosedale, North Shore 0632, New Zealand
(a division of Pearson New Zealand Ltd.)
Penguin Books (South Africa) (Pty.) Ltd., 24 Sturdee Avenue, Rosebank, Johannesburg 2196,
South Africa

Penguin Books Ltd., Registered Offices: 80 Strand, London WC2R 0RL, England

This is a work of fiction. Names, characters, places, and incidents either are the product of the author's
imagination or are used fictitiously, and any resemblance to actual persons, living or dead, business
establishments, events, or locales is entirely coincidental. The publisher does not have any control over
and does not assume any responsibility for author or third-party websites or their content.

PUBLISHER'S NOTE: The recipes contained in this book are to be followed exactly as written. The
publisher is not responsible for your specific health or allergy needs that may require medical supervi-
sion. The publisher is not responsible for any adverse reactions to the recipes contained in this book.

MURDER IS BINDING

A Berkley Prime Crime Book / published by arrangement with the author

PRINTING HISTORY
Berkley Prime Crime mass-market edition / April 2008

Copyright © 2008 by The Berkley Publishing Group.
Cover art by Teresa Fasolino.
Cover design by Diana Kolsky.
Interior text design by Laura K. Corless.

ISBN: 978-0-425-21958-4

BERKLEY® PRIME CRIME
Berkley Prime Crime Books are published by The Berkley Publishing Group,
a division of Penguin Group (USA) Inc.,
375 Hudson Street, New York, New York 10014.
The name BERKLEY PRIME CRIME and the BERKLEY PRIME CRIME design
are trademarks belonging to Penguin Group (USA) Inc.

PRINTED IN THE UNITED STATES OF AMERICA

10 9 8 7

For Valerie Bartlett

*Thank you for introducing me to
the wonderful world of mystery novels.*

ACKNOWLEDGMENTS

Many generous friends (most of them members of my Sisters in Crime chapter, The Guppies), helped me with this first book in the Booktown Mystery series. Deb Baker, Marilyn Levinson, Nan Higginson, and Doranna Durgin were invaluable first readers during the proposal stage of *Murder Is Binding*, and Nan and Marilyn gave wonderful feedback on the final version of the book. My thanks to Elizabeth Becka for forensic information. Michelle Sampson, Wadleigh Memorial Library Director, Milford, New Hampshire, supplied me with local color, as did Nancy Cooper.

Hank Phillippi Ryan volunteered the services of her husband, Jonathan Shapiro, Esquire, for legal advice (any mistakes in that regard are entirely my own). Go Hank and Jonathan! Local bookseller Rebecca Budinger at the Greece Ridge Barnes & Noble was invaluable for sharing information on booksellers. Sharon Wildwind continues to amaze me with the depth of her knowledge and her willingness to share it.

My local critique partners Gwen Nelson and Liz Eng are tireless cheerleaders. They've been with me through thick and thin. (Don't go away, guys, I need you!) Thanks, too, to my tireless IM buddy, Sheila Connolly (also known as Sarah Atwell) for her marvelous brainstorming and cheerleading ability.

Thanks also go to my editor, Tom Colgan, and his assistant, Sandy Harding, for making the process run so smoothly. And most of all I'd like to thank my wonderful agent, Jacky Sach, without whom this book would never have been written.

ONE

"I tell you, Trish, we're *all* victims."

Victims? In the town voted safest in all of New Hampshire? Tricia Miles raised an eyebrow and studied the septuagenarian bookseller before her over the rim of her cardboard coffee cup. *Here it comes*, she thought with dread, *the pitch.*

Doris Gleason would never be called subtle. Everything about her screamed excess—from her bulky frame clad in a bright pink polyester dress, her dyed, jet-black pageboy haircut, to the overlarge glasses that perched on her nose. She leaned closer over the oak-and-glass display case, making Tricia glad she'd taken refuge behind the antique register as a way of guaranteeing her personal space. Too often Doris was in her face.

"If we all negotiate together, we can beat that bastard."

Tricia drained her cup and sighed. "I assume you're referring to Bob Kelly, our mutual benefactor?" President of the local chamber of commerce and owner of Kelly Realty, Bob had recruited Doris, Tricia, and all the other booksellers to relocate to the picturesque village of Stoneham, New Hampshire.

"Benefactor my ass," Doris grated, pink spots appearing on her cheeks. She removed her glasses, exhaled on one of the lenses, and polished it with the ribbed edge of her dingy white sweater. Half-moon indentations marred the ridge of her cheeks where they'd rested. "That chiseler owns or has a share in every storefront on Main Street. He controls our rents, tries to control our stock *and* the quality of our customers. I nearly lost my voice after our last shouting match. It was all I could do not to throttle him."

From her perch on a shelf above the register, Miss Marple, the store's resident cat, a regal, gray domestic longhair, glared down at the older woman—disapproving of her temper. Tricia had to agree, yet she understood Doris's anger. Bob Kelly had charged her extra to transform the facade of her shop front even though the changes had incorporated much-needed repairs to the century-old building.

Most of the village revered Bob. Bringing in antiquarian and specialty booksellers—and the tourist dollars they attracted—had saved the little town from financial collapse. His ideas, commitment, and even a bit of sweat equity, had turned a forgotten hamlet on the New Hampshire–Massachusetts border into a tourist mecca for readers in a world dominated by the Internet and other instant-gratification entertainment. The fact that he could also be the most demanding, insufferable bore on the face of the Earth . . .

Tricia forced a patient smile. "Now, Doris, you know we can't participate in collective bargaining. None of our leases come up at the same time."

Doris pulled off her glasses, set them on the counter as her lips twisted into a sneer. "I *knew* you wouldn't cooperate. The rumors about you must be true!"

Tricia felt her face start to burn. "What rumors?"

"That you're incredibly rich. That you don't *have* to worry about paying your rent. You don't *have* to worry about stock or overhead." Doris glanced around the well-appointed store, the richly paneled walls decorated with prints and photos of long-dead mystery authors, the expensive upholstered armchairs and large square coffee table that made up the seating nook and allowed patrons the comforts of home while they perused Tricia's stock of vintage first-edition mysteries and newly minted best sellers.

A fat lot Doris knew. Tricia struggled to quell her ire. "I have the same worries as you and every other bookseller in the village. This store isn't a hobby for me. I resent the implication that I conspired against you and the other booksellers. I didn't know Bob Kelly before I came to this town, and I'm sure my rent is probably triple or quadruple what you're currently paying."

"That's my point," Doris insisted. "If you hadn't agreed to pay such an exorbitant price, the rest of us wouldn't be in this mess."

It was true Tricia hadn't done much haggling before she signed on as the village's newest bookseller, but then she'd been used to the idea of Manhattan rents and the contrast made the deal she'd been offered seem like a steal.

"I'm sorry, Doris," Tricia said and disposed of her disposable coffee cup in the wastebasket beneath the counter, "but I really don't see how I can be of any help."

Doris straightened, her contempt palpable. "We'll see." She turned and plodded for the exit, wrenched open the door. The little bell overhead gave a cheerful tinkle, an absurd end to an unpleasant conversation.

"Don't tell me the old crab was in here carping about her rent again."

Tricia turned. Ginny Wilson, a lithe, twentysomething redhead and Tricia's only employee, staggered under the weight of a carton of books and dumped it on the counter. "Word is that Daww-ris"—she said the name with such disdain—"has been all over town, badgering the merchants to hop on her 'let's save the Cookery' bandwagon. She claims she's going to have to go out of business if she can't negotiate a better lease." She waved a hand in dismissal. "I say good riddance."

A glance around the area proved at least one of the shop's regular patrons, Mr. Everett, a silver-haired elderly gent who showed up at opening and often had to be chased out at night, had been eavesdropping on the conversations. Tricia placed a finger to her lips and frowned.

"You never had to work for her," Ginny hissed and removed a sheathed box cutter from the pocket of her hunter green apron, opened it, and slit the tape on the carton. Haven't Got a Clue, the bookshop's name, was embroidered in yellow across the apron's top. Pinned to the neck strap was Ginny's name tag.

Tricia, too, wore a tag, but not an apron. She wanted some distinction made between the owner and the help—not that she didn't do her share of the hefting and carrying around the store, though she tried to do it after business hours. Slacks and sweater sets were her current dress code, and today she'd chosen a raspberry combination, which seemed to accent her blue eyes and complement her light brown hair.

"Oh, before I forget," Ginny said, dipping into her apron pocket once again. "I found this in a copy of Patricia Cornwell's newest release."

Tricia took the small folded piece of paper and sighed: another religious tract. Often visitors would hide them in books, hoping to spread the good word, but as she scanned the text Tricia's eyes went wide. "Nudists?"

Ginny grinned. "Is that weird or what?"

Tricia crumpled the leaflet and tossed it, too, into the wastebasket. "We'd better be on the lookout. If we find one, there's usually ten more hidden amongst the stock."

The circa 1935 black telephone by the register rang. Tricia picked up the heavy handset, noticing Doris had left her glasses on the counter. "Haven't Got a Clue—Tricia speaking. How can I help you?"

"Darling Trish. I'm so glad it was you who answered. I despise speaking to that little helper of yours. She never wants to put me through to you."

The apprehension Tricia had felt when talking with

Doris blossomed into full-fledged dread as she recognized her sister's voice. "Angelica?"

"Of course it's me, and I've been trying to get ahold of you for a week. Doesn't that girl ever give you messages?"

"It must have slipped her mind." Which was a lie. Tricia had given Ginny orders to screen calls and to never put Angelica through. It wasn't that the sisters couldn't get along; it was just that Tricia chose not to. Growing up in Angelica's shadow had been painful enough; putting up with her in adulthood was simply out of the question.

"You should give me your cell number," Angelica badgered.

No way! "We're really very busy today, Ange; can I call you back later?" Another lie. The store was practically empty at only ten fifteen on a Tuesday morning.

"Oh no, you're not cutting me off again. I only called to tell you that I've booked a room in the sweetest little bed-and-breakfast in Stoneham, the Brookview Inn. I hear it's very quaint."

Hardly. The Brookview was Stoneham's finest show palace, boasting a French chef, spa facilities, and catering to a very exclusive clientele. Angelica had the money, of course, but the rest of her personal résumé was definitely lacking. Okay, maybe that was untrue, otherwise how would she have attracted so many husbands? Still, being near her sister seemed to bring out the worst in Tricia.

"What do you want to come here for? It's deadly dull. The shopping isn't up to your usual standards. There's nothing to do here but *read*. You'll only be bored."

"I'm coming to see you, dear—and your *little* shop."

Tricia ground her teeth at the descriptor.

"I had Drew pull up your website on the computer," Angelica continued. "You know how challenged I am when it comes to anything electrical. The pictures are just darling, and you look so stunningly slim and successful, as we all knew you would be."

Tricia cringed at the second dig. On the other side of the counter, Ginny suppressed a giggle. Tricia's gaze swiveled and she pointed to a puzzled-looking patron standing by one of the shelves. Ginny gave a resigned shrug and left the counter. Tricia balanced the heavy receiver on her shoulder and took over emptying the box Ginny had started. "This really isn't a good time, Ange. We're already gearing up for the Christmas rush."

"It's only September," Angelica growled. "One would almost think you're trying to discourage me from coming."

"Don't be silly. I love it whenever you visit." And love it more when you leave. "When are you arriving?"

"This afternoon—I'm already en route." In the back of a limo, no doubt—zooming up I-95 even as they spoke. "I can't wait to see you. I should be arriving before dinner. I'll give you a ring. Now how about that cell number?"

"I'm sorry, I'll be right with you," Tricia said to a non-existent customer. "Excuse me, Ange—I really have to go."

"Oh, all right then. Kiss, kiss—see you tonight."

Tricia slammed the phone down and turned, startling the handsome, middle-aged man with a full head of sandy hair and dressed in the dark business suit who stood before her. "I'm so sorry, I didn't see you there. How can I help you?"

The man thrust his hand forward. "Mike Harris. I want to be your next selectman and I hope you'll consider voting for me."

"Tricia Miles." She shook hands, immediately noting the absence of a ring on the fourth finger of Mike's other hand. "The general election isn't for another two months."

"It's never too soon to meet my future constituents." Mike's white-toothed smile dazzled, making Tricia feel giddy. She giggled. It had been a long time since a man had inspired that reaction in her. Far too long.

Mike relinquished her hand and passed her a glossy color folder with his left, his expression growing serious. "I understand leases are an issue with the booksellers. I'd like to better understand the problem in case I can be of some assistance. I'm no attorney, but as an independent insurance agent I've read my share of pretty complicated contracts."

Tricia studied his face, noted the fine lines around his eyes, the slight graying of his fair hair around the temples. He was maybe five years older than herself—putting him in his mid-forties, but without the girth so often associated with his age group. She'd escaped middle-age spread herself, thanks to inheriting genes from the paternal side of the family—about the only perk of growing up a Miles. Angelica hadn't fared so well and had never forgiven her for it.

She shook away thoughts of her sister, focusing again on the man before her. How had she gone six months in this town without meeting this feast for the eyes?

"I'm afraid the leases aren't an issue with me. You might want to visit my neighbor to the north over at the Cookery. She can give you all the facts as she perceives them."

Mike frowned. "I've already spoken with Ms. Gleason. She has . . . an interesting perspective on the subject."

"Yes." Tricia left it at that.

"I take it you're new to our little village?" Mike asked.

"I've been here almost half a year. But I can't say I've seen you in my store before."

"I'm not much of a fiction reader," he admitted. "But I've spent a bundle over at History Repeats Itself. I'm fascinated by anything to do with World War Two, military aircraft being my special interest. As a kid I wanted to be a fighter pilot. That is until I figured out I have a fear of heights."

Tricia laughed. "I can recommend some wonderful novels that take place during the war. Books by J. Robert Janes, Philip Kerr, and Greg Iles. And I'll bet I've got most of them in stock." She indicated the tall oak shelves surrounding the walls and their lower counterparts that filled the center of the long, narrow store.

Mike dazzled her with his smile again. "Some other time, perhaps. I'm taking a day off work to introduce myself to all the merchants on Main Street. Very nice meeting you, Tricia. I'm sure I'll be back." He offered his hand again, this time holding on longer.

"I'll look forward to it." Tricia held on, too. Their gazes locked and she dazzled him with a smile of her own.

Tuesday night: the slowest night of the week. Like most of the other merchants on Main Street, Tricia closed an hour early. That meant that she might actually get a chance to eat a decent dinner or truck on over to nearby Wilton to see a movie if she felt so inclined—which she usually didn't. More often than not she'd retire to her third-floor loft apartment, select a variety of CDs for the player, heat a frozen pizza, settle in her most comfy chair, and *read*. Since her divorce a year earlier, she hadn't often felt a need for male company. Then again, when she thought of Mike Harris's smile . . .

Angelica's arrival in Stoneham, however, had put a damper on her usual Tuesday-night routine.

Ginny had hung up her apron and grabbed her purse to leave. "You're going to be late meeting your sister, Tricia."

"I know," she said and sighed. "I didn't get to vacuum or anything." She retrieved her purse from the cabinet under the display case, slipped past the register, and noticed Doris's glasses still sitting on the counter. "You would've thought she'd miss these," she said and stuffed them into her bag. "I better drop them off on the way to meet Angelica."

"Better you than me—on *both* accounts."

"I'll give you a hundred dollars—cash—if you do both."

Ginny laughed and shook her head. "Maybe for a hundred thousand, but nothing less."

Miss Marple meowed from her perch on the shelf above the register. "Don't worry, you'll get your dinner when I come home." Miss Marple rubbed her head against the security camera. "And stop that. You keep messing up the camera's angle."

Miss Marple threw her entire eight-pound body against it, knocking it out of alignment, and purred loudly.

"I told you so—I told you so," Ginny sang. Yes, she had told Tricia the camera wasn't high enough on the wall. But it would've interfered with the decorative molding if it was mounted any higher.

Tricia scooped up the cat and set her on one of the comfortable chairs. "Stay down," she ordered.

Miss Marple tossed her head, dismissing the command.

Tricia rolled her eyes and headed for the door once again. She locked it, then realized she hadn't lowered the window shades. She'd have to do it on her return.

The lights in the Cookery bookshop were already dimmed, but Tricia could see Doris still standing behind the sales counter.

"See you tomorrow," Ginny called brightly and headed down the street toward the municipal lot where she'd parked her car.

Tricia gave a wave and turned back for the door, giving it a knock. Doris looked up, had on another pair of outsized specs, but motioned Tricia to go away before she bent back over the counter again. Tricia retrieved the glasses from her purse and knocked once more. This time, she waved them when Doris looked up.

The annoyed shopkeeper skirted the sales counter, lumbered to the door, and unlocked it.

"I'm glad you're still here. You left these in my store this morning," Tricia said.

"So that's where they went. I'm always losing them. That's why I keep an extra pair here at the shop." She pocketed them in the same ugly sweater she'd worn earlier in the day, but the rest of her attire had changed. Dressed in dark slacks and a red blouse, she looked pounds lighter, years younger, and, except for the sweater, almost elegant.

Tricia had never actually been in the Cookery before. It seemed like all her encounters with Doris had been in her own shop. Since all the storefronts were more or less the same—give or take a few feet in width—the Cookery was set up in the same configuration as Haven't Got a Clue, except that where the mystery store had a seating area, the cookbook store housed a cooking demo area: a horseshoe-shaped island with a knife block, complete with ten or twelve chef knives, a small sink, burners, and an under-the-counter refrigerator. Overhead hung a large rectangular mirror so that an audience would see the hands-on instruction. A thin film of greasy dust covered the station, which obviously hadn't been used in a while.

"Nice store," Tricia said.

"It ought to be," Doris groused. "I put a lot of money into it, and if Bob Kelly and I can't come to an agreement on it tonight, I'll lose it all."

The cost of doing business, Tricia thought, but didn't voice what would obviously be an unpopular opinion.

Doris glanced at the big clock over the register. "Bob should've been here ten minutes ago—the inconsiderate jerk."

Atop the main sales counter sat an oblong Lucite container that housed what looked like an aged booklet. The little hinged door sported a sturdy lock. "The prize of your collection?" Tricia asked, her curiosity piqued.

Doris's eyes lit up, and for the first time Tricia saw beyond the sour expression to the woman's true passion. "Yes. It's *American Cookery*, by Amelia Simmons, the very first American cookbook ever published back in 1796. A similar copy recently sold for ten thousand dollars at auction."

Calling the little, yellowing pamphlet a book was stretching the definition.

Doris exhaled a shaky breath, her expression akin to a lovesick teen. "I wish I could keep it myself, but—"

Tricia knew that "but" only too well. Like every other collector she, too, had coveted the holy grail for her own collection. She'd been close a few times, but had never been able to obtain an original copy of *Graham's Lady's and Gentleman's Magazine* containing Poe's short story "The Murders in the Rue Morgue."

"What are you asking for it?"

Doris hesitated. "I haven't actually set a price. I only obtained it a couple of weeks ago. The lockbox arrived just yesterday. But I couldn't resist putting it on exhibition." She gazed fondly at the booklet. "Of course I have a facsimile of it at home and have read it many times, but to actually hold an original copy in my hands has been the thrill of a lifetime."

Tricia nodded.

Doris shook her head. "It's sad how few people really appreciate a well-written cookbook. Most of the slobs who come in here are looking for the latest Food Network star's most recent atrocity. And I can't tell you how much money I make on old Betty Crocker books from the fifties and sixties. Not even first editions, mind you. I can sell a tenth or twelfth edition for twenty bucks." She shuddered. Clearly, the woman hated the books, but she'd sell them to pay her rent—it was something else Tricia understood.

"How did you score such a find?" Tricia asked.

Doris's expression curdled. "Private sale."

The fact that she wouldn't elaborate must've meant the former owner had since had an inkling of what the booklet might be worth.

Tricia forced a smile. "I'd better get going."

"Thank you for returning my glasses," Doris said, her tone still clipped.

"No problem."

Doris followed Tricia to the door and locked it behind her without even a good night.

Tricia headed down the sidewalk with no thought to the snub—now to face Angelica. Of the two, she ruefully admitted that she'd probably rather spend time with Doris.

She'd parked her own car in the municipal lot earlier in the day. By this time it was mostly empty. Now that school was back in session, the bulk of the summer tourist trade had evaporated. That would change when the autumn leaves began to turn and tour buses and crowds would return for another few weeks of superior sales. Thank goodness for the cruise ships that moored in Portsmouth and

Boston harbors, which often brought in more customers. Once winter arrived they, too, would be gone. Still, the business slowdown would give Tricia time to establish a storefront in cyberspace, something she'd been meaning to do since she'd opened some five months previous.

Stoneham wasn't very large and it only took a minute or two for Tricia to drive to the Brookview Inn, lit up like a Thomas Kinkade painting with warm yellow light spilling from every window. Soft pink roses flanked steps leading to the entrance, the last of the summer's offerings crowding against white-painted wrought-iron railings. Tricia hesitated, taking in the delicate scent. No doubt Angelica would have doused herself in the latest overpriced perfume with a celebrity's name attached to it.

Stop it, she ordered. Yet she'd spent her whole life finding fault with her older sister. Was it natural that even as an adult she hadn't been able to let go of her childhood animosity? If she was honest with herself, she should blame their mother for fostering such an unhealthy atmosphere.

Then again, Mother never took the blame for anything.

Tricia took a breath to control her anxiety. It was really her own reactions to her sister that upset her. Angelica wasn't likely to change anytime soon. It was up to Tricia to ride out the visit and not let it turn her into the jealous child she thought she'd long outgrown.

The Brookview had given Tricia shelter for three weeks during the time when the apartment over the store was being made habitable. She could've opted for one of the efficiency bungalows behind the inn itself, but had been seduced by the sumptuous bedding and other pampering amenities, finding the inn a serene haven during the demolition and chaos of the store's renovation. And she'd tried to replicate some of that ambiance in her own much more humble abode. So far she'd only managed to acquire the four-hundred-thread-count sheets and fluffy down pillows. Tricia missed the cuisine and the friendly staff, but admitted she still preferred the privacy of her own home and the company of her cat and her precious books.

Bess, the plump sixtysomething night clerk, looked up from her keyboard behind the reception desk, a smile lighting her face. "Welcome back, Ms. Miles. And what brings you to the Brookview tonight?"

"My sister, Angelica Prescott, is a guest."

"No doubt at your recommendation," Bess said and beamed.

Tricia smiled, pushing down the guilt.

"I think you'll find her in our dining room. The special tonight is hazelnut-encrusted salmon." Bess closed her eyes in a moment of pure ecstasy. "It *is* to die for."

"Sounds heavenly. But I've already eaten." Her dinner had consisted of a burger on a soggy bun that Ginny snagged at the Bookshelf Diner down the street from the shop. "I'll just pop in and see if Angie's there."

"You go right ahead, dear." Bess gave a little wave and returned her attention to her keyboard.

Tricia crossed the foyer to the opened double doors at the far end of the lobby. The Brookview's elegant dining room, with its crown molding, traditional furnishings, and lamp-lit oil paintings of Revolutionary War heroes, welcomed her. And at the best table, holding court, sat Angelica, leaning forward, manicured index finger wagging to make a point with her guest. She was blond again, cut short and stylish, and what looked like a recent weight loss was evident in her face. She'd always been the family beauty, and so far age had not worked against her. Even with his back turned toward her, Tricia recognized the man who sat opposite her sister: Bob Kelly. Two of the three people on the planet who irritated Tricia the most, and now she had to deal with both of them—together.

The fact that Bob could've passed as her ex's twin— albeit a decade older—may've been responsible for part of Tricia's dislike for him. Did he have to be so drop-dead handsome? Tall, muscular, with a head full of wavy dark hair that had never seen a colorist, and those deep green eyes. Yes, except for the eyes, he could have been Christopher's double.

Dinner had been cleared and only demitasse cups and crumb-littered dessert plates remained on the linen-shrouded table.

Tricia took a breath, plastered on a smile, and charged forward. "Angie!"

Angelica looked up, a look of true pleasure lighting her expression, reinforcing the guilt Tricia felt. "Darling Trish." She rose, arms outstretched.

The women embraced and Tricia quelled the urge to cough. Angelica did indeed smell like she'd been dipped in a vat of perfume. A couple of air kisses later, Tricia pulled back. "You look fabulous. You've lost weight."

"Twenty pounds," Angelica admitted proudly. "I've just returned from this divine spa in Aspen, and—"

Bob Kelly cleared his throat. Tricia hadn't noticed that he'd also stood. She nodded, dropped her voice. "Hello, Bob. I see you've met my sister."

"Yes, and what a delightful surprise."

Tricia gave the empty chairs around the table a cursory glance. "Where's Drew?"

Angelica scowled. "Obviously not here." She abruptly changed the subject, taking her seat once again. "Order some dessert, Trish, and we'll all have a nice conversation."

Bob remained standing. "I'm afraid I have a business meeting this evening."

"So late?" Angelica asked.

"The downside of being a successful entrepreneur, I'm afraid."

Tricia fought the urge to gag. By now Doris would be furious—and that's probably exactly what Bob wanted.

Bob offered Angelica his hand. She took it. "Thank you so much for the dessert. I'd love to take you to dinner some time during your visit."

"And I'd love to accept. Do call me."

"I will. Ladies." And with a nod, Bob excused himself.

"Isn't he just a doll," Angelica whispered once he was out of earshot.

Tricia took Bob's abandoned seat and forced yet another smile. Her cheeks were already beginning to ache. "What brings you all the way to New Hampshire, Ange? This really isn't your style at all."

Angelica sighed. "I can't keep anything from you, can I?"

Tricia's stomach tensed. Bad news? Angie's twenty-pound weight loss . . .

Angelica played with the chunky diamond ring on her engagement finger. Her wedding band was gone. "Drew and I . . . well, our trial separation proved successful. We're finished."

Tricia relaxed. Not a total surprise. Drew was Angelica's fourth husband. He was a quiet, studious type, whereas Angelica was boisterous and liked fun and crowds of people. Sedate New Hampshire was much more Drew's sort of refuge. "I'm so sorry." And she was. She and Drew could talk books for hours, much to Angelica's chagrin.

"No, actually, I've come to help you with your little store," Angelica charged on. "I'm a successful business-woman in my own right and quite naturally I assumed you'd need my help."

Tricia gritted her teeth and grimaced. Angelica had worked in a boutique in SoHo for all of five minutes some twenty years before. It had closed within weeks of opening. "No, but . . . thank you anyway."

"Nonsense. I'm here and I'm dying to see the little place." Angelica raised a hand in the air and within seconds a waiter appeared. "Please add the dinner to my account."

"With pleasure, ma'am." The black-suited man bowed and made a discreet exit.

Angelica rose. "Come, come," she ordered and, like a well-trained dog, Tricia jumped to her feet to follow.

Already the evening was not going as Tricia had planned.

Minutes later, Tricia steered her Lexus onto Main Street and under the banner strung across the road that proudly proclaimed Stoneham the Safest Town in New Hampshire.

She pulled into the empty parking space in front of Haven't Got a Clue, cut the engine, and waited to hear the inevitable insult disguised as a compliment.

"Oh, Tricia, it's lovely," Angelica breathed, and she truly sounded awed.

All the brick-faced buildings along Main Street sported a different pastel hue, except for number 221. The bottom floor's white stone facade resembled a certain Victorian address in London, while Tricia had had the brick of the top two floors sandblasted to reveal its natural state. The door, beveled glass on the top and painted a glossy black on the bottom, looked impressive with glowing period brass lanterns on either side. The gold-leafed address numbers 221 shone brightly on the Palladian transom above. The plate-glass display window to the right did sort of spoil the effect, but the effort Tricia had made to approximate the beloved detective's home hadn't been lost on the majority of her customers.

"Surely the address is wrong," Angelica said. "Shouldn't it be 221B?"

"I didn't know you'd read Dr. Watson's stories."

"Please! Grandmother bored me to tears with them before you were born."

Tricia had never been bored when Grandmother had read her Sir Arthur's stories. As a child, she hadn't always understood them—but she'd loved the sound of all those wonderful words and her grandmother's voice.

"Come on in and I'll give you the fifty-cent tour."

Tricia opened her car door and stepped out onto the pavement. She held up her keys, selecting the proper one as Angelica got out of the car.

"Do you smell something burning?" Angelica asked.

"No." The truth was, after being sealed in the car with Angie's perfume, Tricia wondered if she'd ever be able to smell anything again.

"Something's definitely burning . . . or maybe smoldering," Angelica insisted. Shading her eyes, she peered into the mystery bookshop's large plate-glass window, then turned her head from right to left and sniffed loudly, her nose wrinkling.

Tricia watched as her sister moved a few steps toward the Cookery. "Trish, I think it's coming from the mail slot next door."

Sure enough, a thin veil of smoke drifted from the painted flap in the door.

Tricia jammed her keys back in her purse, scooping up her cell phone, and hurried to Angelica's side. "Dial nine-one-one," she ordered, shoving everything into her sister's hands. She grasped the Cookery's door handle, shocked when it yielded to her touch.

The smoke was thick, but with no sign of flames, Tricia took a deep breath and plunged inside. Grabbing the heavy rubber doormat, she searched in the dim light for the source of the smoke and found a section of carpet glowing red.

Swinging the mat, she beat at the embers until they were extinguished, then rushed outside for a much-needed breath of air.

The Stoneham Fire Department was only a block or so away and already Tricia could hear their sirens.

"Think there's anybody in there?" Angelica asked.

"I didn't see anyone, but I'd better look, just in case."

Back she dipped into the stinking building. The smoke seemed to hover, but already it wasn't as thick as it had been only a minute or so before. "Doris?" she called and coughed. "Doris, are you in here?"

Grateful for the security lighting that hadn't winked out, Tricia searched behind the sales counter. No sign of Doris. But a glance to her right showed that the little Lucite case that less than an hour before had housed Doris's treasured cookbook was no longer perched on the top of the shelf. Had someone tried to burn the place down to hide the theft of the book?

"Doris?" she called again, trying to remember if Doris inhabited an apartment over the shop or if she lived elsewhere.

Tricia stumbled over something and fell to her knees. The air was definitely better down here. Righting herself, Tricia pivoted to see what had tripped her. She gasped as she focused on the still form half protruding from behind the horseshoe-shaped kitchen island, noting the carving knife that jutted from its sweatered back.

TWO

 Miss Marple wrinkled her little gray nose, sniffing the cuff of Tricia's slacks before giving a hiss of fear and backing away.

"I couldn't agree more," Angelica said and aimed a squirt of perfume in Tricia's general direction.

"Please, don't—I'd rather smell like smoke," Tricia complained, waving her sister off.

Chagrined, Angelica returned the atomizer to her handbag.

Outside the bubble-gum lights of a patrol car flashed upon the walls and shelves of stock, reminding Tricia of a carnival ride—one that, as a child, had made her violently ill.

"Let's go through it once again," Sheriff Wendy Adams said.

Until that night, Tricia hadn't had an occasion to meet any of the county's law enforcement community. The sheriff's uniform shirt buttons strained against her ample cleavage, her large hips accentuated by the cut of her standard-issue slacks. But it was mostly Sheriff Adams's

19

no-nonsense countenance that made Tricia feel so uncomfortable. It probably worked well in police work. Good thing the woman's livelihood didn't rely on retail, where a no-nonsense attitude was the kiss of death.

Tricia sighed and repeated for the third time the events leading up to her discovery of Doris Gleason's body.

Sheriff Adams scowled. "Wouldn't you know, I'm up for reelection in two months and now I've got a murder on my hands. Did you know we haven't had a killing in Stoneham in at least sixty years?"

"No."

The sheriff continued to scowl. "How much was that missing book worth?"

Tricia sighed. "My expertise is in mystery novels—not cookbooks. But Doris told me a copy recently sold at auction for ten thousand dollars. It's all subjective: an antique, book or otherwise, will only sell for what a buyer is willing to pay."

"Whatever," Sheriff Adams muttered. "Did Mrs.—or was it Miss—or Ms.—Gleason have any enemies?"

Tricia's eyebrows rose, her lips pursing as she gazed at the floor.

"Is that a yes?" the sheriff asked impatiently.

"Doris was negotiating a new lease for her store," Tricia explained. "She felt the new terms were . . . perhaps a little steep."

"And who was she negotiating with?"

"Bob Kelly."

"Oh," Angelica squealed. "I just had dessert with him at the Brookview Inn. Very nice man, and oh, those lovely green eyes of his are heavenly."

The sheriff turned her attention to Angelica. "What time was that, and for how long?"

"Surely you don't suspect the town's leading citizen?" Angelica said.

"How do you know his status?" Tricia asked.

Angelica shrugged. "Bob told me, of course."

It took all Tricia's resolve not to roll her eyes.

As if on cue, a worried Bob stuck his head around Haven't Got a Clue's unlocked door. "Wendy, what's going on?"

"There's been a murder, I'm afraid."

Stunned, Bob's mouth dropped open in horror. "Murder? Good grief! Ten years of Stoneham being named the safest town in all New Hampshire . . . down the drain." A parade of other emotions soon cascaded across his face: irritation and despair taking center stage. "What'll this do to my real estate business?"

"That's nothing compared to what Doris Gleason lost— her life," Tricia said, disgusted.

"Doris?" he repeated in disbelief.

The sheriff rested a hand on Bob's shoulder, turning him around. "Let's take this outside," she said and led him out the door and onto the sidewalk for a private chat.

Angelica inhaled deeply, bending lower until her nose was inches from Tricia's hair. "Ooooh, you stink."

Tricia sniffed at her sweater sleeve. "I was only in the Cookery for a minute at most."

"Believe me. You stink."

Tricia's heart sank. "If I smell this bad, think about all those poor books. I wonder if they can be salvaged."

Angelica shook her head. "Only you would think about such a thing."

"Me and every other book lover on the planet."

The sheriff returned with Bob in tow. "Are you okay, Tricia?" Bob asked.

Tricia nodded, suddenly feeling weary.

The sheriff consulted her notebook once again, then spoke to Angelica. "Mrs. Prescott, you said you're staying at the Brookview Inn?"

"Yes, and isn't it just lovely?"

"For how long?"

Angelica gazed down at Tricia. "I arrived just this afternoon and I'll be in town for as long as my sister needs me."

Tricia rocketed from her chair, belatedly wondering if her clothes had already imparted their smoky scent to the upholstery. "I'm fine, Angie. You don't have to hang around on my account."

"Nonsense. What's family for?"

So far emotional support hadn't been a Miles family trait.

"Ma'am," said a solemn voice from the doorway. A fire-fighter, his scarlet helmet emblazoned with the word CHIEF stenciled in gold and white, motioned to the sheriff. "All the smoke detectors in the Cookery were disabled. Who-ever did this didn't want the crime discovered too quickly. However, it appears there was no accelerant used."

Did that mean whoever murdered Doris hadn't planned the killing? Yet they'd been clearheaded enough to try to cover their tracks—however inefficiently.

"Let's keep this discussion private," Sheriff Adams said, and she and the fire chief moved to stand out of earshot on the sidewalk.

Angelica rested a warm hand on Tricia's shoulder. "Trish, dear, you must come and stay with me at the inn. I won't sleep a wink tonight knowing you're here all alone in such a dangerous place. You could've died if that fire hadn't been discovered."

"If *you* hadn't discovered it. Besides, I wouldn't have died. My smoke alarms work—and I have an excellent sprinkler system."

"You discovered the fire?" Bob asked, zeroing in on An-gelica.

She waved a hand in dismissal. "It was nothing, really. I only wish we could've saved that poor woman."

"It wasn't *nothing*," Bob said. "The whole block could've gone up, and then the village would've—" He let the sentence fade, his face blanching. No doubt he was already thinking about the upcoming zoning board meet-ing, and how he could force through new rules for fire safety. The costs would no doubt be passed on to the lease owners. Tricia knew that, like Doris, several other book-store owners were already living on the precarious edge of profitability with the possibility of folding. And trust Bob

Kelly to care more for the buildings than the potential loss of a human life.

Bob's gimmicky idea of basing the village's economy on used bookstores luring in tourists had been inspired by the town of Hay-on-Wye. That little Welsh town had been in the same financial boat as Stoneham: picturesque but fallen on hard times. The original leases had been written in favor of the booksellers, but as Doris had found out, success came with a price. The signs were already evident that Doris's business was on the slide. Fewer food-prep demonstrations and the fact her best-selling product was at the low end of the profit spectrum.

That will not happen to me, Tricia thought. For years she'd daydreamed about every aspect of her store, from the stock to the décor. She'd written and rewritten her business plan, had goals for expanding the business and a timetable to do it. Her divorce a year earlier had presented her with the money and all the time in the world to pursue her lifelong dream of entrepreneurship. After five months in business, Tricia was exactly where she expected to be: paying her rent, her employee, covering her overhead, and making a modest profit. Only time would tell if word of Doris's murder would have an impact on the whole village's revenue stream. The thought depressed her.

As though anticipating her owner's solemn thoughts, Miss Marple appeared at Tricia's side. She gave a muffled "yow," and dropped her favorite, rather ratty-looking catnip sock at Tricia's feet.

"Oh, thank you, Miss Marple," she said, patting the cat's furry gray head. "You are a very thoughtful kitty." Miss Marple purred loudly.

"Darling Trish. You must come back with me to the inn. I'm sure they can move some kind of cot into my room. You're much too upset to drive, so give me your keys," Angelica insisted once again.

"That won't be necessary. This is my home and I'm staying put. And I'm not upset," she lied. "As soon as the sheriff is finished, I'll drive you back to the inn."

"Nonsense," Bob interrupted. "I'd be delighted to escort you back to the Brookview, Mrs. Prescott."

Angelica turned slowly to face Bob. "Call me Angelica," she said, her voice softening, her blue eyes lowered coyly.

Bob smiled, practically oozing with gentlemanly charm.

What was this effect Angie had on men? And what was wrong with these two? A woman had been murdered mere feet from where they all stood. Then again, if Bob managed to get Angelica out of Tricia's hair, she might be inclined to ignore some of his other annoying attributes.

Sheriff Adams returned, looking bad-tempered. "I guess that's all for tonight, folks. But I'll be needing official statements from all three of you. I'll send a deputy by sometime tomorrow to take them. In the meantime, please don't leave town without notifying the sheriff's department."

As if, Tricia was tempted to sniff. Then it occurred to her what Sheriff Adams was really saying: that perhaps she didn't believe their accounts as they'd given them.

Miss Marple hadn't appreciated an early wake-up call, but the image of Doris Gleason with a knife in her back kept Tricia from restful sleep; her dreams had been shadowed by dark menacing images she could only half remember. She'd showered, dressed, and fed herself and her cat before trundling down the stairs to her shop. Next on the list: vacuuming, tidying, and all the other chores she hadn't accomplished before leaving the night before. It was while resetting the security system she noticed the cord from the wall-mounted camera dangling loose, with the unmistakable indentations from feline teeth.

"Miss Marple. Didn't I tell you not to mess with that camera?" she admonished.

The cat jumped to the counter and rubbed her head against Tricia's arm.

"Oh no, you don't. I am not your friend right now."

Miss Marple swished her tail and jumped down, sashaying across the carpet without a backward glance.

Before Tricia could call the security company, the phone rang and she let the answering machine kick in. "The Haven't Got a Clue mystery bookstore's hours are ten a.m. to seven p.m. on Mondays, Tuesdays ten to six; Wednesday through Saturday ten to seven, and Sunday noon to three. Please leave a message at the tone."

Beep!

"Bernie Weston, *Nashua Telegraph.* Looking to interview Tricia Miles about last night's Stoneham murder at the Cookery. Please call at—" He left a number.

That was one phone call Tricia was determined not to return. True, talking to the press would get the shop's name in the newspaper, but a murder—even next door to a mystery bookstore—was negative publicity, and she preferred not to believe that even negative publicity was good publicity.

She wiped the message from the machine and dialed another number.

"We're swamped," said the harried male voice at Ace Security. "I might be able to get someone out to you by the end of the week, but I can't make any promises. If the rest of your system's intact, you shouldn't have too much of a problem."

Let's see: murder, theft, and arson had occurred just feet from Tricia's doorstep. Why wouldn't she feel secure with a third of her system on the blink? As a small-business owner, she'd wanted to patronize other local businesses, but now wondered if she'd regret that decision.

She hung up the phone, put a soothing Enya CD on low, and commandeered her sheepskin duster. Taking care of her beloved books always had a calming effect on her psyche. And she needed that calm, for in the next half hour the answering machine took four more calls from newspapers, radio stations, and/or television stations in Concord, Nashua, and Manchester. Screening calls was the order of the day. Stoneham's small-town gossip mill was bound to be in full force, and the best source of information showed up ten minutes after Haven't Got a Clue opened.

A bleary-eyed Ginny scowled as she snagged a cup of coffee from the store's steaming pot before she'd even hung up her jacket. "Sheriff Adams was waiting for me when I got home last night. Let me tell you, being interrogated by a cop can really put a crimp in your love life. Brian hightailed it out of my place so fast I almost got windburn."

"What does *he* have to hide?" Tricia asked.

Ginny glowered. "I think his car's inspection sticker might be a little overdue."

"A little?"

"Okay, by two months."

"What did the sheriff ask you about?"

Ginny's answer was succinct. "You."

Tricia started. "Me?"

"Apparently, you were the last person to see Dawwris"—she again dragged the name out—"alive."

"Except for the killer, you mean."

Ginny shrugged, warming her hands on the store's logo-emblazoned cardboard cup. "I suppose."

Tricia hoped her only employee had been a little more aggressive in defending her when speaking with the sheriff.

"I told her I was in Doris's shop for perhaps five minutes, just to return her glasses. We talked briefly about her expensive little cookbook, then I went to the inn, picked up my sister, and we were back here within thirty—maybe forty minutes."

"I'm sure you have nothing to worry about," Ginny said, gulped her coffee, and got up to cash out the first of the day's customers.

But Tricia did worry about it—to the point of obsession; it only got worse after she'd given her statement to the young deputy who'd stopped by. She rang up sales incorrectly, punching in three cents instead of thirty dollars for a slightly water-stained dust cover on a first edition of Josephine Tey's *The Singing Sands*, and asked a customer to pay three hundred ninety-five dollars for a laminated bookmark. And still the telephone kept ringing.

"You ought to take a break," Ginny advised, after soothing the latest irate customer. "Go for a drive in the country. Take your sister shopping in Manchester."

"Being with Angelica is the last thing I need. No, here is where I belong."

Ginny shrugged. "You're the boss."

A gray-haired woman with big sunglasses presented a book for purchase. Ginny rang up the sale and Tricia picked it up to place in the store's plastic bag. A slip of paper fell out and hit the floor. Tricia bent to pick it up and silently cursed: another nudist tract. She shoved it into her slacks pocket and handed across the book and bag to her customer. "Thank you for shopping at Haven't Got a Clue," she said cheerfully, hoping her irritation hadn't been apparent. The woman smiled and headed for the exit.

"Another one?" Ginny asked.

Tricia nodded, removing the paper from her pocket. Ginny pulled more leaflets from her apron pocket, handing them over. "You were right when you said we'd find more."

Tricia read over the text extolling the benefits of a natural lifestyle free from restrictive clothing: "a healthy lifestyle that encouraged body acceptance and self-confidence." Still, she wondered how many people caught cold or cut their toes while romping around in the altogether.

Tricia balled up the leaflets, tossing them in the trash. "Let's hope this is the end of it."

The bell over the door jangled and a dark-haired, middle-aged man in faded jeans and a Patriots sweatshirt charged in. He was a couple of weeks late on a haircut, and his Nikes had seen much better days, although Tricia supposed he was good-looking, in a rustic sort of way.

"Looking for the owner, Tricia Miles," he said.

Tricia raised a hand. "That would be me."

The man offered his hand. "Russ Smith, editor of the *Stoneham Weekly News.*"

The name sounded familiar. "I believe we spoke on the phone just after my shop opened. You ran a paragraph or two back in the spring, telling the community about the store."

"Oh, yeah." He'd obviously forgotten. "You probably guessed that I'm here about the murder at the Cookery. It's the biggest news to hit Stoneham in—"

"Sixty years, apparently." Tricia's muscles went rigid. She hadn't counted on the local fish wrapper to come calling. The top story in the last issue had been squirrels chewing through the village gazebo's roof. "Mr. Smith, finding Doris was pretty upsetting. I really don't want to talk about it."

He cocked his head. "Why? Did you kill her?"

Tricia gasped and blinked. "Of course not."

"Then why not take the opportunity to tell the whole village so?" He grasped her by the elbow, maneuvered her around the sales counter, and led her to the nook, where three of the four upholstered chairs were empty. He pushed her into a seat and took the adjacent chair. Tricia hadn't noticed that he'd carried a steno notebook in his left hand, which he now opened. He came up with a pen, too.

He looked at Tricia over the rims of his gold-toned glasses. "I've got the facts from Sheriff Adams. You want to give me your take on the murder?"

"I really don't think I should talk to the press. I mean, what if I say something that compromises the sheriff's investigation?"

Mr. Everett, the shop's most regular customer and seated in another of the nook's chairs, peeked over the top of the book he held unnaturally close to his face. At Tricia's pointed stare, his eyes disappeared again.

Smith read through his notes. "You found the body at approximately six forty-eight p.m. Put out the smoldering fire—"

"It was the other way around. I put out the fire first, then found poor Doris."

"Were you two enemies?" he cut in, his eyes narrowed.

Tricia recoiled. "No."

"Talk is the two of you argued last night."

"We did not! She wanted to enlist me in her crusade to renegotiate the booksellers' leases. I told her I couldn't help her. My lease doesn't come due for more than two years."

"Do you think Bob Kelly is responsible for her death? It's known she argued with him, too," he said.

Tricia took a calming breath and straightened in her seat to perch on its edge. "I was not privy to their conversations. I only know she had an appointment to speak with him again last night. Apparently he was delayed." Gosh, she sounded formal. Would that make her sound even more guilty to this Jimmy Olsen wannabe?

"Kelly was delayed by your sister, an—" He consulted his notes. "An Angelica Preston. Was their meeting something you engineered? Something to keep Bob Kelly from meeting Ms. Gleason?"

Tricia stood. "I don't appreciate your inference, Mr. Smith, and I wish you'd leave."

Smith's calculating scowl tempted Tricia to slap him; only her clenched fists and sheer willpower kept her from doing it. He took his time closing his notebook, clipping the pen onto its cover. Finally, he stood. "I think you'll wish you were a bit more candid, Ms. Miles."

"Is that a threat, Mr. Smith?"

He shook his head. "I'm just stating facts." With that, he turned and moved toward the door. It slammed shut behind him.

Tricia glanced down at Mr. Everett, whose eyes were once again peering over the top of his book. Seeing her, he quickly ducked down again.

Too upset to interact with customers, Tricia grabbed her duster and headed for the back shelves, hoping to work off her anger.

As she ran the fleece over the topmost shelf, she puzzled over the sudden void she felt from Doris's death. The woman hadn't been known as the friendliest person on the planet. Her quick-to-judge temperament and an acid tongue hadn't served her well in business and from what Tricia could tell her personal life, either.

What was so special about the cookbook that had been stolen? Yes, it was a rare first edition, but Doris's reluctance to discuss where she'd obtained the book now seemed more sinister than circumspect.

Or was it only paranoia that kept Tricia's thoughts on that circuit? Somebody had killed Doris, had stolen a rare book, and had committed arson to try to hide the crimes.

And just who among the denizens of Stoneham was capable of such wanton acts?

There was only one way to find out. Talk to them. And she knew just where and with whom to start.

THREE

Stoneham's chamber of commerce resided in the former sales office of a company offering log homes. Tricia had passed it hundreds of times, and though she'd been a member since before the actual day she'd opened her store, she'd never had time to visit the office.

She stood out on the sidewalk admiring the charming little pseudohome with its stone chimney, folksy rockers on the front porch, and the double dormers poking through the green-painted metal roof. Someone had a green thumb, judging by the welcoming baskets of magenta fuchsias, pink begonias, and colorful pansies that hung suspended along the porch's roofline.

Tricia climbed the steps and entered through the glossy, red-painted door. Like every other business in Stoneham, a little bell tinkled as she entered. Inside, the cabin was just as charming, with its chinked walls and timbered rafters. The outside had hinted of a second floor, but the cathedral ceiling was a good twenty feet above her and sunlight streamed through the dormer windows. A sitting area, furnished in comfortable leather couches and chairs with a rustic flair, gave way to racks of local brochures, file cabinets, and other utilitarian office equipment.

"Howdy!" came a female voice with a thick Texas twang. "How can I help you?"

Tricia stepped up to a counter, where a thin woman with close-cropped, gray-streaked brown hair, with a face wrinkled by years of smiles, and wearing a baggy crimson-and-white Hawaiian shirt awaited. "I was hoping to find Bob Kelly here. His real estate office is closed and I thought—"

"I don't usually see much of Bob during the workday. He tends to catch up on chamber business on evenings and weekends. Today's an exception. He's been doing damage control; interviews with the media and such. We've got ourselves a little PR crisis here in Stoneham after last night's events."

So now Doris's death was an event?

"Is there something I can help you with?" the woman asked again and went back to chomping on her gum cud.

"My name is Tricia Miles, and—"

"I know you! You're the lady runs that mystery store. Let's see, joined in late March this year. Haven't made one of our luncheons at the Brookview Inn, yet, have you? Best grub in town, that's for sure."

"Uh, no," Tricia said, wondering if this woman was for real or putting on an act.

The woman extended a calloused hand. "Hi. Frannie Mae Armstrong, but folks just call me Frannie. Named after my grandma on Daddy's side."

Tricia blinked, but took her hand. "How nice."

Frannie's handshake was as strong as any man's though not crushing. "How's the book business? Doin' real well, are ya? I read romances myself. Love that Nora Roberts—but not those J. D. Robb ones she writes." Frannie leaned closer, lowered her voice confidentially. "They're set in the future, ya know, and that's just plain weird."

"Can't say as I've ever read any of her work."

"You're missing out on some real entertainment. Since

that Have a Heart romance bookstore opened, my TV watching has dropped by half."

"You'd seem to be one of the few locals who patronize us."

Frannie nodded sagely. "Oh, there's a few of us out there. Maybe you should try starting a reader group—maybe team up with the library on that. They supply the warm bodies, you supply the books."

"That's a good idea. Thanks."

"But you're right about one thing: there does seem to be an us-verses-them sort of rivalry going on among the merchants. There's also no doubt that bringing in the booksellers has revitalized Stoneham. Some of the old-timers—that's what I call those businessmen who were around before the booksellers came—resent you newcomers. What for?" she asked, her hands flying into the air. "They didn't want to be located on Main Street anyway—it was falling apart. Most of 'em moved to the edge of town to be near the highway. And the bookstores bring in lots of money. Saved 'em all from bankruptcy if you ask me." She shook her head.

"Have you lived in Stoneham long?" Tricia asked, genuinely interested.

"Must be going on twenty years, now." She laughed and the windows rattled. "It's my accent, huh? I *am* a long way from home," she admitted, "but I've come to love the changing seasons. That is until I retire, then I'll be off to Hawaii. They call it paradise, ya know." She straightened, her face losing some of its animation, all business now. "Now just what was it you wanted to ask of old Bob?"

Tricia had almost forgotten why she'd stopped in. "I had some questions concerning Doris Gleason's murder."

Frannie shook her head, her left hand rising to clasp the side of her face. "Lord, isn't that just awful. And I heard you found her, you poor little thing."

"Yes, I did. Did you know Doris?"

"No. She wasn't a chamber member. I called her several times to ask if she wanted to join, but she was just the most ornery woman I ever did speak to. Told me to stop bothering her or she'd report me to the state's attorney general as a telemarketer."

"But being a chamber member is great, even if you only use it to promote your store."

"I know, and I tried to tell her that, but she hung up on me. I don't see how she stayed in business as long as she did. And now she's dead. Well, I guess she annoyed someone one time too many, don'tcha think?"

Tricia shrugged, afraid to agree—especially as it appeared she was the prime suspect. "Doris told me she had an appointment to meet with Bob last night, but apparently he didn't make it over to the Cookery to see her before she was killed."

Frannie crossed her thin arms across her equally thin chest. "Well, that's Bob for you. He's always overbooking himself. Thinks he's Superman." Frannie laughed again, and Tricia feared for the window's mullions. "I know he had a dinner meeting at the Brookview Inn. Must've fallen behind schedule."

"I saw him there last night. When he left, he said he was late for an appointment. I assumed he meant with Doris, but he didn't show up for at least another hour after he left the inn."

"Do tell," Frannie said and cocked her head. She paused in her gum chewing, looking thoughtful. "I wonder . . ." But she didn't articulate exactly what it was she pondered. Long seconds went by before she shook herself and seemed to remember Tricia stood before her. "Do you want to leave Bob a message?"

Tricia shook her head. "I'll call him later."

"You want his cell number? He doesn't mind taking calls when it comes to protecting the good name of Stoneham. Business is business, ya know."

"I don't want to bother him." That wasn't exactly true . . .

"Well, I'll tell him you stopped by. If there's anything the chamber can do for you, you just give us a holler, ya hear?"

Discussion over.

Tricia managed a wan smile. "Thank you, Frannie, you've been most helpful." Not.

She headed for the door with Frannie calling a cheerful good-bye behind her. Once outside, Tricia stood on the porch for a few moments, wondering what it was concerning Bob that Frannie hadn't wanted to talk about.

Since she'd gone inside, a crew had arrived to take down the Safest Town banner from the north end of the street. Had they already removed the one from the south end?

A sheriff's cruiser rolled slowly past, its driver taking in both sides of the street. Was it just the cool breeze that made the hairs on the back of Tricia's neck prickle or was it the idea the deputy might be watching her?

Two hours later, Tricia was positive she did not suffer from paranoia. Even Ginny remarked about the sheriff's cruiser making a regular circuit up and down Main Street, and that too often its occupant's attention seemed to be focused on Haven't Got a Clue.

When she ducked out to take the previous day's receipts to the bank, Tricia noticed a patrol car parked in the municipal lot. Inside it, a deputy's gaze was trained on Stoneham's main drag. It made Tricia want to look over her shoulder, keeping an eye out for the real murderer. Then again, Doris's killer could be just about anybody. Since there was no sign of forced entry and the door had been unlocked, it was likely Doris had opened it to let in her killer. Meaning, she'd probably known the person—and Tricia wasn't about to let anyone think that person might be her.

What would Miss Marple, Hercule Poirot, or any other self-respecting protagonist in a Christie novel do in this situation? Ask questions.

Tricia took a detour on the way back to her shop, stopping at the Happy Domestic, a boutique specializing in new and gently used products, consisting of how-to books, gifts, and home décor. She'd met the owner, Deborah

Black, at an auction several months before where they'd shared coffee and local gossip, and they had continued to look out for each other at every other sale. Deborah loaded up on glassware and bric-a-brac while Tricia had scoured box lots for interesting titles.

Thirtysomething Deborah, her swollen belly straining against a maternity smock, wore a plastic smile that never waned until the customer she'd waited on had exited her store. "Oh God," she exhaled and collapsed against her sales counter. "Sometimes I think I'll kill myself if I have to coo over another satin pillow with the words 'Do Not Disturb' cross-stitched on it."

Tricia laughed. "Only a few days more and you'll have a vacation from customers. You're due next week, aren't you?"

"And, boy, am I ready. Jim Roth over at History Repeats Itself has a parlay going. He says I won't make it until my due date on Monday." She looked down at herself and laughed. "And he may be right." ·

"Hey, nobody told me about the parlay."

"I think there's a few squares left, if you want to get in."

"I may just visit him when I leave here."

Deborah studied Tricia's face. "Betting on my baby's birth is not why you came to visit today—not during work hours. You're here about Doris, right?"

"That obvious, huh?"

"Well, her murder *is* the talk about town." She bent down to pick up a cardboard carton.

"Let me get that," Tricia said and lifted the box onto the counter. "So, tell me what you know about Doris," Tricia prompted.

Deborah untucked one of the box's flaps and withdrew a paper-wrapped package, talking as she worked. "She was a nasty piece of work. The rest of us avoided her at all costs. Never a positive word. Never contributed to the United Way. Never wanted to do anything positive for the village or the community at large. Her view in life seemed to be 'What have you done for me lately?'"

"So the rest of the shop owners won't be mourning her."

Deborah shook her head, tossing her long brown hair back across her shoulders. "You know what she was like."

How pathetic, Tricia thought, not to be mourned at all. Surely Doris had had some redeeming qualities. She voiced that question.

Deborah shook her head, unwrapping the first of the bundles, a delicate pink, etched water goblet. "Not that I noticed. You might want to talk to some of the other booksellers. Most have been around here longer than me. But if you expect heartfelt tributes, you're wasting your time." She held up one of the glasses to the light. "Aren't these just the prettiest crystal?"

Tricia nodded and counted the remaining bundles. "Only seven."

"If nothing else, I can sell them as a set of six. I'll set up a whole new display around them. Lots of pink, girly items. It'll be gorgeous."

"Did you pick these up at the last auction?"

She shook her head. "No. I got them from Winnie Wentworth."

"Who?"

Deborah laughed. "The village eccentric. A combination bag lady/antiques picker. I'm surprised you haven't met her. She sells to all the shop owners."

Tricia inspected one of the goblets. "Is the quality of her merchandise always this good?"

"Gosh, no. She sells mostly junk—but occasionally she comes up with a few prizes. I learned to inspect most items pretty thoroughly for chips, nicks, and repairs before I part with any money."

Tricia set the glass back down on the counter. "I'm sure you've heard the gossip going around town. Doris had an appointment with Bob Kelly, but no one wants to look at him as a possible suspect. You've been here longer than me—what do you know about him?"

Deborah sobered. "Definitely a man who focuses on results. It's no wonder he's been single all these years. He

lives and breathes the real estate business. But he has been
good for the village."

Another testimonial for Saint Bob.

"Doris complained about her new lease," Deborah continued, "and it's made me look at my bottom line as well.
I'm already trying to budget for a substantial increase when
it comes time for me to renew."

"Can you afford it?"

"It'll be a stretch, but the village—and Bob in
particular—gambled on me and all the other booksellers
when we first came aboard. Most of us have done okay.
And it may be that Bob was tired of dealing with Doris's
complaints. He may have simply demanded a higher price
to get rid of her. I don't know, and anyway it's moot. Doris
is history. Now he can rent the place to anyone he pleases."

Tricia's thoughts exactly.

The door opened and a couple of women entered the
store. "Can I help you?" Deborah asked cheerfully, abandoning the glassware.

"Thanks for the chat." Tricia clasped her leather brief-
case and Deborah gave her a quick wave as she headed for
the door.

Tricia's next stop was the Coffee Bean, a heavenly shop
that sold exotic blends and decadent chocolates, where she
bought a five-pound bag of fresh-ground Colombian coffee. Too many customers clogged the shop for her to en-
gage the owner in idle gossip, and she'd intended to head
straight back for her own store, but a new enterprise on the
block caught her attention. She made one more diversion.

A red-white-and-blue poster, with patriotic stars across
the top, heralded Mike Harris's selectman campaign office.
Tucked between two shops—Stoneham's Stoneware and
History Repeats Itself—it had to be the most narrow storefront on Main Street. No wonder it had remained empty
since Tricia's arrival. It really was too small for a retail establishment.

Tricia opened the door and entered the crowded room.
Boxes and cartons stacked along the north wall awaited

unpacking. Two desks and assorted chairs seemed to be in place, but none of the usual office accouterments yet occupied them. A fake ficus stood in the corner, looking decidedly forlorn.

Footsteps sounded from a back room.

"Hello!" Tricia called.

Mike Harris stepped into the main room. Dressed in jeans and sneakers, shirtsleeves rolled up to his elbows, he looked ready to tackle the towering boxes.

"Looks like we're neighbors," Tricia said.

"Hey, thanks for stopping by."

Tricia glanced around at the freshly painted walls and the stacks of printed literature in one of the only opened boxes. "No offense, but I wouldn't have thought the race for selectman warranted a campaign office."

"Ordinarily I'd agree with you. The lease on my current office is about to run out and Bob Kelly offered me a great deal. Besides, I intended to open shop here in the village after the election anyway."

Tricia glanced around. "By the look of things, you haven't been here long."

Mike nodded. "I moved in last evening."

"Before all the chaos?"

He frowned. "I heard what happened to Ms. Gleason, but I didn't see anything." He shook his head. "Her death could become a campaign issue."

Tricia frowned. "How?"

"Not all our citizens are happy with the way development has been handled in Stoneham. They think the village is growing too fast and want a moratorium on new businesses until an impact study can be done." That echoed what Frannie had said about the unofficial divide between the old-timers and newcomers.

"Sounds like a waste of taxpayer funds. From what I understand, the influx of money has paid for a new a library and sewer systems—things the village sorely needed. What's so bad about that?"

Mike crossed his arms over his chest, sobering. "When

the tax base expands, so does the cost of maintaining it. That new sewer system is just one example."

He had a point, but it didn't make sense. The newcomers had taken over the crumbling Main Street while the old-timers had fled the village for the outskirts of town, presumably building new structures along the way. No wonder there was animosity between the two camps.

Still, how sad was it that Doris had been reduced to a campaign issue.

"I hope you've registered to vote."

"Yes, as a matter of fact I have."

He grabbed a brochure from the stack. "That's what we need in this town. Voters who care about Stoneham's future."

She took the paper from him; he must've forgotten he'd given her one the day before. "I'll read through it carefully. Why don't you stop by my shop for a welcome-to-the-neighborhood coffee later?"

"Sounds great. Thanks."

"See you then," she said and backed toward the door.

Mike waved. "Stop in anytime."

The line at the register was three deep when Tricia arrived back at Haven't Got a Clue. Wispy hairs had escaped the pewter clip at the base of a harassed Ginny's ponytail. "Where have you been?" she scolded Tricia under her breath. "A bus came through and these people have to be back on it in ten minutes."

"Sorry. I had no idea. I had to make a few stops after the bank." While Ginny rang up two pristine early Dick Francis first editions and an Agatha Christie omnibus, Tricia bagged the order, first checking the books for nudist leaflets before tossing in the current week's stuffers and a copy of the bookstore's newsletter. Within a couple of minutes everyone had been served and the door shut on the last customer's back.

Ginny sagged with relief and headed straight for the coffee station and a caffeine fix. She collapsed onto one of the store's comfy chairs and, still feeling guilty for leaving her alone during a rush, Tricia didn't have the heart to remind her it was against store rules for the help to sit in the customers' reading nook.

Ginny took a gulp from her steaming cup and stretched her legs out before her. "Winnie Wentworth stopped by to see you."

"Finally," Tricia said, circling around to face her employee.

"You want to meet her?" Ginny asked, puzzled.

"Deborah Black told me about her just a while ago. I wondered why she hadn't been offering me merchandise."

"Her stock isn't as good as most of our regulars. She only seems to go to tag sales to find books and other stuff to resell to the shop owners. Her car's a rolling junk mobile. She's been coming around the last couple of weeks. I've tried to discourage her, but today she was adamant; she wants to deal only with the owner—you—and said she'd be back."

"What's she trying to sell us?"

"Mostly crappy old paperbacks—things you wouldn't even put on the bargain shelf. There were too many customers in the store, and I just didn't want to deal with her."

The shop telephone rang and Tricia grabbed it. "Haven't Got a Clue, Tricia speaking."

"Trish, dear, where have you been all morning? That little helper of yours kept saying you were out of the store."

Tricia grimaced, her already haggard spirits sinking even lower. "Sorry, Ange, I was running errands."

"You sound tired. Is everything okay?"

"I got back in time for a rush of customers."

"Good, then you're flush. Let's go shopping. I hear there's an outlet mall not too far from this sleepy little village of yours."

"I can't leave the shop."

"Every time I've called, you've been away from the store. I've been running all over town myself; I'm surprised I didn't run into you." Her sarcasm came through the phone lines loud and clear.

Tricia ignored it. "Yes, well, Ginny was inundated with customers because I have been out most of the day."

"If you can't leave now, can you at least get off early?" Angelica pressed.

"No. Ange, this is *my* store. It's up to me to—"

Angelica cut her off with a loud sigh. "Have you never heard the word *delegation*?"

"Yes, and I'm also familiar with the words *responsibility* and *ownership*. Pride of ownership," she amended.

"No shopping today?" Angelica whined.

"Sorry."

"How about dinner tonight?"

Tricia's turn for the heavy sigh. "At the inn?"

"Goodness no. I'm going to cook for you. I'll come by at seven with everything I need. Have you got a bottle of red in the fridge?"

"Yes."

"Good. I've got loads to tell you. See you then."

The phone clicked in Tricia's ear. She hung up.

First Angelica showed up for an extended visit. Now she wanted to cook for her little sister. Something about this whole visit didn't feel right. Angelica was a confirmed chatterbox, yet she'd barely spoken of—nor seemed unduly upset about—her impending divorce, merely saying she and Drew would remain good friends. Still, it was unlike Angie to be so *nice* to Tricia. Something was definitely up, and Tricia was afraid to find out just what Angelica might be plotting.

Winnie Wentworth had her own car, so she didn't actually qualify as a "bag lady." Then again, from the looks of the contents of the backseat of her bashed and battered 1993 Cadillac Seville, maybe she did live in her car.

Winnie raked a grubby hand through the wiry mass of gray hair on top of her head. Her threadbare clothes were gray, too, either from repeated washings or from not being washed at all. She watched, eagle-eyed, as Tricia sorted through the offerings in her trunk. Book club editions, creased and well-thumbed paperbacks, all good—mostly contemporary—authors, but not the kind of stock Tricia wanted to carry at Haven't Got a Clue.

Desperate to find something of worth, Tricia pawed through the books a second time. "I understand you sell to all the local bookshop owners. Did you ever sell to Doris Gleason?"

Winnie pulled back a soiled scrap of old blanket from around another stack of books. Six copies of different Betty Crocker cookbooks peeked out. "She was my best customer. Now what am I going to do with all these stupid books? Nobody else in this town will touch 'em." Eyes narrowed, she scrutinized Tricia's face. "And you don't want any of my books, either, do you?"

Tricia hesitated for a moment. "Did you see the Amelia Simmons cookbook Doris had in her special little case?"

"See it? I sold it to her. She gave me five bucks for it."

"Did you know it was worth much more?"

"Everything I sell is usually worth more than what I can get for it. But I don't have the overhead you people do." She nodded at Tricia. "I don't wear no froufrou clothes. I don't got no fancy house. Maybe she coulda given me more, but then I was only gonna ask a couple a bucks for it anyway. Most people didn't like Doris, but she was always fair to me."

Perhaps Doris would be mourned after all.

"Do you remember where you bought the book?"

Winnie shook her head. "I don't remember where I get stuff, let alone who I get it from. I buy from tag sales, estate sales, and auctions." She leaned forward, squinting at Tricia, who got a whiff of the woman's unwashed body. "But mark my words—whoever I got it from musta seen it in her shop. Outside of the fancy shops, ain't many books like that in and around Stoneham."

Did Winnie realize the implications of what she'd just said? "Doris was murdered by someone who wanted that book. I think you should be careful. That person may think you can implicate him or her in Doris's death."

Winnie waved a hand in annoyance. "Nah. Everybody around here knows I got a mind like a sieve. I ain't worried. Now are you gonna take any of these books or not?"

Tricia selected three and paid Winnie five dollars in cash.

"Don'tcha wanna see what else I got?" Winnie folded back another end of the blanket. A small white box contained a tangle of costume jewelry: bright rhinestones of every color of the rainbow adorned brooches, clip and screw-back earrings, and necklaces. Other metals glinted dully under the trunk's wan lightbulb. Tricia picked through the offerings. She loved the colorful brooches in the shapes of flowers, butterflies, and snowflakes, but they were out of date, not something she could really wear herself. But one little gold pin drew her attention.

"That there's a scatter pin, and an oldie," Winnie said with pride.

Tricia examined it closely. About an inch long and maybe three-quarters of an inch wide, it was made of gold—solid gold—with an old-fashioned clasp. Its face was etched with delightful leaves and curlicues. A faded memory stirred in Tricia's mind. "My grandmother had a pin like this."

"It'd look real nice on a jacket or a hat," Winnie said, smelling a sale.

Tricia held the little pin in her hand, rubbing her thumb in circles against its surface. Grandmother Miles had worn her scatter pin on the collar of a snowy white blouse. As a little girl Tricia had sat on her grandmother's lap, playing with the pin while Grandmother would read to her. Whatever happened to that plain little adornment?

"You can have it for five bucks," Winnie offered.

Tricia's gaze rose from the pin to the old woman before her. Winnie's wispy hair was rustled by the breeze, her eyes red-rimmed but bright at the prospect of another sale.

Tricia gave her ten.

Back inside the shop, Tricia tossed the paperbacks into the trash barrel and headed for the sales counter and a group of waiting customers. She opened the cash drawer and deposited the scatter pin in the left-hand, empty change hole before ringing up the next sale.

Winnie was foolish if she thought her poor memory would keep her safe from whoever had killed Doris Gleason. It might be something Tricia should report to Sheriff Adams.

And she did.

But her warning came too late to save Winnie.

FOUR

Sheriff Adams squinted down at Tricia, her piercing gaze sharper than a stiletto. "Two people have died in the last twenty-four hours after speaking with you, Ms. Miles. Why do you think that is?"

Tricia exhaled a slow breath through her nose, surprised steam wasn't escaping from her ears. "I talked to a Deputy Morrison in your office only minutes after speaking to Winnie, warning that she could be in danger from the same person who killed Doris Gleason."

The sheriff consulted her notebook. "That was at eleven-oh-three this morning. And have you left the premises since that time?"

"No, she hasn't," Ginny answered curtly.

A flush of gratitude warmed Tricia. Ginny just earned herself a twenty-five-cent-an-hour raise.

Sheriff Adams frowned. "Odd all the same."

"How did Winnie die?" Tricia asked.

"Car accident. She hit a bridge abutment and wasn't wearing a seat belt. No skid marks. I'm having the car's brakes checked."

"You think they were tampered with?"

"It's possible."

"Well, Tricia certainly didn't cut the lines," Ginny said hotly. "Look, there's not even a pill on her sweater, let alone a speck of dirt or grease."

Tricia fought the urge to show Sheriff Adams her grease-free fingernails.

This is ridiculous, she thought. *I am not responsible for anyone's death.* Yet the heat of Sheriff Adams's scrutiny had caused sweat to form at the back of her neck.

"Will there be an autopsy?" Tricia asked.

"To rule out drug and alcohol use. It's also possible she had a heart attack—or simply blacked out while behind the wheel. Who knows if she even ate regularly?"

"Then why come here and practically accuse Tricia of murder?" Ginny demanded.

Tricia laid a hand on her assistant's arm. "Now, Ginny, I'm sure Sheriff Adams is only doing her job." *Which should include clearing me!* "Are there any leads in Doris's murder?"

"Not so far." Sheriff Adams slapped her notebook closed. "I'll be in touch."

Tricia and Ginny, along with the six customers who'd been eavesdropping on the conversation, watched as the sheriff got into her double-parked cruiser and took off.

"The music has stopped," Tricia told Ginny, trying not to focus on all those pairs of eyes. "Let's put on something cheerful. Maybe Celtic?"

"You got it." Ginny crossed the room for the CD player and the customers went back to perusing the shelves.

Miss Marple jumped up on the sales counter, rubbed her little warm face against Tricia's hand. "Good girl," she murmured, and yet even the comfort of petting her cat couldn't ease the knot of apprehension that had settled in Tricia's stomach. Two deaths less than twenty-four hours apart and both connected to that antique cookbook. Had the sheriff started looking for it on online auction sites or had she or one of her deputies called Sotheby's? Would the killer be dumb enough to try to sell it or would he or she now dump the book to avoid drawing attention to themselves? Perhaps a third party would be enlisted to sell it in a year or two.

Tricia's gaze was drawn to the clock on the wall. Twenty minutes until closing, and then Angie would show up to cook her dinner—and no doubt spoil what was left of her day.

With one last scratch behind the ears, Tricia left Miss Marple to begin her end-of-day tasks.

Main Street was bathed in shadows as the last of the customers departed, with Mr. Everett bringing up the rear. "Good. All gone," Ginny said, turning the sign to CLOSED and throwing the dead bolt. She diverted on her way to the register to close the blinds over the shop's window. "Another good day."

"That depends on your point of view," Tricia said, thinking about Winnie, although she knew Ginny meant the cash drawer stuffed with bills, checks, and credit card receipts.

Ginny stopped before the counter and fished in her apron pocket.

"Don't tell me—" Tricia said, dreading what she knew she was about to see.

"Yep. I found a lot more. And I've got a theory," she said, slapping ten or more of the nudist leaflets on the sales counter. "Somebody's been hiding these things in a lot of books. Pretty much everybody who comes in here is a stranger, except for—"

"Mr. Everett?" Tricia said, aghast. She shook her head. "No, I won't believe that sweet old man—"

"Runs around in the buff?" Ginny finished. She thought about it and shuddered. "Have you got any ideas?"

"No," Tricia admitted. "I wonder if we're the only business being targeted."

"We'll have to make some calls tomorrow to find out. If we have time." Ginny hit the release button on the cash drawer, which popped open. "Look at all that wonderful money!" She grinned.

Tricia took out the day's receipts, counted them, and placed them in the little blue zippered bank pouch. By then Ginny had retrieved her jacket, said a cheery good-bye, and departed. Tricia locked the money in the safe; that left only the nudist leaflets on the counter.

She tried to imagine prim and proper Mr. Everett in his birthday suit and, thankfully, failed.

She trashed the leaflets.

The clock ticked. Miss Marple had parked herself at the door leading to the back stairs and the loft apartment and cried, impatient for her dinner. "I'm hungry, too, but we have to wait for Angie."

Miss Marple turned her back on Tricia, licked the pads on one of her white boots.

The street lamps glowed and most of the parked cars had disappeared when the sound of an engine drew Tricia to draw back the shade on the front window to see Angie's rental car pull up in front of the store. She got out, waved a hello, and opened the car's rear door, crouching down for something. Tricia headed for the shop's door to intercept.

"Here, take this," Angelica said, handing Tricia a large, heavy Crock-Pot along with funky chili pepper potholders. Tricia set it on the sales counter, heading back to the door to hold it open for Angelica, who juggled her large purse and a big brown grocery bag, with a crusty loaf of Italian bread poking over its rim.

"How much food did you bring?"

"You can freeze the leftovers. Besides, you're much too thin. I'll bet you haven't had a decent meal in months. Now lead me to the kitchen, and then you can tell me how it is you became Stoneham's jinx of death."

Miss Marple sat before her now-empty food bowl, daintily washing her face. After a brief tour of the loft apartment, with its soaring ceiling and contemporary décor, which Angelica had declared gorgeous, she'd commandeered the kitchen, demanding various utensils that had gathered dust from months of disuse. The pasta water was already bubbling on the stove when Tricia located her corkscrew and opened the wine. She poured, handing a glass to Angelica.

"Just who in town thinks I'm a jinx, and how are you privy to that kind of gossip? You've only been in town one day."

Angelica shrugged theatrically. "It's my face. People feel they can unburden themselves to me."

Tricia frowned. She'd never felt so inclined.

"You know, I never saw the appeal of small-town life," Angelica began and took a sip of her wine. "But everyone's just so friendly and they *love* to talk."

"About me, apparently." Tricia said, growing impatient.

Angelica waved a hand in dismissal, put down her glass, and stirred the sauce once more. "It's just an odd co-incidence. I'm sure the sheriff's department will take care of everything within a few days and someone else will be the object of everyone's curiosity." She tasted the sauce. "Mmm. Maybe it could use a little more oregano." She started opening cupboards.

"The one by the sink," Tricia said. "And just what is it everyone's saying?"

Angelica squinted at the row of jars. "I told you. That you're a jinx. Don't be surprised if the locals cross the street as you approach. Set the table, will you? The pasta is almost al dente."

Tricia dutifully gathered place mats, plates, and cutlery. "Who did you meet? How did you meet them?"

Angelica sprinkled on the herb and stirred it in. "I took a walk around your new little hometown. It's very cute. I can see why you love it here. Let's see, I spoke to most of the other booksellers, or at least their sales staff. Do you realize there isn't one shoe store in this entire town?" She slapped her forehead. "Like I need to tell you. Look at your feet."

Tricia glanced down at her thick-soled loafers. "What's wrong with my shoes?"

"Honey, between them and those sweater sets, you are

in dire need of a fashion intervention. I have not arrived a minute too soon."

"I have to stand for ten hours a day. I need comfortable shoes."

"If you say so. I also noticed that besides the Brookville Inn, there isn't one decent restaurant in Stoneham."

"We've got the Bookshelf Diner."

"As I said, there isn't one decent restaurant," Angelica deadpanned. "Where do regular people go for food that isn't dripping in grease?"

"I eat in a lot."

"Good thing, too. It's a lot healthier." She stirred the pasta. "Now, do you want to hear the results of Doris Gleason's autopsy, or are you squeamish?"

"Give me a break, Ange. I've been reading mysteries and thrillers since I was in grade school."

Angelica snagged her glass and drank. "As expected, the knife wound was fatal—sliced up something terribly vital. She died almost instantaneously, that's why there wasn't much blood."

Hardly a gory account. "Tell me something I didn't know."

Angelica sobered. "The poor woman had pancreatic cancer, which she either didn't know about or had chosen not to have treated. Without immediate treatment, it's likely she would've died within months."

Doris couldn't have known, otherwise she wouldn't have been worried about renegotiating her lease. "That poor soul."

Angelica frowned. "I suppose that depends on your point of view. A quick death with little fear or pain, or lingering in agony: I'll take the former any day."

Tricia reached for linen napkins from a drawer. "How did you find out about Doris's autopsy?"

Angelica went back to work on the salad as she spoke. "Didn't I tell you? Bess, the Brookview Inn's receptionist, has a cousin who works for the county health department, who has a direct pipeline to the medical examiner's office.

Isn't it amazing how already I've met the most eclectic assortment of people here in Stoneham? Not many of them seem to know you."

"That's because nearly all my customers are from out of town."

"And I'm sure the fact that—except for today, apparently—you rarely leave the store also has a lot to do with it." She paused in slicing a tomato and looked over at her sister. "I'm worried about you, Trish. You need to have a life outside your bookstore."

"I'm doing just fine."

"Have you made any friends?" Angelica asked, abandoning her knife to add spices to a little bowl of olive oil.

"Of course I have," she said, thinking of her conversation earlier in the day with Deborah.

"All booksellers, no doubt. They probably work themselves to death, too, with no real social outlets. Then again, you were right; aside from reading, there isn't much else to do in this burg."

"It's the main draw. How I and all the other booksellers make our living. And in a world with so many other distractions, it's getting harder and harder to find new readers."

Angelica shook her head sadly. "How typical you'd choose a dying trade."

Tricia ignored the jab. "Have you spoken to any of the locals about Bob Kelly?"

"Of course. He's a fascinating man and I want to know all about him. Although I've noticed people either seem to love him or hate him."

"And you're choosing to love him?" Tricia asked.

"Don't be silly. I only met the man last night. But it seems something's going on in town."

"Oh?" Tricia thought back to Frannie, who hadn't wanted to let on what she thought about Bob's meeting the night before.

"There's talk of a big box store wanting to open up right on the edge of town."

"And just who's saying this?"

"People." She didn't elaborate. "It's a hot topic, and I wouldn't want to get in between someone who's for and another who's against the idea. You could lose your life. Some of the locals don't like all these tourists in town and don't want to encourage any more change. If a big store came in, they might have to actually add a traffic light on Main Street." She rolled her eyes.

"Is Bob negotiating for the village?"

Angelica checked the wine level in her glass, then topped it up. "He's apparently exploring the idea, although I don't know if he's doing it for himself or the Board of Selectmen."

"Who told you all this?"

Angelica's smile was sly. "I told you, I'm sworn to secrecy."

Tricia frowned, growing grumpier by the moment. "That pasta will be gummy if you don't serve it soon."

"Oh, right." Angelica switched off the burner and drained the penne. She placed the salad bowl, sliced bread, and dipping sauce on the table and within another minute had heaped their plates with pasta, ladling the sauce on thick. Tricia had to admit it smelled divine. Angelica took her seat across from Tricia, sighed, and smiled. "Isn't it great to be back in each other's lives again?"

Tricia's fork stopped inches from her mouth, cold dread encircling her heart. "How long were you planning on visiting?"

"Oh, didn't I tell you? I've decided to move to New Hampshire."

FIVE

Tricia nearly choked on her wine. "You what?"

Angelica picked up her napkin, smoothed out the folds, and placed it on her lap. "I don't like the idea of you living up here all on your own. Murders happening right next to your place of business." She shook her head. "Mother and Daddy would be heartsick if they thought I'd abandon you in such a violent community. I feel it's my duty to stay here with you at least throughout the crisis."

Tricia sat back in her chair. "There is no crisis. This is the first murder in Stoneham in over sixty years. It's not likely to happen again."

"What about that poor woman who crashed her car?"

"You heard about that, too?"

"I told you, people here like to talk."

"Well, there's no proof she was murdered. I'll bet she didn't maintain that old rust bucket she drove."

Angelica picked up her fork, speared a chunk of tomato. "Surely that's what yearly car inspections prevent."

"Let's get back on topic, which is you moving to Stoneham. There's nothing for you to do here. There's no shopping, no art galleries, no museums, no gourmet restaurants—and as you pointed out, no shoe stores."

Angelica toyed with a piece of pasta. "Perhaps it's my destiny to bring culture and a sense of style to this little backwater."

"Stoneham is my home. Don't call it a backwater. It has history and charm and it doesn't need outsiders coming in with an agenda to change it."

"Au contraire. You yourself are an outsider. Bob Kelly told me the majority of booksellers were all recruited from out of state to come here. And you just said yourself that most of your customers are out of towners."

"Yes, but—"

"Most of the villagers don't mind you little guys opening shop, but they don't want malls and big box stores moving in and changing the area's character, not to mention all the people from Boston crossing the state line just because it's cheaper to live here."

"Tell me something I don't know."

"Change happens, Tricia," she said, pointedly. "Whether some people want it or not."

Tricia's temper flared. "You do not need to live here in Stoneham."

Angelica swirled the wine in her glass. "And I may not stay long. Just long enough to see you through this ordeal." And then she did something that totally startled Tricia; she laid one of her hands on Tricia's. "I may not have been the best big sister in the past, but I intend to make up for that now."

Flabbergasted, Tricia could only sit there with her mouth open. Then she shut it. Angelica had never before displayed even a hint of altruism. Something else was behind her visit, and her newfound sisterly love.

How long would it be before she revealed her true intent?

Being labeled the village jinx didn't seem to have an impact on customers at Haven't Got a Clue. A busload of bibliomaniacs on a day trip from Boston had unloaded an hour earlier, and business had been brisk. It was easy to tell the townsfolk from the transients. The villagers paused at the shop's windows, faces peering in to see the jinx on display like at a zoo, judgment in their eyes. Tricia braved a smile for each of them, but the faces turned away.

Tricia rang up a three-hundred-dollar sale for a British first edition of Agatha Christie's *Why Didn't They Ask Evans?* and carefully wrapped the book in acid-free tissue before placing it in one of the store's elegant, custom-printed, foil-stamped shopping bags. No plastic for an order of this magnitude.

"Please sign our guest book," she suggested as she handed over the purchase to a dapper old gent.

"I will, thank you."

The phone rang and Ginny stepped up to the counter, taking the next customer. Tricia answered on the second ring. "Haven't Got a Clue, this is Tricia speaking, how can I help you?"

"Hi, Tricia, it's Mike Harris." Aha—one friendly voice remained among the locals. "Scuttlebutt about town is that you've developed into the village jinx. How's it feel to be raked over the coals?" Then again . . .

Tricia sidled over to the front window, looked across the street to Mike's campaign office. "I'm feeling the heat but so far haven't been burned."

"How'd you like to escape the pressure cooker for an hour or two? I know a little bistro up on the highway that serves a mean lobster bisque, and their sourdough bread is the stuff of legends."

"Right now that sounds heavenly."

"Fine. I'll pick you up at eleven thirty."

"I'll be here." Tricia hung up the phone and turned to find Ginny at her elbow.

"A date?"

"It's not a date."

"That'll be thirty-seven fifty," Ginny told the elderly male customer. "Then what do you call lunch with a handsome man?"

"An escape. Can I help you find something?" Tricia asked a matronly woman in a denim jumper.

Six sales and fourteen more nudist tracts later, Tricia glanced at the shop's clock. The Care Free tour bus had picked up its passengers and there was sure to be a lull in foot traffic, assuring Tricia she needn't feel guilty for leaving Ginny alone in the shop.

At precisely eleven thirty a sleek black Jaguar pulled up in front of Haven't Got a Clue, its powerful engine revving. Ginny gawked and inhaled deeply. "Ooh! I smell money."

"Behave," Tricia scolded and grabbed her purse. "I'll try to be back within—"

"Take your time. I'll be fine here," Ginny said. "But you'll have to report on everything the two of you talk about."

"No promises," Tricia said, suppressing a smile as she headed for the door. Then on impulse, she stopped, went back to the counter, and fished one of the nudist leaflets from the trash, stuffing it in her handbag. "See you later," she told Ginny as the door closed behind her.

In celebration of the beautiful early autumn day, the Jag's windows were wide open, and Tricia bent down to see Mike's smiling face. "Hop in."

Tricia opened the door and slid onto the cool, black leather seat. "What a beautiful car. The insurance business must be booming."

"Not bad if I say so myself."

Tricia pulled shut the door and buckled her seat belt as Mike eased the car back into traffic. Her gaze momentarily lighted on the Cookery, the yellow crime tape still attached to the door frame reminding her of Doris Gleason's murder. She shook the thought away and concentrated on the Jag's dashboard, with its GPS screen and rows of buttons and switches. It reminded her of the cockpit of a jumbo jet. She wiggled her shoulders deeper into the leather, remembering she had once been used to this kind of luxury in the early days of her marriage to Christopher. She glanced across the seat, caught Mike's eye. He looked fabulous in a gray pin-striped suit, crisp white shirt, and a pale yellow silk tie—and nothing like her ex. "You're dressed to the nines. For my benefit?"

"I'd love to say yes, but I've got a speaking engagement later this afternoon. There's always next time." Again he flashed those perfect white teeth.

Next time. That sounded nice. Maybe Angelica had been right. In pursuing her goals to get the bookstore up and running Tricia had neglected to factor in time to build a social life.

"Is this little restaurant in Milford?"

"Just east of there. It's only twenty minutes down the road. Don't worry, I'll have you back to your store before the Red Hat Society bus comes in."

Tricia stifled a laugh. "Do you have all the tourist bus schedules memorized?"

"I'm making an effort. Stoneham's economy has rebounded thanks to tourism. I want the business owners to know how much I appreciate their efforts to keep the village in the black."

"Happy potential constituents mean a landslide victory?"

"Something like that."

"Forgive me, but I thought the village voted for these kinds of things in the winter—not on traditional election day."

"That's right. This is a special election at the next town meeting to fill the spot left by Sam Franklin, who had a heart attack and died a few weeks back. My opponent and I are pretty much evenly matched."

Tricia couldn't remember seeing any other literature for the selectman campaign, realizing she didn't even know the other candidate's name.

"What made you decide to run?"

"Too many former Stoneham selectmen have been outsiders who came to the area after retiring. They fought against the idea of tourism, wanting Stoneham to remain a quaint little—dead—village. They were also lawyers," he said with contempt. "They didn't have a clue how to bring life back to the village. It was people like Bob Kelly who turned Stoneham around. The board begged him to take the job of village administrator, but he said he couldn't afford to take the pay cut."

"Oh?"

"It's only a part-time job, but Bob felt it would take away from running his real estate empire. Besides, he wields his own power as president of the chamber of commerce."

"Yes, he does seem to, doesn't he?"

"We could use a couple more Bob Kellys in Stoneham. I intend to follow his lead in a number of areas. We need to boost the tourist trade by offering more than just the lure of used books. We need more restaurants; maybe attract some kind of light industry."

"And do you insure buildings suited for light industry?"

Mike flashed his pearly whites. "How did you guess?"

"Is there anything in the works?" she asked, thinking about the rumors of a big box store coming to town.

He kept his eyes on the road. "There might be, and that's all I'm at liberty to say about it."

"You're a tease."

"And you're beautiful."

That wasn't true . . . but she liked hearing it anyway.

She cast around for something else to talk about. "I've noticed the locals don't seem too interested in supporting the booksellers. Why do you think that is?"

He shrugged, his gaze fixed on the road ahead. "You don't sell what they need."

"Which is?"

"That's something I need to learn," he admitted. "Rare and antiquarian books and expensive baubles—those are for collectors and people who don't know what to do with their money."

Hurt and irritation suddenly welled within Tricia. "Is that how you feel about us?"

Mike momentarily tore his gaze from the road. "Of

course not. But that's what a lot of the villagers think. Surely you've at least considered that."

"Yes," she grudgingly admitted.

The Jaguar slowed and Mike pulled into the parking lot of a little ramshackle building, its white paint peeling, the bands of color on the lobster buoys decorating it bleached to pastel hues. A hand-painted sign with red lettering proclaimed ED'S.

"Oh," Tricia said, trying—and failing—to hold her disappointment in check. "It's a clam shack."

"Don't let the outside fool you. They serve the best chowders and bisques on the eastern seaboard."

Except that they were at least fifty miles from the ocean. Tricia painted on a brave smile. "And I can't wait to try it."

The décor inside Ed's consisted of nets studded with lobster buoys, lobster traps—complete with plastic lobsters—starfish, and shells. Picnic tables were covered in plastic tablecloths with lighthouse motifs, and each had bottles of ketchup, vinegar, salt and pepper shakers, as well as bolts of paper towels on upright wooden holders.

"Nothing too fancy," Mike conceded. "But you won't be disappointed. Sit down while I go order."

Tricia nodded, her smile still fixed.

She chose a table near the rear of the tented patio. Attached to the wall was a large gray hood with a heater inside, presumably used to keep the makeshift dining room habitable during the colder months. Several other couples munched on fried clams and fries served on baker's tissue set in red plastic baskets, washing it down with cans of soft drinks or bottles of beer.

Settling at the table, Tricia ran her fingers across the tablecloth, thankful to find it wasn't sticky. Still, she tore off four sheets of paper toweling, fashioning two crude place mats.

Mike returned with napkins and plastic cutlery. "It'll only be a few minutes." He settled on the bench across from her and tied a lobster bib around his neck, settling it over his suit coat. "Don't want to spill soup on my tie. Have to look presentable for my speech this afternoon."

"What are you talking about? Who are you speaking to?"

"A group of seniors at the center on Maple Street. Thanks to my mother's difficulties, I have a unique perspective on the kinds of problems they have, what with the cost of medicine, health care, and the realities of living on a fixed income."

"You mentioned your mother's difficulties," she began, interested, but not wanting to appear too nosy.

"I probably wouldn't have returned to Stoneham last year if it weren't for Mother. Alzheimer's," he explained succinctly.

Something inside Tricia's chest constricted.

"At first she seemed safe enough to leave on her own, but her mind has really deteriorated in the past year," Mike continued. "I had her moved into an assisted living facility almost six months ago. The next step is probably to a locked ward in a nursing home."

"I'm so sorry." Head bent, Tricia looked unseeing at the table in front of her. Mike's words had triggered a plethora of unhappy memories for her. She'd watched her former father-in-law go from a funny, loving man to a sometimes violent, empty-eyed soul. It had torn Christopher's immediate family apart, putting a strain on her own marriage. A strain that contributed to shattering it.

"Let's talk about something more pleasant," Mike suggested. "Like books. They're your specialty. I've slowly been cleaning out mother's house, and I don't have a clue about what to do with her lifelong collection of books."

Though not a true change of subject, it was something Tricia was much more interested in discussing. "What kinds of books did she have?"

"A little bit of everything. Strike that: a *lot* of everything. Mother was on the village board when Bob Kelly came up with the idea of bringing in all the used booksellers. I'm sure she was one of the booksellers' best customers."

"Can she still read?"

Mike shook his head, grabbed the pepper shaker, and set it in front of his place.

How sad to lose the thing that means the most to you, Tricia thought. Of course her scattered family was important to her—she even grudgingly loved Angelica, and couldn't forget dainty little Miss Marple—but to be deprived of her favorite pastime would be akin to stealing a portion of her soul.

"Would you like me to have a look at the collection?"

Mike tore his gaze from the paper towel place mat he'd been playing with. "Would you? I'd like to see every one of them go to a good home, but that just isn't practical. I've already called libraries within a hundred-mile radius; they aren't interested. Booksellers are my last hope before I resort to a Dumpster."

"Never say that word to a bookaholic," Tricia warned. "And yes, I'd love to have a look. But it'll have to be on a Sunday. That's the only day my shop has limited hours. What's best for you, morning or evening?"

"Morning. Campaigning has eaten a lot more of my time than I'd planned. I'm afraid I'm falling behind in my work with deadlines looming."

"How does nine o'clock this Sunday sound?"

"Perfect. I'll give you the address later."

A portly, fiftysomething man with a white plastic apron over a stained white T-shirt and a paper butcher's cap covering his balding head approached the table and plopped down a couple of bottles: a Squamscot black cherry soda and a straw for her, and a bottle of Geary's pale ale for Mike. Retrieving a church key from a chain on his belt, he opened Mike's beer. "Be right back with your soup," he grunted.

"Ed?" Tricia guessed.

Mike laughed. "You got it. He's a client of mine. Saved him a lot of money when I took over his insurance accounts. Let me know if you'd like me to take a look at your contracts. I'll bet I could offer you lower rates, too."

Always the salesman, she thought. "I'll consider it."

Mike took a swig of his beer and smacked his lips. "Great stuff."

Tricia wrestled with the cap on her bottle, before giving it up for Mike to open. Uncovering the straw, she popped it into the bottle and took a sip. "Oh, this is nice." She examined the label. "Ah, a local product."

Mike held up his beer in salute. "I think I've patronized every microbrewery in New Hampshire, Massachusetts, and Maine."

"A real pub crawler, eh?"

Mike dazzled her with another of his smiles. "In my youth. Those wild and carefree days are behind me now."

"But you never settled down."

"With a family? Not yet, but there's still time," he said and winked.

Tricia sipped her soda. A couple rose from a nearby table and walked in front of them to deposit their trash in a bin. The man's pants were slung low around his hips, exposing the top of his rear end and reminding her of the nudist tract in her purse. She'd meant to call other shop owners this morning but hadn't had time. She opened her purse and removed the leaflet. "Have you seen any of these around town?"

Mike took the paper and squinted at the text. Then he laughed. "This is a joke, right?"

"I'm afraid not. I've been pulling them out of books for the last couple of days."

He turned it over and frowned. "My guess is this is the first in a series."

"What do you mean?"

"It's just a basic message to get an idea across. The next in the series will give more information. It's been done hundreds of times. The U.S. and British troops dropped thousands of pounds—probably tons—of leaflets on the enemy back in World War Two. It's still done today in war-torn countries."

"How do you know so much?" she asked, then remembered their conversation the first day they met. "Didn't you say you were a World War Two buff?"

"Yeah. I've even got a few examples of propaganda

leaflets that I bought off the Internet. It's a fascinating subject. They tried dropping them by hand—only to be sucked into the plane's air intake—and in bombs that exploded at a predetermined height above the ground. The Brits were famous—and very successful at reaching their targets—by sending them up in balloons."

"You sound like an expert."

He shrugged. "It's just a hobby."

Ed returned with a tray laden with steaming bowls and a basket of chunky bread, which he placed before them. "Eat hearty."

Tricia picked up her plastic spoon and stirred the thick soup, turning up large pieces of lobster, potatoes, and onions. "Smells wonderful."

Mike grinned. "Dig in. I guarantee you'll feel like you've died and gone to heaven."

SIX

The Jag pulled smoothly to the curb on the west side of Main Street, and Tricia got out. "See you soon," Mike called and pulled away, heading south. Tricia didn't even have a chance to look for oncoming traffic before her gaze was drawn to the front of the Cookery. The yellow crime scene tape that had been there less than two hours ago was gone. A huge kelly green poster, decorated with shamrocks and screaming FOR LEASE— KELLY REALTY and a phone number, took up several square feet of the front window. The door was wedged open, and the scene of Doris Gleason's death less than forty-eight hours before was now a hive of activity. Double-parked nearby was a Becker's Moving van. Two guys in buff-colored coveralls emerged from the store, carrying boxes and loading them into the van.

Tricia hurried across the street. "What are you doing?" she asked. "You can't take those books. Who said you could—?"

"Don't talk to me, lady. Talk to him." The mover jerked a thumb over this shoulder just as Bob Kelly emerged from the inside of the store. His nose and mouth were covered with a dust mask, and he held a clipboard in his left hand, making notes with his right.

Tricia marched up to him. "What's going on?"

Bob looked up, pulling his mask down below his chin. "I'm clearing out my property. I need to get it professionally cleaned and painted if I'm going to rent it out in the next couple of weeks."

"Doris hasn't even been buried yet and already you're emptying her store? What kind of an unfeeling monster are you?"

Bob's glare was arctic cold. "I am a businessman. This is my property. The terms of the lease were immediately negated at the time of Doris Gleason's death."

"What are you going to do with all her stock?"

"Put it in storage. I've rented a garage over at the self-storage center on Bailey Avenue. I'll bill the cost to her estate."

"But it's not right!" she cried. "If the rent was paid till the end of the month—"

Bob's gaze, and his voice, softened. "You're getting all emotional over nothing, Trish. Doris is gone. What she left behind has no meaning for her now. The sheriff gave me the okay to enter the premises and I'm well within my rights to take care of my property in any way I see fit."

She had no doubt of that. It was just such a cold-blooded move—and typical of the man. "Those books are smoke damaged, but they're still salvageable if they're taken care of properly."

"That's not my concern."

"Well, it ought to be. You're cheating Doris's heirs out of what's rightfully theirs."

"The sheriff has been unable to locate any heirs. And besides, I'm not taking anything away from the heirs. Just relocating it. According to the terms of the lease—"

"Oh, give it a rest, Bob." Fists clenched, Tricia turned on her heel and stalked into her own shop. Ginny was in the midst of making a fresh pot of complimentary coffee for their patrons, while Miss Marple dozed on the sales counter. The sight of such normalcy instantly lowered Tricia's anxiety quotient by half. That still left the other half to bubble over.

Tricia stowed her purse under the counter. "Did you see what's going on next door?"

"How could I miss it?" Ginny said. "The truck pulled up only a minute after you left for lunch. I guess that means the police have finished their investigation, otherwise Bob Kelly wouldn't be allowed inside."

"I've read a lot of true crime and police procedurals and I've never heard of a law enforcement agency abandoning a crime scene so quickly," Tricia said.

"Wendy Adams will figure it out. She's supposed to be good at her job," Ginny offered.

"Maybe, but she's never had to solve a murder before."

"But as she also pointed out, it's an election year. That'll give her plenty of incentive."

Tricia nodded thoughtfully.

The phone rang. Tricia grabbed it. "Haven't Got a Clue, Tricia speaking. How can I help you?"

"Trish? It's Deb Black. I wanted to let you know a deputy's been canvassing Main Street, asking questions of all the shop owners."

"Let me guess: asking questions about me."

"More like planting suspicions." She sounded worried.

Tricia swallowed. "Thanks for the heads-up." She remembered the nudist tracts. "Deb, have you had a problem with leaflets about—"

"Nudists!" she cried. "Yes, and it's really, really tacky. I offer quality merchandise and these horrid little pieces of paper are just plain vulgar. I called the sheriff, but she told me she's too busy with a murder investigation to bother with something so trivial. And besides, they're not illegal, just a nuisance."

"That's what I was afraid of."

"I've got customers. See you Tuesday night at the auction—that is if I don't have the baby before then."

"You got it. See you then." Tricia hung up.

"More bad news?" Ginny had obviously been eaves-dropping.

Tricia shrugged. Movement outside caught her eye. One of the movers placed another carton in the back of the truck and closed the hinged doors, throwing a bolt. "There goes the first load." Tricia's thoughts returned to the Cook-ery. "Bob said Sheriff Adams hadn't located any of Doris's heirs. That doesn't mean there aren't any. I'm sure the sheriff has already searched Doris's home for that kind of information . . . insurance policies . . . whatever."

Ginny nodded. "It's not much of a home, really. More like a cottage."

Tricia looked up. "You've been there?"

"A couple of times. Once when we had a celebrity au-thor come in, Doris forgot some paperwork she needed and sent me over to her house." She lowered her voice. "I know where she hid an extra key to the back door."

"And?" Tricia whispered.

"Maybe it wouldn't hurt for an interested party—someone the sheriff seems to want to pin this murder on—to go over there and have a look."

The thought repelled yet fascinated Tricia. "But that would be breaking and entering."

"Not if you've got the key," Ginny said. "You could go tonight."

"You'd have to come with me."

"Can't. Brian's taking me to Manchester for a Red Hot Chili Peppers concert—we've planned it for months. Which reminds me, I'm going to need to leave a little early tonight. Is that a problem?"

Tricia shook her head.

"You could go on your own to Doris's. You can park in the back. No one will see your car from the road. No one will ever know you were even there."

"Maybe," Tricia said.

"Think about it. In the meantime, why don't you have a

nice cup of coffee and tell me all about your lunch date."
Ginny handed Tricia a cup, just the way she liked it.

"He took me to some little clam shack that served the
best lobster bisque in the entire world."

Ginny smiled. "That would be Ed's."

Tricia laughed. "Does everyone know about this place
but me?"

"You're still relatively new here."

Tricia sipped her coffee, her thoughts returning to the
conversation she'd had with Mike. "You're a lifelong resident of Stoneham; do you know Mike Harris's mother?"

Ginny shook her head. "Not my generation. I suppose
my mom or grandmother might. If I think of it, I'll ask."
She considered Tricia's question for a moment. "Why do
you want to know?"

"Mike wants me to have a look at her book collection.
Give him some ideas on disposing of it."

Ginny frowned. "Makes it sound like the books are
nothing but garbage."

"I know. The idea seemed to bother him, too."

"What do you expect to find?"

Tricia sighed. "Nothing of particular value. Cookbooks,
book club editions of bygone best sellers . . ."

"And no doubt the dreaded *Reader's Digest* condensed
books."

Tricia shuddered. "Please—don't blaspheme in the
shop."

Ginny laughed.

A gleaming white motor coach passed by the shop on its
way to the municipal lot to disgorge the latest crowd of
book-buying tourists.

Ginny brightened. "Get ready for the ladies of the Red
Hat Society. It's showtime!"

Soon after Ginny left for the evening, the store emptied
out as well. All except for Mr. Everett, who sat in his

favorite chair in the nook, nose buried in a paperback copy of John D. MacDonald's *The Scarlet Ruse*, being careful not to crease its binding. Tricia lowered the shades, closed down the register, and counted the day's receipts, locking them in the safe before disturbing him. "Closing time," she said.

Mr. Everett looked up, glanced at the clock, which read 7:05. "I'm sorry, Ms. Miles. I was so entranced . . ." He slid a piece of paper inside the book to hold his place, and stood, about to replace it on a shelf.

"Just a moment," Tricia said and took the book from him. As she suspected, his bookmark was indeed one of the nudist tracts. "You wouldn't know anything about these, would you, Mr. Everett?"

Mr. Everett looked both embarrassed and aghast. "Certainly not. But I will admit to finding more than a dozen of them in the last day or so."

"You haven't seen who it was who put them inside the books, have you?"

"No, but I have been watching the customers in an effort to put an end to it. I'm sorry to say I haven't caught the culprit. I know everyone in the village and can't say I've seen any come in, so it must be an outsider."

"My sentiments exactly." Tricia turned for the sales counter and a little basket holding author promotional bookmarks. "We'll save your place with one of these, okay?"

Mr. Everett lowered his head, his cheeks reddening. "Thank you, Ms. Miles."

"See you tomorrow?" she asked.

"Bright and early," he promised, the hint of a smile gracing his lips.

Tricia walked him to the door, closed and locked it, spying a sheriff's cruiser slowing, its driver craning his neck to check out her shop. Her cheeks burned as she lowered the shades on the windows and commenced with the rest of her end-of-day tasks, tidying up and running the carpet sweeper across the rug. With Ginny gone early, every task seemed to take extra time, or maybe she was just dragging her feet. The idea of violating the sanctity of Doris Gleason's home bothered her. Then again, it bothered her more that the sheriff still seemed to think she was the prime suspect in the murder and might be staking out her store.

Maybe the deputy had been checking out Doris's shop, not Haven't Got a Clue. But if that was true the driver should've speeded up when he'd passed the Cookery, not slowed down.

Miss Marple patiently waited at the door to the apartment stairs. Tricia cut the lights and headed for the back of the shop when a furious knock at the door caught her attention. Miss Marple got up, rubbed eagerly against the door, and cried.

The knocking continued.

"Now what?" Tricia groused. Guided by safety lighting, she crossed the length of the shop, ready to tell whoever was at the door that she was closed. Pulling aside the shade, she saw Angelica balancing a tray on her knee, holding on to her huge purse, and about to knock again. Tricia opened the door. "Ange, what are you doing here?"

"I brought you dinner." She bustled into the shop, leaving behind the scent of her perfume. "Why is it so dark in here?"

"The store is closed. And you don't have to bring me dinner every night." She took a sniff—bread? Sausage? Heavenly!—and realized that her bisque lunch had been many hours before. "Let me take the tray. Follow me, and don't step on Miss Marple when we get to the door."

Angelica muttered something about "that damn animal," but followed. Tricia hit the light switch and the little gray cat scampered up the steps ahead of them, with Angelica complaining about the three-flight trek and the lack of an elevator.

Tricia balanced the tray and opened the apartment door, hitting the switch and flooding the kitchen with light. She set the tray down and lifted the dishcloth covering the evening's entrée. It looked like a meatloaf-shaped loaf of bread. "Stromboli?" she asked.

A breathless Angelica nodded. "And a thermos of the most amazing lobster bisque you're ever likely to eat."

Tricia stifled a laugh. "You don't say. Where did you get it? At a clam shack?"

"I made it." Angelica set down her gargantuan purse on the counter and leaned against it, still panting.

"I really appreciate you feeding me, Ange, but I don't want to make you wait until after my shop closes just to eat dinner."

"Darling, on the Continent they don't dine until nine or ten."

"And where are you cooking all this stuff, anyway?"

"At the inn. I've made friends with the executive chef, François. He's learned a few things from me, too." She turned to her suitcase-sized purse and withdrew a bottle of red wine. "Where's the corkscrew?"

"No wine for me. I'm going out later."

Angelica set the bottle down, shrugged out of her suede jacket, and hung it on the coatrack just inside the door. "Where are we going?"

"Not we, *me.* Besides, I'm not sure what I've got planned is exactly legal."

Angelica's eyes flashed. "Ooh, this sounds like fun. What've you got in mind?"

"Someone told me where to find the key to Doris Gleason's house. I'm hoping I might find something the sheriff could use in her investigation."

"And what makes you think you could do a better job than the sheriff?"

"Well, I have read thousands of mysteries."

"That's true. I'll bet you've got so much vicarious experience you could open your own investigation service."

Tricia frowned. "Sarcasm doesn't become you."

Angelica advanced on the stove, turning on the oven. "Well, just listen to yourself. Got a cookie sheet handy?"

Arms crossed over her chest, Tricia nodded toward the cabinet next to the stove. Already acquainted with some other portions of the kitchen, Angelica found aluminum foil in another cupboard, tore a sheet, and pressed it over the tray. "The stromboli should only take ten minutes to re-heat. Why don't you set the table?"

Why don't you stop ordering me around in my own kitchen? Tricia felt like shouting. Instead she gathered up plates, bowls, and spoons. Miss Marple sat beside her empty dinner bowl and complained loudly. "And you, too," Tricia hissed and picked up the dish, putting it in the sink to soak.

By the time she'd fed the cat, Angelica had popped the bread into the oven and was pouring the soup into a copper-bottomed pan to reheat as well. "Did you know there was a sheriff's car parked down the street from here? Looks like they've got you under surveillance."

The heat returned to Tricia's cheeks. "That's why I want to go to Doris's house. The sheriff still has an unnatural fixation on the idea that I might've killed her."

"Or they could just be watching her shop—maybe wait-ing for the killer to return to the scene of the crime."

"There's nothing to return to. Bob Kelly emptied the place out this afternoon."

"I heard about that."

Was there nothing the local gossip mill missed?

The yeasty aroma of bread filled the kitchen, and Tri-cia's stomach gurgled in anticipation. Angelica leaned against the counter. "You can't go out the front door with-out the deputy seeing you, so I think it best if I leave first, swing around and pick you up in the alley behind the store."

"Wait a minute, you're not going with me."

"How much investigating do you think you can pull off with a tail?"

"How do you know so much about police procedure?"

Angelica rolled her eyes. "I do have a television, you know. I've seen enough crime shows over the years to have as much investigative experience as you."

"Television? Please. The scientific blunders alone have every jury in the country believing you can pull forensic evidence out of thin air, and they expect it in minutes when the reality is that most police departments are understaffed, and most labs underfunded and overworked, and—"

"What's that got to do with us checking out Doris Gleason's house?" Angelica turned, plucked a wooden spoon from the utensil crock on the counter, and stirred the soup.

"*We* are not going to do it. *I* am. Do you realize how much trouble I'd be in if I was caught? What kind of sister would I be to put you in that same situation?"

"Then who's going to act as your lookout? You can't search the place if you're looking over your shoulder every minute."

Tricia hadn't considered that. She changed tacks. "I don't know if the house is on a well-lit street, if the neighbors would be watching. I'm not even sure I can go through with it. I just thought I'd drive out there and take a look."

"Then there's no harm in me going with you. Here, try some of the soup." Angelica held out the spoon.

Tricia tasted it, surprised at its robust flavor. She took another taste. It was even better than the bisque at Ed's— something only hours before she would have thought impossible. "Where did you learn to cook like this?"

Angelica shrugged. "Let's get back to the subject of searching Doris's house. Do you have any latex gloves? We don't want to leave a bunch of fingerprints."

"We don't need gloves. It wasn't a crime scene. I have no intension of committing a misdemeanor by breaking in if I can't find the key."

"Party pooper."

"Why are you so hyped to come along, anyway?"

Angelica smiled coyly. "Because it just might be fun."

SEVEN

Doris Gleason's little white cottage had seen happier days, as evidenced by its peeling paint, rusty metal roof, and the overgrown privet that adorned the west side of the property. As Ginny promised, a gravel driveway circled to the back of the dark house, affording the perfect cover for Angelica's rental car. She killed the lights and the yard was engulfed by the night. The engine made tinking noises as the sisters waited for their eyes to adjust to the darkness.

Angelica spoke first. "The woman didn't have a whole lot in her life, did she?"

Tricia shook her head. "I wonder if she owned the place or if it was a rental. She probably spent more time at the Cookery than here anyway."

"How long are we going to sit here?" Angelica asked.

"Give me a minute," Tricia said, looking over the darkened yard. Now that they were here, poking around the dead woman's home seemed like a bad idea—more than that, creepy. Okay, the house was isolated, its nearest neighbor at least a quarter mile in either direction. With the drapes pulled shut there was little chance they'd be seen by passing cars, but just what did Tricia hope to find? A big red sign pointing to a will or an insurance policy?

Tricia reconsidered their quest. "I think we'd better go."

"Oh, come on," Angelica urged, "where's your sense of adventure?" She reached behind her and dragged out the convenience store bag, extracting the big orange flashlight they'd stopped to buy along the way. She fished out the D batteries and filled the empty compartment, switching it on. An ice white beam of light pierced the car's darkness.

"Not in the eyes," Tricia complained, putting a hand up to shield her face.

"Sorry. Now where'd you say the extra key was hidden?"

"It's supposed to be under a fake rock by the back door."

"Right." Angelica opened her door, but Tricia's hand on her arm stopped her.

"Before we do anything else, here." She reached into her jacket pocket and pulled out a pair of latex gloves and handed them to Angelica. "I changed my mind. I decided you were right and we shouldn't leave any fingerprints behind."

"Whoa. That's a first. Me, with a good idea? Can I stand the compliment?"

"You're making me paranoid."

"Where did you get them?" Angelica asked, pulling a glove over her left hand and flexing her fingers.

"The hardware store. I bought them for a refinishing job I never got around to doing." Tricia put on her own set of gloves, got out of the car, and marched toward the darkened house. Angelica followed, their feet crunching on the gravel drive. Good thing it wasn't raining. Tricia didn't want to track in any detritus and leave any other evidence that they'd been there.

The flashlight's beam whisked back and forth around the steps. "I don't see any fake rocks. How long ago did your little helper say it was that she used it?"

Tricia went rigid. "I never said it was Ginny."

"Don't give me that look," Angelica chided. "Who else would it be? You don't talk to anybody from around here except her. I'm assuming she either once worked for Doris or moonlights as a burglar."

"Yes," Tricia reluctantly admitted, "she worked for Doris for a couple of months before she came to work for me." She explained why Ginny hadn't accompanied her on this little expedition.

Drooping perennials and overgrown grass along the back of the house made it difficult to search for the pseudorock. "Be careful," Tricia whispered. "Don't step on the flowers. If the sheriff comes out here again, we don't want her to know someone's been snooping around."

"I think I've got it," Angelica said.

Tricia hurried over. Using the flashlight, Angelica held back a swath of grass. A little white plastic rock sat sheltered by the greenery. She lifted it up and a fat worm recoiled at being disturbed.

"Oh, ick!"

"Grow up," Tricia warned, still whispering. The key was embedded in the dirt, bringing a small clod with it as Tricia picked it up. "Nobody's used it for a long time."

"Why are we whispering?" Angelica asked.

Tricia cleared her throat. "Come on."

She wiped the dirt from the key, stepped up to the back door, and inserted it in the lock. She turned it, grasped the handle, and let herself in. Fumbling around the door, Tricia found the light switch, flipped it, and a meager glow emanated from the kitchen's single, overhead fixture.

Angelica crowded against her. "Move over."

The tiny off-white kitchen was tidy with signs of a life interrupted. A newspaper sat neatly folded on the white painted table. A solitary coffee-stained mug occupied the dry stainless-steel sink. A stack of opened mail on the counter awaited consideration. Dusty footprints marred the otherwise clean, but dated dark vinyl floor—no doubt those of the sheriff and her deputies.

"Prisons look homier than this," Angelica offered.

She was right. Not a picture, an ornamental hanging plate, or even a key rack decorated the bland walls. No curtains, just a yellowing blind hung at half-mast over the room's only window. Tricia fought the urge to pull it down completely.

"Creepy," Angelica muttered.

"My sentiments exactly. And how would I feel if this were my home being violated by a couple of strangers?" Tricia wondered aloud. Still, she swallowed down the guilt and stepped into the darkened, narrow hallway, with Angelica so close on her heel she could feel her sister's breath on the back of her neck.

The light overhead flashed on, and Tricia's heart pounded. She whirled to find Angelica with her hand still on the switch. "Sorry."

Tricia ground her teeth, hoping her glare would scorch.

"Looks like a bedroom here," Angelica said, poking her head into a darkened room. She found that light switch, too. The smell of old paper and leather permeated the space. A twin bed wedged into the corner was made up, the patchwork quilt covering it the only splash of color in the room. On the small nightstand next to it was an open book and a pair of reading glasses, looking like they awaited their owner. The walls were floor-to-ceiling bookshelves stuffed with old tomes, while stacks of homeless books stood in front of the bottom shelves. Tricia stepped closer to examine the titles nearest her.

"Are they cookbooks?" Angelica asked eagerly.

Tricia shook her head. "No. But wow—!" She picked out a dark volume, holding it reverently as her trembling fingers fumbled to turn the pages for the copyright information. She let out a shaky breath, throat dry, making it hard to speak. "It's a first edition."

"Of what?"

"Dickens. *A Tale of Two Cities*."

"Must be worth a few bucks, huh?"

Tricia turned on her sister, ready to lecture, but the passive expression on Angelica's face told her she didn't have a clue about antique books, their intrinsic value, and there was no way she could readily explain it, either. "Yeah, it's worth a few bucks." She drank in some of the other titles, their brittle leather covers and the gold lettering on their spines making her catch her breath. Alcott, Alger, Emerson, Hawthorne, Melville, Thoreau, Twain, Whitman—the quintessential collection of nineteenth-century American authors. The only author missing was Edgar Allan Poe—and a good thing, too, or Tricia might have been tempted to—

"My God, if they're all first editions, there's a fortune in this room alone."

"I thought you said Doris only sold cookbooks."

"That's what her store was dedicated to, but obviously her taste in literature was much more discerning."

Angelica shrugged. "If you say so," and she trotted out of the room. Tricia fought the urge to touch each and every one of the spines, and backed out of the room, turning off the light and silently closing the door with a respect usually held only for the dead.

A trail of lights led to the living room. Angelica stood in the middle of the worn and dingy, putrid green wall-to-wall carpet, sizing up the space, which, like the bedroom, was primarily a storage place for books, though the shelves here seemed to hold mostly contemporary fiction. "Lousy taste in furniture," she said at last, her gaze fixed on the olive drab sofa, its lumpy cushions and sagging springs declaring it a reject from the 1960s. "You'd think with all those valuable books, she'd live in a space to show them off."

"Maybe that was the point," she said. "She could only afford them if she lived like this."

Angelica shook her head. "Not my life choice."

Nor Tricia's. Still, it was a choice she could understand. "I'll take the desk. You want to investigate the rest of the house?"

"Sure."

Tricia was glad to note the drapes were heavy, effectively blocking the light so it wouldn't be visible from the street. Knowing that gave her more confidence to inspect the cherry secretary that stood defiantly against the west wall. It was tall, topped with a glass cabinet that held an antique glass compote, several more old books, and a silver mercury glass vase with hand-painted roses. Tricia grasped the pulls and opened it. The cubbies inside were stuffed with envelopes, a checkbook, and other assorted papers—not Doris's doing, as evidenced by the tidiness of the rest of the house. Had the sheriff been in a hurry when going over the house's contents? Maybe she'd found what she was looking for and had shoved everything back in the pigeonholes with more speed than efficiency.

Utility bills, bank statements, magazine subscription notices, but no last will and testament. Abandoning the top section, Tricia opened the first drawer. Extra checks, a phone book, pens and pencils, paper clips, scissors—typical desk fare.

The next drawer held more receipts and the minutiae of a busy life. She sorted through the papers and found a stack of five or six paper-clipped statements from New England Life Insurance Company. Tricia glanced over the information. Policy Number 951493. Insured's Name: Doris E. Gleason. Plan of Insurance: Whole Life, issued six months previous. Nowhere on the statement did it list who the beneficiary was, probably for security reasons. Tricia took the oldest one, folded it, and slipped it into her pocket, then replaced the others.

She opened the last drawer without enthusiasm. In it were a little pink photo album and a bulging string envelope. The album drew her attention. She picked it up and opened to the first page to find a fuzzy black-and-white photograph of a baby. In fact, the book was dedicated to the child, whose features quickly changed from nondescript to the all-too-familiar features of Down syndrome.

The string envelope contained receipts and canceled checks, each of them referencing the Anderson Developmental Clinic Group Homes, located in Hartford, Connecticut. The letters referred to a Susan Gleason as "your daughter."

"Oh boy." If Doris had no other living relatives, who

would take on the responsibility for her mentally disabled child? Would the young woman—oh, no longer young, she realized—lose her spot in a group home? End up on the streets, homeless?

"Trish! Come and see all these wonderful old cookbooks," Angelica called.

Tricia replaced the album and envelope, closed the drawer, and wandered toward the back of the little house. She found Angelica, book in hand, in another small room crammed with boxes and shelves.

"Look, it's the *Household Bookshelf*, an all-in-one cookbook from 1936. Grandmother had a copy of this in her kitchen. I remember how I loved to read the recipes in it. See this, they used to call bread stuffing bread *force-meat*. There must be a dozen variations." Angelica looked up at Tricia, her eyes aglow with the same kind of pleasure Tricia had felt in Doris's other book storage room. "Wouldn't it be a kick to try them all?"

Tricia had thought Angelica's infatuation with meal prep had been a recent development. Why hadn't she known her older sister had been interested in cooking even as a little girl?

Angelica closed the book, replacing it on the shelf before her. "Wow, there's—" She ran her fingers along the row of books. "Twelve copies of it. Where did she get them all?"

"Estate sales, tag sales—pickers. Doris might've been collecting them for years."

"It's too bad she's dead," Angelica said wistfully, "I'd love to buy a copy of it from her. And look at all these others. *The Boston Cooking-School, The Settlement House.* I've always wanted an old copy of the Fannie Farmer cookbook. I've only got a softcover edition." She sighed and looked away, embarrassed. "Did you find any sign of heirs? Maybe they'll have an estate sale and I can get copies of some of these old books."

"Looks like her only living relative is a retarded daughter living in a group home. I couldn't find anything to the contrary."

"Oh no. That poor woman."

Did she mean the daughter, Susan, or Doris?

"Find anything else of interest?"

Tricia shook her head. "You didn't happen to see a copy of *American Cookery*, by Amelia Simmons, did you?"

"That was the book stolen from the Cookery. Why would it be—? Oh, you think the killer might have brought it back here, hidden it amongst all her other stock?"

"He or she can't very well sell it. Not without drawing attention to themselves. Let's take a minute and look. Then we'd better get out of here before our luck runs out."

It took longer than a minute, more like fifteen, but it wasn't until she'd scanned nearly every title in the room that Tricia was satisfied Doris's precious treasure was not buried among her less valuable stock.

Ready to go, she found Angelica's attention had returned to one of the copies of the *Household Bookshelf*. "You okay, Ange?"

She nodded. "It just seems so sad to leave all these old books here alone, knowing their owner will never come back. They might never be loved again."

Touched, Tricia leaned in closer to her sister. "I've never heard you talk about books that way before."

Angelica's expression hardened. She sniffed and threw back her head. "Ha!" She pushed past Tricia, heading back for the kitchen. "Probably something I picked up from you these last few days. I'm sure it'll wear off."

With one last look around the crowded room, a frowning Tricia turned off the light and pulled the door closed, just the way it had been when they'd arrived.

EIGHT

Deception wasn't Tricia's strongpoint. Not when she'd been seven and blamed Angelica for a vase she'd broken, nor when coming up with excuses to avoid dating high school jocks who couldn't spell, let alone comprehend, Sherlock Holmes.

She paced her kitchen, cell phone in hand, until the clock on her microwave read 9:01. Did a cell phone number come up on caller ID and would it also reveal her name as well? She didn't think so, which was why she'd decided not to use her regular phone. She punched in the number, listened as it rang three times.

"Good morning. New England Life, this is Margaret. How can I help you?"

No long wait on hold? An actual American, not a native of some foreign land earning pennies an hour?

"I . . . I—" Tricia hadn't come up with a plausible story, so she told the truth. "I need to find out a beneficiary on one of your policies."

"Do you have the policy number?"

"Yes." She read it off, heard the tap of a keyboard in the

background. "Doris E. Gleason. Did you wish to report her death?"

"Uh, yes. She died three days ago."

"Are you authorized to act on her behalf?"

"Um . . . yes."

"You'll need to provide us with a copy of the death certificate and copies of letters of administration. Are you Ms. Gleason's executor?"

"Not exactly. I'm a friend. I need to track down her next of kin and I thought—"

"I'm sorry. Privacy laws prohibit our giving out sensitive information of this nature. Please have Ms. Gleason's attorney or executor contact us with the necessary paperwork and we will inform the beneficiary the death has occurred."

"Oh. Okay."

"Thank you for calling New England Life."

Click.

Rats!

No sooner had she turned off the cell when her apartment phone rang. "Hello."

"Trish, it's me, Angelica."

"How did you get this number?" Was it too early to already feel so annoyed?

"I figured you'd never give it to me so I read it off the phone and wrote it down last night." Very smart, and she sounded oh so smug.

Tricia examined her empty coffee cup and poured herself some more. "Isn't this awfully early for you to be up, Ange?"

"I've mended all my evil ways. Age does that to you."

Hadn't Mike said something similar? Always a bookworm, Tricia had never had any evil ways to mend.

"Besides," Angelica continued, "I know you're only free during the hours the store isn't open. This is my only window of opportunity to talk to you until tonight."

"So what do you want to talk about?"

"Nothing really. I just wanted to tell you I had a great time last night. I felt like one of the Snoop Sisters."

"You remember that old TV show? It couldn't have lasted more than one season, and we are both far younger than any of its characters."

"I do admit I was a mere infant, but it was one of Grandmother's favorite shows. And anyway, you know what I mean." She actually giggled.

Tricia glanced at her watch and sighed. "What else do you need, Ange?"

"When are you going to call Doris's insurance company?"

"I already did. It was a bust."

"You're kidding."

"No, I'm not."

Silence for a few moments. "Give me all the info," Angelica demanded.

"What for? They told me I needed a death certificate and all kinds of other documentation before they'd give me any information. And they only want to talk to Doris's attorney or executor."

"Just let me try."

"Fine. If you've got time to waste, be my guest." She pulled out the old insurance statement and read off the pertinent information.

"Hmm. This could take some time," Angelica admitted, ruefully. "I may have to call in a few favors. I'll get back to you." She hung up.

Tricia drained her cup and replaced the handset. "Good luck."

As usual, Mr. Everett was waiting outside the door of Haven't Got a Clue at 9:55 a.m. on that gray Friday morning. He liked to be the first customer inside the door every day, although "customer" was a misnomer since so far in the five months the shop had been open he hadn't bought a thing. But he usually only drank one cup of Tricia's free coffee and, despite hanging around for most of the day, he ate only one or two of the complimentary cookies that she laid out for the paying clientele. And if she and Ginny were busy with customers, Mr. Everett had been known to make a recommendation or two and could knowledgeably talk about any book they had in stock.

Tricia unlocked the shop's door. "Good morning, Mr. Everett."

"Morning, Ms. Miles. Looks like rain today."

A glance at the sky proved the clouds hung low. "Ah, but rain is good for retail. It brings in customers who spend. And there's no better weather to settle down with a good book."

"Obviously you haven't yet seen one of our winters."

She laughed. "You've got me there."

Mr. Everett didn't share in her mirth, nor did he move to his customary seat in the nook; instead he looked down at the folded newspaper in his hands. "I brought you a present, but I don't think you're going to like it." He handed her an obviously read copy of the *Stoneham Weekly News*. The 72-point headline screamed "A Murderer Among Us?"

"Oh dear," Tricia breathed.

Mr. Everett patted her arm. "Why don't I make the coffee this morning?"

Tricia nodded dumbly and headed for the sales counter. She laid the paper flat and immediately Miss Marple jumped up to investigate. The swishing of her tail and rubbing of her head against Tricia's chin made it difficult to follow the text. By the time she'd reached the end of the first column, Tricia had removed a miffed Miss Marple and set her on the floor. She looked over at Mr. Everett, who'd taken shelter behind the side counter and the coffeemaker. He averted his gaze.

For a moment Tricia wasn't sure if she'd been libeled or slandered. She finished the article, then read it again. And again. Russ Smith was a careful writer, so suing him was definitely out. It wasn't so much what he said, but what he didn't say that inferred her probable guilt. Her lack of answers to his questions and the fact that Sheriff Adams had no other suspects in Doris Gleason's murder painted an unflattering picture.

Bob Kelly hadn't been mentioned at all. The editor knew Bob had an appointment with Doris the night she was killed, knew the two of them had argued about the leases, but instead he'd intimated that Tricia was suspected of murder—no one else.

Ginny arrived just as the phone rang. Tricia had no intention of answering it. She let the answering machine take it as Ginny hung up her coat. Then she folded the newspaper and put it under the counter.

The door opened and a couple of women entered. "Good morning, ladies, and welcome to Haven't Got a Clue."

Dressed in jogging attire, they didn't look like tourists, and they didn't have that *we're here to spend* look in their eyes. One of the women giggled. "This is a mystery bookstore, isn't it? You sell *murder* mysteries, don't you?"

Tricia swallowed, forced a smile. "Yes."

"I hope you don't *murder* your customers," the other woman said and snickered.

Ginny returned in her shop apron with the look of a mother tiger out to save her cub and insinuated herself between Tricia and the women. "Mrs. Barton, Mrs. Grant, thanks for stopping by. This must be your first visit to Haven't Got a Clue. Can I help you find a book?"

"No, thanks, we just came by to look the place over," one of them said, bending to look around Ginny and catch a glimpse of Tricia.

Tricia turned her back on the women and found some busywork at the counter. She tried not to listen to the rest of the conversation, but noted Ginny's words were not delivered in her usual, friendly tone.

Eventually the door opened, the bell tinkled, and the door closed. Footsteps approached. "You okay?" Ginny asked.

Tricia turned, braved a smile. "Sure."

"Everybody's talking about Russ Smith's front-page article. I wouldn't be surprised if more of the villagers dropped by just to have a look at—" She stopped, looked embarrassed.

"Look at what?" Mr. Everett asked, still standing at the coffee station.

"The, uh, jinx," Ginny said in a tiny voice.

The muscles in Tricia's calves ached from being so tense. "We'll just have to welcome them, if they do. Maybe I should get another couple of pounds of coffee." She almost managed to keep her voice steady.

"You're being a lot more generous than I could be," Ginny said.

"I won't let idle gossip run me out of town. I'm here for the long haul."

Ginny's smile was tentative. "You go, girl."

With a small tray in hand, Mr. Everett appeared behind Ginny. "Coffee, ladies?"

Tricia and Ginny each took a cup, and Mr. Everett took one, too. "I propose a toast. To Haven't Got a Clue, the best bookshop in all of Stoneham. Long may we read!"

Tricia swallowed down the lump in her throat.

"Here, here!" Ginny agreed, and the three of them raised their cardboard coffee cups in salute.

Like most Friday afternoons, this one was busy, and the forecasted rain did bring out paying customers. Stoneham was a favorite day trip for senior groups from Vermont, Massachusetts, and from within New Hampshire itself, a happy happenstance for every business owner in the village. And while most seniors took the trips to alleviate boredom, a lot of them actually were avid readers. However, when four or five buses converged at once, the result was chaos.

Ten or twelve customers hovered like angry bees around the sales counter in Haven't Got a Clue. "Our bus leaves in less than ten minutes," someone from the back of the crowd growled.

"It won't leave without you," Ginny said reasonably, as she stacked wrapped books into a plastic carrier bag.

"Well if it does, you'll be paying my hotel bill for the

night," snapped a thin, bleached blonde in a beige cashmere sweater set and pearls. An idle threat. There were no hotels or motels in or around Stoneham. Just the Brookview Inn.

Tricia's fingers flew over the cash register's keys, and not for the first time she wished the store had a laser checkout system. Though tagging the books would be great for inventory purposes, the resale value on the older, most expensive books would plummet.

"As soon as the last bus rolls down the road and out of town, we'll break open that pound of Godiva I've been saving," she muttered to Ginny, who smiled gratefully. Lunchtime had come and gone several hours earlier, but they'd been too busy to even stop and grab a bite.

The shop door opened and the little bell rang as Tricia accepted a copy of Dorothy L. Sayers's *Gaudy Night* from a pair of outstretched hands. She turned to ring it up when from beside her Ginny let out a stifled scream. Mouth covered with one hand, with the other she pointed at the apparition standing just inside the door.

Tricia, too, gulped at the sight of the seventysomething plump, but smartly dressed woman who stood in the doorway. She took in the tailored red pantsuit, white turtleneck shirt, and large red leather purse, designer glasses, and severely short, dyed jet-black hair. Unable to find her voice, Tricia mouthed the name: "Doris?"

The woman charged forward with an energy the living Doris Gleason had never possessed. "Hello, I'm Deirdre Gleason. Doris was my sister." The voice was a shade deeper, her words spoken more slowly. "What on Earth happened to Doris's shop? Why is it empty? Where is all her stock?"

"Excuse me, but I was here first," said the woman in a damp trench coat, elbowing her way forward.

Tricia looked from her customers to the doppelganger in front of her. "Can you give us a couple of minutes? We're a little overwhelmed right now, but I'd be glad to tell you everything I know as soon as things calm down." She gestured toward the coffee station. "Help yourself and then we'll talk."

The woman's lips pursed, but she nodded and skirted the crowd at the sales counter.

Once the initial shock had passed, Tricia had little time to think about Deirdre Gleason, who wandered the store during the rush. Nine customers and three hundred dollars later, the shop was nearly empty and Ginny gave Tricia a nudge in the direction of the mystery woman who had finally settled in the sitting nook. "I believe in ghosts," she whispered. "Make sure she isn't one of them, will you?"

A curious Miss Marple had perched on the coffee table in front of the woman. The cat wasn't spitting or acting odd, so Ginny's fear of specters was no doubt unfounded.

Tricia sat down on the chair opposite Deirdre and offered her hand. "Hello, my name is Tricia Miles. I own this store and—"

"You found my sister's body." A statement, not an accusation.

Tricia swallowed, pulling her hand back. "I'm so sorry for your loss."

The woman shrugged, her creased face ravaged by the effects of gravity and sorrow. "The coroner said poor Doris was sick with cancer and probably didn't even know it. I would've lost her anyway. I'm just sorry I never got a chance to say good-bye."

Tears threatened and Tricia's throat closed. Angelica was a gigantic pain in the butt, but she had always been in Tricia's life. Sometimes lurking, sometimes in her face, but always her big sister. The thought of her suddenly gone . . .

"I'm sorry there's nothing I can tell you that will ease your pain. Someone killed your sister and I believe it had to do with a rare cookbook that was stolen the night she died."

"The sheriff told me all about it. I'm not sure she believes it."

Not good news, but not totally unexpected, either. "I

didn't know Doris had a sister, although I did know about her daughter."

Deirdre's left eyebrow arched. "Doris wasn't one to chat about her personal life."

Tricia quickly adopted a wide-eyed and, what she hoped was, innocent expression. No way was she going to say how she knew about Doris's daughter. Deirdre's penetrating gaze was as unforgiving as her late sister's.

"Why is the Cookery empty? What happened to all the stock? I spoke to Doris last Monday and she didn't say anything about closing the shop. In fact, she said she was negotiating a new lease."

"That's true. Uh . . ." Tricia stalled, trying to come up with a tactful reply. "The landlord apparently didn't realize Doris had any heirs. I think he—"

"Jumped the gun at emptying the store?"

"I'm afraid so."

The woman sighed, shook her head, irritated.

Tricia became aware that her palms, resting on her knees, had begun to perspire. She wiped them on the side of her slacks and sat back in the comfortable chair, feeling anything but comfortable. "He had all the books and display pieces moved to a storage unit. I'm afraid they may be smoke damaged."

"Would you happen to know where I can contact this . . . this landlord person?"

"Yes. As a matter of fact, I believe I have one of his business cards."

Ginny, who had been unabashedly eavesdropping, spoke up. "I'll get it. It's here in the register." She opened the drawer, lifted the cash tray, and came up with the card. In seconds she'd handed it to Deirdre.

"Thank you." She stowed the card in the pocket of her jacket. "It was always my intention to move to Stoneham to help Doris with the shop. Her death has just hastened my entry into the world of bookselling." She opened her purse, took out a tissue, and bowed her head, looking ready to cry. "I've been a very selfish woman. I should've been there for her in her time of need. I knew she was having cash-flow problems; I knew she wasn't feeling well. And I knew she'd had employee problems—"

At this, Ginny stepped back, looking guilty. She'd quit the Cookery to take the job with Tricia. Doris had never replaced her.

Deirdre faced Tricia once again. "I was always too busy, wasting money on travel and clothes when I should've been here helping my sister."

Tricia wasn't sure how or if she should reply. Deirdre made it easy on her and rose from her seat.

"What will happen to Doris's daughter?" Tricia asked, and also stood.

"Susan is now my responsibility." Deirdre pursed her lips, an effort that failed to stop them trembling. "It wasn't Doris's way to let on that she cared—about anything. But she loved that girl. It broke her heart when Susan had to go live in the group home. But apparently she's happy there. Doris told me she has friends and a job. I don't know how I'll tell her she'll never see her mother again."

The three women stood there, all of them fighting tears for several long moments. Finally Deirdre cleared her throat and straightened, her expression once again impassive. "Thank you for answering my questions. It was traumatic to hear of Doris's death. Finding her had to be even more so."

Odd, Tricia thought, except for Frannie, Deirdre had been the only other person to acknowledge that she might've felt traumatized by the experience. This morning's newspaper story had brought it all back in vivid detail, but it had also bolstered Tricia's determination to clear her name. And yet, she had no clue how to go about it.

"Yes, it was. If only I'd arrived a few minutes sooner."

"You mustn't blame yourself. If you had arrived sooner, Doris's murderer might've killed you, too."

Deirdre's words, spoken with such casualness, made Tricia go cold.

NINE

"Good night, Mr. Everett," Tricia said, shut the door, turned the sign on it to CLOSED, and was about to shut and lock it when she saw the familiar rental car pull up in front of the shop.

Ginny was still tidying up, but she, too, saw the car, turned off the vacuum, and began to wind up the cord. "You don't mind if I leave, do you?" she said, already shoving the cleaner toward the utility closet. "Sorry to say, but your sister really hates me for all the times I screened your calls."

"I know, and I'm sorry. I never thought you two would ever face each other." Tricia crossed to the register, opened it, lifted the money tray, and withdrew an envelope— Ginny's paycheck. "I didn't get a chance to tell you before, but I've given you a raise. Sorry it couldn't be more."

Already shrugging into her jacket, Ginny paused, her surprise evident. "But you gave me a raise only last month."

"Well, you've been so supportive these past few days I figured you'd earned another."

Ginny accepted the envelope. "Thank you, Tricia. I've worked for three booksellers here in the village in the past four years, but you are by far the best." She gave Tricia a quick hug.

"Can somebody help me?" came a muffled, annoyed voice from behind the shop's locked door.

Tricia crossed the store to open the door, letting in Angelica, who scowled as Ginny went out, calling cheerfully behind her, "See you tomorrow."

Once again Angelica was weighed down with a grocery bag full of ingredients. "That girl," she muttered and dumped the sack on the nook's coffee table.

"Ange, I hope you don't think you have to come here every evening and cook for me," Tricia said, although the thought of the leftovers now residing in her freezer was a comfort.

"You work so hard, and it's the only part of the day you have time for me." She patted one of Tricia's cheeks and simpered, "I do so miss my baby sister. We've still got years and years to catch up on."

Tricia didn't reply. It was the memory of Deirdre Gleason's sorrow at the loss of her sister that made her keep quiet. She would try to be a better sister to Angelica. She would.

She turned for the door.

"I've got it," Angelica said, triumphantly.

"Got what?"

She pulled a piece of paper from her jacket pocket and waved it in the air. "Doris's beneficiary."

With everything else going on, Tricia had completely forgotten her quest from earlier in the day. "Don't tell me. Susan Gleason, but in some kind of trust with Deirdre Gleason in control."

Angelica's face fell. "Who told you?"

"I met Deirdre a couple of hours ago. She came into the shop, wanted to know why the Cookery was empty."

Surprise turned to pique. Angelica exhaled sharply. "If you only knew how much trouble I went through to get this."

"Sorry, Ange. I figured you'd come up against the same brick walls I did." Avoiding her sister's gaze, Tricia reached for the door.

"Don't lock it—I've asked Bob Kelly to join us for dinner," Angelica called, rummaging through the grocery bag. "Oh dear. I hope you've got an onion. I don't think I picked one up at the store."

"I wish you'd asked me first."

"Doesn't everyone keep onions?" Angelica asked, looking up from her supplies.

"I mean about inviting Bob. I told you he isn't my favorite person."

"Like you, that poor man is a virtual workaholic. Why I'll bet he hasn't had a home-cooked meal in ages."

"What are you making?"

"Stroganoff."

Like Pavlov's dog, already Tricia anticipated the aroma of one of her most favorite entrées. "Well, next time please let me know when you're going to invite guests to *my* home."

"That's why I invited him. If I'm going to be staying in Stoneham for the winter, I'll need a place to live. I considered staying in one of the inn's bungalows, but I really want more space and I've heard Bob is the best person to talk to about the local real estate market." And with that, Angelica picked up the sack and headed for the door to the upstairs apartment, where she paused. "Why don't you like Bob, anyway? What's he ever done to you?"

"Have you taken a close look at his face?"

"Yes, and he's a very good-looking man."

Tricia crossed her arms over her chest. "Exactly. And who does he remind you of?"

Angelica thought about it for a moment. "Christopher?"

"Duh! My ex-husband."

"Well, that's certainly not Bob's fault," Angelica said with a shrug and turned. "I'll go get dinner started. Don't let me keep you from whatever you have to finish up."

From her perch on the shelf above the register, Miss

Marple looked from Tricia to Angelica. The squeak of the door's hinges promised food, and the little gray cat jumped down to follow.

"Traitor," Tricia hissed, but Miss Marple took no heed and scampered up the steps.

It was another ten minutes before Tricia finished her evening chores, all the while stewing about Angelica's threats to make Stoneham her new hometown. She'd emptied the wastebaskets, cleaned the coffee station, straightened books on the shelves, and aligned the mystery review magazines on the nook's big, square coffee table, and still there was no sign of Bob. They'd never hear the bell from the third-floor apartment, so she was forced to wait until he showed up.

Her irritation escalated to smoldering anger with every passing minute. She peered out the shop windows. Nothing. She wondered if she should give him a call, but then remembered Ginny had given her only copy of his business card to Deirdre. She went in search of the phone book and remembered she'd let the answering machine take at least one call this morning. She'd been too upset to answer it after reading the *Stoneham Weekly News*.

Tricia played the message.

"Tricia? Hi, it's Mike Harris. In case you haven't already seen it, the *Stoneham Weekly News* has a scathing report about the murder at the Cookery. I wanted to let you know that Russ Smith is a jerk, and the whole village knows it. He'll sensationalize anything to sell copies of that rag. Don't take it seriously. My day is pretty full, but I'll try to get over to see you later this afternoon or early tomorrow. We're still on for Sunday morning, right? Talk to you later."

Tricia's finger hovered over the delete button. Well, at least one citizen in the village thought she was innocent.

A knock on the door caused her to look up. It came again and Tricia went to the door. Shoulders hunched inside his jacket, Bob Kelly looked as peeved as Tricia felt.

"Hello, Bob," she greeted without enthusiasm.

"Tricia," he grunted and stepped inside the shop.

"Angelica's upstairs."

He grunted again, waited as she locked the door, then followed her across the shop. "This way," she said and started up the stairs at a brisk pace.

As she hit the top-floor landing, Miss Marple was there to admonish her. "Did you give the cat anything to eat?" Tricia asked.

Angelica looked up from a pan on the stove. "I don't know what to feed a cat."

Miss Marple rubbed against Tricia's ankles, looked up at her with hope in her green eyes.

"Where's Bob?" Angelica asked.

Tricia looked down the staircase. Bob was nowhere in sight. "I thought he was right behind me." Annoyed, she started back down the stairs, with Miss Marple right at her heels. Bob rounded the second-floor landing.

"Sorry. Had to tie my shoe," he said. "What smells so delicious?"

Tricia waited for him to catch up, then turned back for her apartment, with Miss Marple sticking to her like glue. Bob was breathing hard by the time they reached the apartment.

"There you are," Angelica called from her station at the counter. Already a heavenly aroma teased the senses. "Trish, take Bob's coat," she scolded.

Tricia did as she was told, stowing Bob's jacket on the coat tree.

He took in the changes she'd made to the third-floor loft—he hadn't been there since she'd signed the lease. "It's beautiful, Trish. You've done a wonderful job converting the space into a home."

She had. But everything was modular—from the pickled maple cabinets to the granite-covered island that doubled as a breakfast bar. Should she ever decide to relocate she could remove everything, leaving the space as she'd found it—an empty shell.

"Have a glass of wine and relax, Bob," Angelica suggested. "Or would you like something a little stronger?"

"Wine is fine," he said, settling on a stool at the breakfast bar.

Again Angelica proved she knew her way around Tricia's kitchen. She took another couple of glasses from the cabinet and poured, setting the merlot before Tricia and Bob. Then she grabbed a pot holder, took a tray out of the oven, and settled the contents onto a waiting platter.

"The seafood around here is pretty good. I hope you like crab puffs." She offered the plate to Bob, who took one of the golden savory pastries. He popped it into his mouth and chewed.

"These are delicious. Where did you buy them?" he asked, eyes wide with pleasure.

Angelica laughed. "I made them, silly."

Tricia selected one as well. "From scratch?"

"Of course. Have another, Bob," Angelica said, taking one for herself.

"You're going to spoil me," he said, but he took another puff anyway.

Angelica set the platter down within reach of all them, pushed the napkin holder toward her guest, and leaned her elbows against the granite, resting her head on her balled fists. "You look tired, Bob. Tough day?"

Bob snagged a napkin, wiped his fingers. "I've got problems. Who knew Doris Gleason would have a sister bent on keeping the Cookery open?"

Angelica shook her head. "I heard all about it."

From where? Tricia wondered, annoyed. She turned to Bob. "I believe I suggested you wait to take action on the property. It fell on deaf ears."

Bob didn't answer, only glowered at her.

"Tricia, behave," Angelica admonished. "Bob is our guest."

No, he was *her* guest in Tricia's home.

"The worst thing is, this woman—this sister—is making out like *I* might have had something to do with Doris's death, just because I exercised my rights as the building's owner to do some cleanup and maintenance. She as good as accused me of killing Doris so I could lease the Cookery to someone willing to pay a lot more in rent."

Good. At least one other person in Stoneham considered Bob a viable suspect.

"Oh I'm sure she doesn't believe that," Angelica said. "It's just grief. If I lost my only sister"—she looked fondly at Tricia—"I'm sure I'd be just as devastated."

Bob wasn't listening. "She's already called in an attorney. Apparently Doris had sent her sister copies of the current and proposed leases. The sister threatened a lawsuit over my emptying the store. It may be easier for me to cut my losses and extend the current lease—as is—for another year and renegotiate at a later date. That way she would be up and running again in a couple of weeks. No matter what, it's going to cost me." He shook his head. "The damage that woman's death has done to Stoneham's economy will end up being in the millions."

"Don't be ridiculous," Tricia said.

"I'm not. The PR value of being the safest town in all New Hampshire was priceless. Losing it could affect future development here for decades."

Angelica clucked sympathetically, but it took all Tricia's self-control to keep quiet on that account. Instead, she decided to move things along. "How's that Stroganoff coming, Ange? It sure smells good."

Angelica was not about to be hurried and topped both her own and Bob's wineglasses.

Resigned, Tricia tried another topic. "What's this about a big box store coming to Stoneham?"

Bob choked on his wine. Angelica scurried around the island, thumped him on the back. "Are you okay?"

"Who told you that?" Bob asked, anger causing his eyes to narrow.

"I heard it. Around," Tricia offered lamely.

"I did, too, Bob," Angelica said. "Is it true?"

Bob cleared his throat, pounding on his chest before answering. "No. Maybe. I hope not."

"That's not much of an answer," Tricia said.

"All I can tell you is that a nationally known company has put out feelers. That doesn't mean they're actually looking to establish a presence in Stoneham."

"But you are talking to their representatives," Tricia pushed.

"I've been approached, and so has the Board of Selectmen, on a number of proposed projects. That's all I can say."

"Would candidates for selectman know about this interest, too?" Tricia asked. Maybe she could pump Mike Harris for information.

"No," Bob said emphatically and gulped the rest of his wine. Angelica filled his glass again.

So much for that idea.

"Any news on Winnie Wentworth's death?"

"How would I know?" Bob looked up, aggravated.

Tricia shrugged. "You seem to have your finger on the pulse of Stoneham. I wondered if they'd made a determination."

"I have no interest in vehicular accidents unless they pose a threat to commerce."

Talk about coldhearted.

"Winnie was a citizen of Stoneham. Surely, she—"

"She didn't own property. She didn't pay taxes. She was little more than a pest to most of the shop owners, always trying to flog her junk. I had more than a few complaints about her over the years. Everything from vagrancy to harassment."

"Yes, but—" Tricia tried to protest, but Bob cut her off again.

"She was an embarrassment to the village. It's hard to promote tourism when you've got her sort wandering about. She was a nuisance in life and a liability in death. No one's claimed her body. It'll probably be up to the taxpayers to bury her," he finished bitterly and took another gulp of wine. He turned his attention to Angelica. "Now, what kind of house were you thinking about buying or were you just interested in renting?" And Bob launched into his pitch for possible residential rentals and sales.

Taking the hint, Tricia busied herself by feeding Miss Marple and setting the table. Although Bob was her first official dinner guest since moving in, she decided not to use her grandmother's best china and tableware. For someone like Mike, however, she might be persuaded to pull out all the stops.

She would've liked to have returned Mike's call, thanking him for his support. Hadn't he said his mother's book collection included cookbooks? Deirdre Gleason would need additional titles to restock the Cookery. Perhaps Tricia could broker a deal for the books, which would at least keep the lines of communication open with her nearest neighbor.

When the crab puffs were finally gone Angelica declared the entrée ready to serve. She'd whipped up a romaine salad and homemade poppy-seed dressing as well. The three of them took seats at the table.

Bob dug in, chewed, and swallowed. "Unusual flavor. What is it?"

Tricia took a bite and could tell the meat wasn't beef. "Yes, it's different, but it's delicious," she said and took another bite.

"Venison," Angelica said, smug. "Most people won't eat it, but I know how to take out the gamey flavor."

"And how do you do that?" Bob asked, shoveling up another mouthful.

"It's a secret." She sipped her wine. "I'm sorry I had to use store-bought noodles, but there just wasn't time to make them from scratch," she lamented and sighed.

Tricia watched as Bob stabbed another forkful, then savored the taste. "This is absolutely delicious. Have you ever thought about opening a restaurant, Angelica?"

Angelica brightened. "Well, actually, I have."

Bob leaned in closer, his voice growing husky. "I've got a couple of beautiful properties that could be converted into the most exquisite little bistros."

Tricia cringed. Honestly, he sounded like the worst kind of used car salesman.

Angelica didn't seem to notice and fluttered her eye-
lashes. "Do tell."

Tricia cleared her throat, afraid they'd forgotten she was
still there. She'd never seen Angelica turn on the charm for
a man before—and she was sure she didn't want to see a
repeat performance.

"Gee, it's too bad Drew isn't here. As I recall,
Stroganoff was his favorite. And he has such a vast knowledge of architecture and renovation—which would sure be
a big help if you're serious about opening a restaurant."

"Drew?" Bob asked.

Angelica straightened in her chair, her expression sour-
ing. "My soon-to-be ex-husband."

"I'm still hoping for a reconciliation," Tricia said, trying
to look encouraging.

Angelica put down her fork. "Well, I'm not. More
Stroganoff, Bob?"

Tricia studied her sister's face. There was hurt behind
her strained smile. Tricia still didn't know why her sister's
marriage was about to end, and teasing her now, in front of
Bob, really wasn't fair. Although, the last thing she wanted
was for the two of them to start a relationship.

Tricia sipped her wine. Then again, why should she stand
in the way of her sister's happiness even if she'd find it with
someone like Bob Kelly? Wasn't she looking forward to seeing Mike Harris again? The pain of her own divorce was still
fresh, and somewhere in the back of her mind she heard her
mother scolding, *If something happens to Dad and me,
you're all you've got.* Those words held new meaning for
her after finding Doris Gleason's body, and suddenly Tricia
found herself looking at her sister with kinder eyes.

"Tell me more about those hot properties, Bob," Angelica cooed, lashes fluttering again.

Tricia's grasp on her fork tightened. If she didn't end up
killing Angelica first.

TEN

Tricia lay awake half the night, disturbed by dreams of Angelica, radiant in a long white gown, and Bob Kelly in a tuxedo with a green shirt and tie, making goo-goo eyes at each other as they exchanged I dos, and vowing to live a life of wedded bliss *in* Tricia's home. The rest of the night Tricia lay awake, various scenarios of her future—none of them good—circling through her mind.

Regular coffee might not be enough to get her through the day. A double shot of espresso was what she needed, except there was no place in all of Stoneham to get a cup of that black-as-tar brew at this time of day.

After a half hour of running nowhere on the treadmill, a shower, and a Pop-Tart breakfast, Tricia and Miss Marple headed down to the store, if only to soak up its cozy ambiance on that gray morning. Miss Marple settled down on one of the nook's chairs, ready for some serious napping, while Tricia puttered around the shop.

Mr. Everett must've seen the lights on, because he showed up especially early, with his collapsible umbrella

under his arm. Tricia let him in and offered him the first
complimentary cup of coffee of the day.

"Thank you," he said, taking his first sip. He scrutinized
her face. "Is something troubling you, Ms. Miles?"

She shook her head—definitely in denial—then thought
better of it and nodded. "Yes. I keep thinking of all that's
happened in the past few days and I can't quite make sense
of it all."

"Death is never as easy to handle in person as it is in fiction. Yet that's the fascination that inspired all the books
here on your shelves."

"That's true," she admitted, "but it doesn't feel so antisep-
tic, so remote when you've actually known the deceased."

"I agree." He took another sip. "Death is not a stranger
to Stoneham. We lose people all the time to sickness, to accidents. That we've lost one to murder gives us more in
common with our big-city cousins. Not something we as a
village aspire to."

"You're right. When someone dies of natural causes
there's pain, but also a sense of acceptance. But murder
and accidents . . ." She studied the old man's gray eyes.
"Did you know Winnie Wentworth?"

His gaze dipped and he took his time before answering.
"Yes."

"What was she like?"

"In years past she liked honeydew melons, green beans,
and pork rinds and malt liquor on a Saturday night."

Not the kind of details Tricia would've expected. She
laughed. "How do you know that?"

He shrugged. "Just some things I observed over a number
of years. For instance, you don't want customers to know
how passionate you are about keeping the work of long-dead
mystery authors alive. So you carry the current best sellers
and give them some prominence, but when you talk to your
customers, you always recommend the masters."

Of course she did. Like the rest of the booksellers in
town, Haven't Got a Clue offered used and rare books. He
hadn't really answered her question.

"Tell me something else about Winnie," she said, hungry to hear more.

Mr. Everett searched the depths of his quickly cooling coffee. "She had contempt for the written word, or at least reading for pleasure, but she recognized books as way to stay afloat with the changes that came to Stoneham these past few years."

"Then why didn't she offer me more books?" Tricia asked, puzzled. "I didn't meet her until the day she died."

Again he shrugged. "She was eccentric, didn't trust many people. But I do know one thing: she was always careful with her car. It's all she had. She wasn't one to drive recklessly."

"Do you think her death was an accident or . . . something else?"

He glanced around the shop with its thousands of books. "Perhaps I read too much. Yet unless she was ill, it makes no sense that she crashed and died on such a beautiful, sunny day. Especially when she was the only person who knew where the book stolen from the Cookery came from."

Though Winnie denied remembering, Tricia suspected Doris's killer could've believed the same thing. Hearing that theory from another source gave her no comfort.

"Oh dear," Mr. Everett said within minutes of opening a copy of Carter Dickson's *The Punch and Judy Murders.* Even with a Nicholas Gunn CD playing softly in the background, the tone of his voice caused Tricia to look up from opening the morning mail.

Mr. Everett rose from his chair, headed for the sales counter.

Ginny, who'd been helping a customer, excused herself and intercepted him.

The elderly gent handed a folded piece of paper to Tricia. Another nudist tract, but this one was different. Instead of a generic missive on the health benefits and pleasure of a nudist lifestyle, this one was a blatant advertisement. "Free Spirit Inc. presents Full Moon Camp and Resort," Tricia read aloud. The tract went on to list all the amenities, including a pool, hot tubs, therapeutic massage, and—"Why is it nudists are so intent on playing volleyball?" she asked.

Ginny giggled. "Look, there's a website listed. Maybe they've got pictures."

Tricia made the trek up to her apartment, snagged her laptop computer, and was back down to the shop in record time. She booted up and was connected to the Internet within another minute or two. The three of them gathered behind the sales counter. "If there're naughty pictures, I'm shutting it down," she warned.

"We're all grown-ups," Ginny said sensibly, but Mr. Everett bristled at the notion. Still, he didn't walk away.

Free Spirit's home page flashed onto the little screen. No naked people. So far so good. Instead there was a cute little graphic of a squirrel named Ricky, which was apparently the site's mascot. By clicking on various links, Ricky took visitor 120,043 on a tour of the website. First up, the volleyball court, but there were no naked men and women playing the game, only the photo of a well-groomed court. The pool was Olympic-sized, with scores of white chaise longues lined up around it, each with its own clean, neatly folded white towel. That picture was also devoid of people, as was every other photograph on the website. Instead, like any other camping resort, the text stressed the clean, well-maintained facilities at every Free Spirit location.

"It's a chain?" Mr. Everett asked.

"Apparently so." Tricia clicked on the coming attractions page and found what she'd been looking for. "Aha. Listen to this: 'Our newest Full Moon location is scheduled to open next summer in southern New Hampshire.' "

"You think they mean here in Stoneham?" Ginny asked.

"It can't be." Still, there had been the rumor of a big box outfit wanting to locate in the area. No, retail was a year-round moneymaking concern while a nudist resort would, for the most part, only be seasonal.

"There's no reason it would have to be located near here. Saying 'southern New Hampshire' is rather ambiguous. They'd probably want to be near a larger city to make it accessible for travelers," Mr. Everett said reasonably.

"You're probably right," Tricia agreed.

Mr. Everett stepped away from the counter. "I think I'll go back to my reading. Excuse me, ladies," he said, and off to the nook he went.

"I think it would be cool to have a nudist resort right outside of town. Think of all the new money it would bring to the area," Ginny said wistfully. "All those people might get bored with volleyball after a while. Did you see all those lounge chairs? They'd definitely need something good to read while they whiled away the hours working on their tans."

"One can hope," Tricia said. "But, oh, think about the mosquitoes and all the new places you could get bitten." She shuddered and Ginny laughed. "Better be on the lookout for more of these," she said, crumpled up the tract Mr. Everett had found, and tossed it into the trash.

"Could you help me, miss?" asked the customer Ginny had abandoned only a few minutes before.

"I'll keep an eye out for more of those advertisements," Ginny told Tricia, before skirting the counter. "Now, what can I help you find?" she asked the customer.

Tricia clicked on the button for the website's home page once more. Ricky smiled at her with a toothy grin more appropriate to a cartoon chipmunk. Bob hadn't wanted to talk about big box stores. How eager would he be to talk about the possibility of a nudist resort—if she could even catch him at his realty office to ask?

Tricia didn't have an opportunity to find out. Their slow start of a morning suddenly morphed into a busy afternoon of enthusiastic shoppers looking for vintage mysteries. Tricia was deep in conversation with a Mrs. Richardson, a serious collector from the Hamptons, who had already picked out more than a dozen books with authors ranging from Margery Allingham to Cornell Woolrich. She glanced up as the bell over the door jingled and a damp Mike Harris shook the drops from his raincoat onto the mat just inside the door.

Both Ginny and Mr. Everett were also deeply involved in customer service, so Tricia gave Mike a be-with-you-when-I-can smile. He waved a no-hurry hand in response and started browsing amongst the shelves.

The Hamptons woman spent close to seven hundred dollars and left the store a happy customer; likewise, Tricia was a very happy proprietor. A Charioteer tour bus rolled down Main Street, which would hopefully mean another influx of customers. A patient Mike had settled into the nook, thumbing through *Mystery Scene Magazine*. Tricia knew she only had minutes before the store would be flooded with potential customers again.

"I'm sorry it took so long," she apologized, taking the seat opposite him.

"No, I'm sorry. I should've called; but then I wouldn't have gotten to see you."

Tricia felt her cheeks redden. "I wanted to thank you for your call yesterday. I didn't grab it because—"

"If it was me, I'd have been screening my calls after that hatchet job in the *Stoneham Weekly News*."

"I'm afraid that's exactly what I was doing. Unfortunately some people believed every word. A few even came here to gawk at me."

"Don't judge the whole village by a couple of jerks." He changed the subject. "We still on for tomorrow?"

"I wouldn't miss it. Just give me the time and place."

"I know you need to open at noon. Is nine o'clock too early?"

"Not at all."

"Great." Mike pulled a piece of paper from his jacket pocket. "Here's the address. Do you need directions?"

Tricia glanced at the paper. "No, I've driven through this neighborhood before. Very nice houses."

Mike's smile was wistful. "Yes. It's a shame I have to sell it. But Mother's care comes first."

Tricia nodded, remembering the pain of losing Christopher's father to dementia.

The bell over the door jangled as a fresh wave of customers entered the shop.

Mike stood. "I'd better make room for the onslaught." They stood for a moment, looking into each other's eyes, then Mike clasped her hands and drew her close, kissed her cheek. "See you tomorrow."

Surprised but pleased, Tricia watched Mike depart, even going so far as to follow his progress as he crossed the street to his new office and campaign headquarters. She did, however, move away from the window in case he turned. She didn't want him to know she'd been watching him.

At the coffee station, Ginny motioned for Tricia, then proffered the pot. "It isn't even two o'clock and this is the last of the coffee. We're already out of cookies. Want me to go get more?"

Tricia shook her head. "Most of our sales today have been via credit card; we haven't got much cash in the till. I'll go get the supplies and be back within half an hour. Can you manage?"

"I'd be glad to help out if you need me?" said Mr. Everett, coming up behind Tricia.

"I can't keep imposing on you."

"I like to feel useful," said the older gentleman.

"Go on," Ginny encouraged. "We'll be fine."

Tricia grabbed her purse, raincoat, and umbrella and ducked past the hoard of customers for a hasty exit. She waited for traffic to pass before crossing the street. Mr. Everett's help these last few days had been a blessing. As he was at the store on a daily basis, she wondered if she should offer him a part-time job. Her balance sheet was already in better shape than what she'd initially projected and as Ginny had Sundays off, he might be willing to help out then. Granted, it was a slow day, but she could always use his help for shelving new stock. It made perfect sense, and why hadn't she thought of it before?

The Coffee Bean was just as busy as Haven't Got a
Clue, and Tricia took a number, noting there were at least
eight customers ahead of her. Stoneham was really hop-
ping on this bleak, late-summer afternoon.

To pass the time, Tricia distracted herself by examining
the store's stock: coffee cups that ran the gamut from artful
to sublimely silly, packets of gourmet cookies, petit fours,
and chocolate in colorful wrappings, everything so beautifully packaged it enticed customers to spend. But she'd get
her cookies from the village bakery—if they had anything
left this late in the afternoon.

As Tricia read the list of ingredients on a box of Green
Mountain chocolates, she began to feel closed in. Looking
up, she saw editor Russ Smith was standing well within her
personal space. "Excuse me," she said, stepping aside.

"I understand you weren't happy with my article," he
said without preamble.

"Who would be?"

"I owe it to my readers to—"

"Act like a tabloid journalist?"

His eyes flashed. "That's uncalled for."

"So was painting me as a murderer—and without even
circumstantial evidence." Heads turned at her words. She
lowered her voice. "I don't think this is the place to discuss
this."

"Then how about dinner. Are you free tonight?"

Tricia blinked. "You've got to be kidding."

Smith's gaze was level. "No, I'm not. We could discuss
the story, and perhaps a follow-up—among other things."

Tricia replaced the box of chocolates on the shelf. "I
don't think so."

"I'm not your enemy."

"And after what you wrote about me, you're not my
friend, either."

"Number forty-seven," the salesclerk called out.

Tricia glanced down at the crushed ticket in her hand.
"If you'll excuse me, Mr. Smith." She elbowed her way

through the other customers and placed her order, all the time feeling Russ Smith's gaze on her back.

Dodging the raindrops, Tricia clutched her bags of coffee and cookies and hurried down the sidewalk. The big, green Kelly Realty FOR RENT sign was gone from the front window of the Cookery. The door stood ajar and the lights blazed. Poking her head inside, Tricia called, "Deirdre?" A woman in a baggy red flannel shirt and dark slacks, with a blue bandana tied around her hair, turned from her perch on a ten-foot ladder. In her hand she clasped a soapy sponge. A six-foot-square patch of wall had already been scrubbed of soot, showing creamy yellow paint once again.

"You shouldn't be doing that," Tricia admonished. A fall for a woman Deirdre's age could send her to a nursing home—or worse.

"It's got to be done," Deirdre said, in the same no-nonsense voice as her dead sister.

"But surely Bob Kelly ought to be paying someone to do it."

Deirdre dropped the sponge into a bucket and carefully stepped down off the ladder. "We came to an agreement on other more important things." The hint of a smile played at her lips. Perhaps she was a harder bargainer than Doris had been, which had been the reason for Bob's sour mood the evening before.

"How soon do you think you'll reopen?"

"Possibly a week. Then I think I'll hold a grand reopening the first week in October. Doris had already lined up an author signing for that week. It should work out nicely."

"But what about the smoke-damaged stock? It'll take weeks to restore them, and surely some of them won't be salvageable."

"I've got an expert coming in on Monday. Meanwhile there're hundreds of boxes in the storeroom upstairs, which thankfully Mr. Kelly neglected to clear out, and there's a room of excess stock at Doris's house. We'll start with that and fill in with newer titles until we replenish our supply of rare and used books."

"We?" Tricia asked.

Deirdre frowned, her gaze dipping. "Excuse me. I can't help talking about Doris and myself as though we'll always be together. She was my twin. When we were younger we were so very close she used to swear we could read each other's minds."

Tricia felt a pang of envy laced with guilt. She'd never felt that way about Angelica. "It sounds like you've had experience running a shop before."

"I was an accountant until last winter, but I heard so much about the Cookery from Doris I always felt I could step into her shoes and run it at a moment's notice. And now I have." She pursed her lips and swallowed.

Tricia considered carefully before voicing her next question. "Have you made any arrangements for Doris?"

Deirdre's expression hardened. "There will be no service, if that's what you mean. She told me she had no friends here in Stoneham. If there's one thing she hated, it was hypocrisy. I couldn't bear to hear platitudes and regrets from people who had no time for Doris during her life."

Ouch—that stung, but Tricia couldn't blame the woman. No doubt Deirdre would grieve for her sister in her own way and time.

"Have you had a chance to visit with your niece?"

Deirdre shook her head. "Her counselor doesn't seem to think it's a good idea. Doris and I looked so much alike it would only confuse her."

"I was very surprised to hear Doris even had a child."

"How was it you found out?" Deirdre asked.

Again, Tricia adopted an innocent stare. "I can't for the life of me remember. It must've been hard on her—being a single mother with a special child."

"You can call Susan retarded. It doesn't offend me, and it didn't offend Doris."

Tricia wasn't sure what to say.

Deirdre averted her gaze. "Being pregnant out of wedlock was one thing; keeping a Down syndrome child was another. Our family abandoned Doris. All except me," she amended. "I was the only one who cared about poor Doris. The world in general"—she turned back to Tricia—"and Stoneham in particular—always treated Doris shabbily."

"Is that what she told you?"

"It's what I observed. But yes, she did tell me that. We were very close."

"I can't say as I recall seeing you here in Stoneham before this week."

"I was not a regular visitor. We kept in touch by phone." Deirdre turned her back on Tricia, picked up her sponge, and began wiping the grimy wall once again. "Is it my imagination, or is this conversation turning into an interrogation?" She looked over her shoulder with a hard-eyed stare.

"I'm sorry. I was merely curious." Tricia changed the subject. "Tomorrow I'll be looking at a private collection of books; the owner is eager to sell. I'd be glad to look out for any cookbooks."

Spine still rigid, Deirdre gave a curt nod. "Thank you, Ms.—?"

"Call me Tricia. After all, we are neighbors."

Deirdre nodded and stepped closer to the ladder. "I must get back to work if I'm going to reopen next week. Thank you for stopping by."

Tricia knew a dismissal when she heard it. She gave a quick "Good-bye," and headed out the door.

Soft, mellow jazz issued from Haven't Got a Clue's speakers as Tricia reentered the store. Stationed at the sales counter, Ginny flipped the pages of a magazine, while sitting in the nook. Mr. Everett's nose was buried in a book without a dust jacket. Tricia hung up her coat, stowed her umbrella and purse, and headed for the coffee station, where she made a fresh pot and set out a new plate of cookies before heading for the sales counter.

Ginny looked up from her reading, quickly closing the big, fat magazine and turning it over. Tricia leaned close. "What would you think about me asking Mr. Everett to come work for us?"

Ginny's gaze slid to the closed magazine and then up again. "What a great idea. I've always felt bad about you being all by yourself here on Sundays. Business is good and he sure knows his mystery authors. Go for it."

Tricia caught sight of the magazine's name on the spine: *Bride's World.* Was there a wedding in Ginny's future? She nodded and smiled at the thought, also happy Ginny approved of her decision.

Tricia approached the elderly gent. "Mr. Everett?" He made to stand, but Tricia motioned him to stay put and took the seat opposite him. "Mr. Everett," she began again. "You've become a bit of a fixture here at Haven't Got a Clue."

Mr. Everett's eyes widened, his mouth dropping open in alarm. "I don't mean to be a pest, Ms. Miles. I won't take any more of your coffee and cookies, I promise—"

It was Tricia's turn to be alarmed. "Oh no—you misunderstand me. I'm not trying to throw you out. I'd like to offer you a job, Mr. Everett."

Alarm turned to shock. "A job? Me? But what can I do?"

"Sell books. You're very good at it. You know as much as I do—and probably a whole lot more—about our merchandise, and goodness knows you're dependable about showing up every day."

Color flushed the old man's cheeks. "A job?" he murmured in what sounded like disbelief.

"I won't ask you to lift heavy boxes, and your hours would be flexible, but you've already proved to be an asset to Ginny and me when the store is busy. I can't offer you a lot of money, and unfortunately I'm not in a position to give benefits of any kind, but—"

"A job—" he repeated, as though warming to the idea.

"I'd be glad to give you a couple of days to think it over. You wouldn't have to give me your answer until—"

Mr. Everett suddenly stood, a fire lighting his bright eyes. "No need for that. When do you want me to start?"

Tricia laughed. "How about an hour ago?"

The old man's lips quivered, his eyes growing moist. "Thank you. Thank you, Ms. Miles." He shook himself, then his head swiveled back and forth. "What do you want me to do first? The back shelves are in a terrible state. Customers have no sense of order. They take books out and then put them back every which way. Or I could rearrange the biographies in chronological order, versus alphabetical, so that customers would have a better understanding of how the genre grew. Perhaps it should have been done long before this."

Tricia stifled a laugh. "I'm glad you have so many good ideas. But right now I have a different kind of request. Would you be willing to go next door and make sure Ms. Gleason doesn't fall off a ladder? I don't want you to do anything that puts you in a position of getting hurt yourself, but just make sure she doesn't hurt herself in trying to get ready to reopen her sister's store."

"I could do that," he said, sounding less than enthused.

"Great. And tomorrow we'll figure out what your regular hours and duties will be."

Mr. Everett held out his hand. Tricia took it. "Thank you, Ms. Miles. Thank you for making an old man feel useful again. I'll go next door right now and make sure Ms. Gleason stays safe."

"Thank you."

Mr. Everett started for the door, which opened, admitting Angelica, who paused in the entryway, barring Mr. Everett's escape. They did a little dance with muttered "sorry's" and "excuse me's" while they tried to maneuver out of one another's way. At last Angelica stepped over to where Tricia still stood in the nook.

"I've never been here when the store was open," she said, without even a hello. She took in the clusters of browsing shoppers and Ginny at the register waiting on a customer with a stack of books. Angelica nodded approvingly.

"You've created a nice atmosphere here, Trish. And it doesn't stink of old paper like some used bookstores do, either."

Trust Angelica to spoil a compliment. "Thank you. I think. What brings you here so early?"

Angelica picked up one of the well-thumbed review magazines. "I wanted to let you know I can't fix dinner tonight."

Tricia hated to admit it, but in only three days she'd come to enjoy and look forward to one of Angelica's delicious entrées. "What's up?"

Angelica actually blushed. "I've got a date."

Tricia's stomach tightened. "Not with Bob Kelly."

"But of course. I haven't met any other eligible men in this burg."

"Where is he taking you?"

"Some divine little bistro called Ed's. I hear they've got the best seafood and that it's charmingly intimate."

"Charming for sure," Tricia admitted. Intimate as in small. But she didn't want to spoil her sister's anticipation.

"You've been there?"

She nodded. "The food is very good." An idea came to her: Bob and Angelica, dinner, a relaxed social atmosphere . . . "Ange, when you're with Bob tonight, see if you can get him to spill where he went after he left us at the Brookview on Tuesday night."

"I will not," she said sharply.

"Why? Don't you want to help prove me innocent?"

"Of course, but I also don't believe Bob killed the woman."

"Ange, please?" Tricia found herself whining.

Angelica turned away, refusing to meet her sister's gaze, and glanced out the front window and at the street beyond. "I'll think about it."

A couple of women walked past, clutching shopping bags, but they didn't enter Haven't Got a Clue.

"I circled the block three times before I gave up and parked in the municipal lot," Angelica said, annoyed.

"Who owns that car out front with the Connecticut license plates? They've been hogging that spot all morning. Surely you have parking restrictions along the main drag during business hours."

Tricia hadn't noticed the car. "The sheriff's department is pretty busy these days; at least I hope they're busy trying to solve Doris Gleason's murder."

"Mmm," Angelica muttered, her attention still on the offending vehicle. "That's the third or fourth time I've seen it."

"Excuse me, miss, could you help me?" asked a middle-aged woman, clutching a handwritten list. "I'm looking for *Malice with Murder*, by Nicholas Blake. Do you have a copy?"

Tricia gave the customer her full attention. Angelica mouthed, "Later," and wandered off toward the back shelves.

Ginny popped a more lively CD into the player, and between them she and Tricia waited on four more customers who paid for their purchases. The crowd had thinned by the time a puzzled-looking Angelica stepped up to the counter, slapping a booklet onto the glass top. "What are you doing with an old cooking pamphlet on one of your shelves?"

Awestruck, Tricia gaped at the booklet's title: *American Cookery*, by Amelia Simmons. "Good grief, it's the book that was stolen when Doris was murdered."

ELEVEN

 Curious onlookers lurking under umbrellas peered through the plate-glass windows of Haven't Got a Clue, the closed sign and locked door did nothing to deter them from rubbernecking. And despite the lack of customers, the shop seemed crowded with Sheriff Adams, a deputy, Angelica, Ginny, and Tricia, as well as Deirdre Gleason and Mr. Everett, who'd followed along after Ginny had called Deirdre over.

Sheriff Adams's piercing glare was fixed on Tricia. "I thought you said this thing was a book?"

Tricia looked down at the little booklet. "Technically, it is. Its significance is undisputed in the evolution of American cookery books. It's condition and rarity make it extremely valuable."

"This can't be worth ten grand," the sheriff said, poking the pamphlet with the eraser end of a pencil, unconvinced.

"Oh yes, it can," Ginny chirped up. "I looked it up online."

The sheriff shook her head, then took in the four women standing around the sales counter. "Who's touched the *book* since it was found?"

Tricia looked sidelong at her sister, but didn't answer.

The quiet lengthened. "Okay, it was me," an exasperated Angelica said, crossing her arms across her chest. "And what's the big deal anyway?"

"You might've obliterated whatever incriminating fingerprints were on it," the sheriff muttered.

"Oh, don't go all *CSI* on me. Whoever stole that little pamphlet probably wiped it clean before they dumped it here."

"Ange," Tricia warned.

The sheriff turned her scrutiny back to Tricia. "It's very odd that the person who found Ms. Gleason's body should now possess the stolen book."

"And not at all coincidental, if someone is trying to implicate my sister as Doris's killer," Angelica said, her voice rising. "And do we even know this is the same book?"

The sheriff turned to Tricia for the answer. "Given its rarity, it's unlikely there'd be two copies of it in a town this size. And, Sheriff, I assure you I have no idea how it ended up in my store, but I'm not responsible."

"Any ideas on who might be?"

If she had, she certainly would've volunteered that information before now. Tricia shook her head, fought to stay calm. "People wander in and out of here all day long, most of them strangers. Anyone could've planted that book here."

"But it's not likely Ms. Gleason would've let a stranger into her shop after hours."

"She was expecting someone," Tricia reminded the sheriff. "Bob Kelly."

"Trish." It was Angelica's turn to scold.

Sheriff Adams threw back her head and straightened to her full height. "Mr. Kelly has accounted for his whereabouts at the time of Ms. Gleason's death. I'm satisfied with his answers."

It was all Tricia could do not to blurt, "Yeah, but—" The way the sheriff kept glowering at her reinforced her fear that she remained the prime suspect.

"Why wasn't I told my sister expected Bob Kelly on the night of her death?" Deirdre demanded.

"I saw no need to upset you. And as I've just told Ms. Miles here, I don't suspect him."

"And why not? He was determined to force my sister out. The way he cleaned out the store less than forty-eight hours after her death is proof positive."

Sheriff Adams pointed a finger of warning at Deirdre. "This discussion is closed." She looked over her shoulder at the young deputy standing behind them. "Placer, take this 'book' to the office and lock it up. We'll send it to the state crime lab first thing Monday morning."

The uniformed officer stepped forward with what looked like a tackle box, which he opened, and took out a pair of latex gloves. He withdrew a paper evidence bag, shook it open, and picked up the booklet. A yellowed note card fell from it, hitting the carpeted floor.

"What's that?" Angelica asked, bending down.

"Looks like a birthday card," Tricia said.

"Don't touch it," the sheriff warned. "Placer?"

The deputy elbowed his way in and picked up the card, setting it and the booklet back on the counter before stepping aside. The five women crowded around, silently studying the front of the card, with its old-fashioned font and the image of a dozen red roses, the colors muted by the yellowing paper.

"Happy Birthday, to my dear wife," Angelica read.

"Open it up," the sheriff said.

Ginny stepped back so the deputy, with his gloved hands, could do so. The text in black was the usual syrupy wishes for a happy day; it was the peacock-blue-inked script that drew them in. "To my dearest Letty, Happy Birthday, love Roddy."

"What kind of a name is Letty?" Ginny asked.

"Letitia comes to mind. Or it could be short for something else," Tricia suggested. She raised her gaze. "Anybody in town named Letitia or Letty?"

The sheriff shook her head. "Not that I know of. And I've lived here my whole life."

They watched as the deputy carefully placed the book into a paper evidence bag, then put the card in another. With a curt nod to his boss, the officer headed out the door to his double-parked cruiser.

"That book is worth a lot of money. With my sister's passing, it now belongs to me," Deirdre asserted.

"It's part of a criminal investigation," the sheriff said.

"Will I ever get it back?"

"Possibly. But these things take time. Sometimes years."

"Years?" Deirdre repeated, appalled.

"Just what are you going to do to the book?" Ginny asked.

The sheriff bristled. "Normal procedure."

"Wait a minute," Tricia said. "Subjecting that book to black magnetic powder or ninhydrin would ruin it. I suppose iodine fuming might work. It develops prints beautifully. They'd just have to be photographed, not lifted, but it should spare the book. Then again, all that humidity." She shook her head. "CrimeScope. That's the book's best option, though on a porous surface like paper, it might not show a viable fingerprint, either."

"How do you know so much?" Sheriff Adams asked, suspicious.

Tricia waved a hand, taking in the thousands of books on the shelves around them. "I deal in mystery fiction. Not only do I read the classics, I read contemporary authors like Patricia Cornwell, Kathy Reichs, and Elizabeth Becka. You can practically get a degree in forensics just by reading these top authors. But that doesn't change the fact that it's likely only Angelica's prints are on the book, anyway."

"I want a receipt for it," Deirdre said. The sheriff just about rolled her eyes, and Deirdre snorted in outrage. "If any harm comes to that book, I will not only sue the county sheriff's department, but you personally."

"Will you at least ask the state lab to take special care with it?" Tricia pressed.

"I'll ask, but I can't make any guarantees."

"And I can't guarantee I won't immediately speak to my lawyer, either," Deirdre said. "Now about that receipt—"

Tricia provided a pen and a piece of paper. The sheriff scribbled a few lines, handing the sheet to Deirdre, who gave Tricia a nod. "I appreciate you calling me over. Otherwise, I'm not even sure I'd have been told the book was found." She turned on her heel and stalked out the door.

Sheriff Adams was the next to leave, following Deirdre without even a good-bye.

Angelica scowled. "I thought people from New Hampshire were supposed to be extra nice. Isn't that the state motto? Be nice or die?"

"That's 'Live Free or Die,' and don't judge all of us by some people," Ginny said, then, "What am I saying? Sheriff Adams is a good person. I've just never known her to be so cold. She must be getting pressure from somewhere else, like maybe the village board."

"What should I do next, Ms. Miles?" asked Mr. Everett, who hadn't said a word during the entire conversation.

"Why don't you go back and help Deirdre? Ginny and I can manage here." He didn't look happy, but nodded anyway. She glanced up at the clock. Two hours until official closing. Although the onlookers had disappeared, there was no reason she had to stay closed. She followed Mr. Everett to the door, turning the sign back to OPEN, and shut the door behind him.

"I guess I should go, too. Have to get ready for my big date tonight," Angelica said brightly. Shouldering her enormous handbag, she fingered a wave, called, "Ciao," and she, too, was gone.

Tricia and Ginny exchanged glances. "I need a cup of coffee," Tricia said.

"I'd go for something stronger," Ginny muttered.

"Not during work hours—but I agree. Put something cheerful on the CD player and hope we get busy so we don't have to think about what we've just been through."

"You got it," Ginny said.

Tricia poured them both a cup of coffee while Ginny

sorted through a stack of jewel boxes, selecting a jazz pi-
ano CD.

Peace now reigned, but forgetting the significance of
finding that wretched booklet in her store wasn't going to
be so easily accomplished.

The hands on the clock finally crawled around to closing
time. Despite her hopes otherwise, very few customers had
come in during the intervening hours and Tricia and Ginny
had completed all their end-of-day tasks, save for counting
the receipts. Mr. Everett had checked in, assuring Tricia
that Deirdre had left the Cookery for the day, then he, too,
departed. Miss Marple sat patiently at the door to the
stairs, anticipating her evening routine.

Ginny grabbed her coat and purse from the back closet
and headed for the exit. "Night, Trish."

The door opened before she could grasp the handle.
Russ Smith stood in the open doorway. "Are you closed?"

"Yes," Ginny said emphatically.

"Not quite," Tricia said. "How can I help you?" Her
tone was civil, but cool.

"Want me to stay?" Ginny asked.

Tricia shook her head. "Go on. Have a nice day off. See
you Monday."

Ginny looked uncertain, but Tricia waved her off. "It's
okay. Now scoot."

As the door closed behind her, Russ walked up to the
counter. Shoving his hands in his trouser pockets, he gave
the shop the once-over. "I seem to be your last customer."

"Yes, and you're keeping me from my dinner."

"As I recall, I invited you out."

"And as I recall, I turned you down. Come on, you're
only here because you heard the book stolen from Doris
Gleason's store was found here earlier today."

"Actually, I *didn't* know that, but thank you for sharing.
The special over at the diner is meat loaf and real mashed
potatoes."

"How do you know they're real?"

"I wasn't always a small-time reporter. I worked the Boston crime beat for years. And besides, I've seen the peels in their garbage."

Tricia's stomach growled, betraying her.

"See, at least part of you wants to go with me. And what's your alternative: a peanut butter sandwich?"

Had he been scoping out her cupboards and fridge? And although she'd neglected her paperwork for days and needed to catch up, the truth was she really didn't want to be alone tonight and cursed Angelica for having a date.

"Okay," she agreed, "but only if we go Dutch."

Russ shrugged. "Saves me eight-ninety-nine plus tax and tip."

Already Tricia regretted her decision, yet she locked the cash drawer, pocketing the keys. "I have to feed my cat before I can go."

"Do what you gotta do," he said and flopped down into one of the nook's chairs. "I'll wait."

The walk to the Bookshelf Diner had been silent. At least the rain had stopped, but a voice in Tricia's head kept up a litany of "big mistake, big mistake" with every step along the damp pavement.

Russ held the door open for her. A sign on the metal floor stand said SEAT YOURSELF. With only two other booths occupied, they had their pick of the place. Heads turned as the village jinx walked down the aisle, but Tricia aimed for the back of the restaurant with her head held high. She slid across the last booth's red Naugahyde seat and shrugged out of her jacket, folding it and placing it next to her. Russ hung his on a peg and sat down.

A college-age waitress with a quick smile, a pierced brow, and a name tag that said "Eugenia" handed them menus and took their drink orders before disappearing.

Tricia eyed her surroundings. The name over the door did not match the décor. The only books in the Bookshelf

Diner were of the trompe l'oeil variety—and then on a commercial wall covering. The waitress returned, setting the stemmed glass down in front of Tricia and pouring coffee for Russ. After quickly consulting the menu she did order the meat loaf, then practically gulped the well-deserved glass of red wine.

"Tough day, huh?" Russ asked.

"I've had better. And I don't want to talk about it."

"Why should you? The sheriff suspects you of murder. I'm sure it's just lack of motive that's keeping her from locking you up. She'll have to turn up the heat after finding that book in your store."

"She did not find it. My sister did."

"Then she's not doing you any favors, either."

Tricia snatched up her glass, gulping down the rest of her wine, then let it smack back down on the table. "I barely knew Doris Gleason. She argued with Bob Kelly, had an appointment to see him on the night she was murdered. He wanted her out of that store, which is at least a credible motive for murder. He left the Brookview Inn before Ange and I did, but he didn't show up at the Cookery until more than an hour after I found Doris dead. Where was he during that time?"

"You tell me."

"He could have murdered Doris, then showed up later feigning no knowledge."

Russ sat back, folded his arms across his chest. "If I was you, I'd quit harping on Bob Kelly as a possible suspect. For one thing, he would've never started the fire at the Cookery and put his property at risk just to get rid of a tenant. And even so, it wouldn't matter if he were caught plunging the knife in the victim's back. Most people around here consider him a savior for how he almost single-handedly brought Stoneham back to life."

"So someone like me, who's innocent, should take the blame?"

"I didn't say that. But in the sheriff's eyes, so far you are the only 'person of note.' "

Tricia picked up her glass, signaling the waitress for a refill. "I did not kill Doris Gleason. I had no reason to kill Doris Gleason."

Heads turned at the sound of her words.

"I'd start looking for reasons why others might've wanted her dead."

"That isn't my job. You said you were once a big-time reporter; isn't there at least a shred of Clark Kent left inside you? Why don't you take up the challenge, or at least direct one of your minions to do it?"

"Honey, I have a staff of two, one of which spends her time soliciting ads to keep us afloat. My chief reporter is a soccer mom who writes most of her copy after her kids go to bed. I do everything else. You own a small business—you know the drill."

"Do I ever."

The waitress returned with another glass of wine and their dinners.

Russ picked up his fork and stabbed at his mashed potatoes. "Besides, you run a mystery bookstore. You've probably read enough of them to get you started. In fact, you may already have bits and pieces of knowledge about the murder you haven't yet put together. I'd be happy to brainstorm with you about it."

"You'd be the last person I'd bare my soul to. I'd see whatever I tell you in next Friday's edition. It's just as likely whoever killed Doris was a transient. Someone who'd canvassed the Cookery, figured any book worth locking up would be of value, killed Doris, and stole it." She took another sip from her glass.

"Is that you or the wine talking? Don't kid yourself. The fact that book was found in your store means someone wants you to take the blame. You can either keep wandering around in denial or ask yourself some tough questions: like who wants you out of the picture and why?"

TWELVE

When the check arrived, Tricia and Russ ponied up their shares, donned their jackets, and headed for the exit. The wind had picked up and the clouds had departed, leaving the sky clear and star-strewn. "Walk you home?" Russ offered.

They stood outside the Bookshelf Diner. Tricia buttoned her jacket. "I'm not afraid of the dark. And besides, Stoneham is safe."

"I believed that a week ago," he said. "Now I'm not so sure."

Tricia looked down the street and saw the flashing lights of a police cruiser. "Now what?" She started walking, heading south down the sidewalk at a brisk pace.

"Looks like it's parked outside the Cookery," Russ said, as he struggled to keep up with her.

It was, but a deputy stood outside Haven't Got a Clue. Tricia broke into a run, crossed the street, and practically skidded to a halt in front of her shop. The large plate-glass window now sported a gaping hole in its center, with cracks radiating from it in a sunburst array. Inside the shop, what was left of her security system wailed.

"You wanna shut that thing off?" She didn't recognize the deputy, whose name tag read "Placer."

Heart pounding, Tricia fumbled for her key, unlocked the door, and flipped on the light switch. Seconds later, she'd disarmed the alarm and quiet descended. She joined the deputy on the sidewalk. "What happened?" she asked, breathless.

"Looks like a rock," he said, peering into the hole.

Tricia frowned at his blasé attitude. Glass covered Tricia's display of Ross Macdonald's books. Several people had turned up, rubbernecking from behind the back of a parked car.

"So what's the story, Jim?" Russ asked Placer.

"Just what it looks like, petty vandalism."

"How can you be sure?" Tricia asked. "A woman was killed right next door just days ago. This could be tied in."

The deputy shook his head, turned his attention to the clipboard he held and the report he'd already started to fill in. "Probably just kids."

"Did anybody see anything?" Tricia called to the unfamiliar faces in the gathering crowd, but they all shook their heads, huddling in their coats and jackets.

Placer handed Tricia a business card. "These guys can board up the window until you can get it fixed. You want me to hang around until then?" He couldn't have sounded more bored.

"Wait a minute. Aren't you going to check out the shop?"

"The door was locked—you opened it yourself. Did you see any other damage or anything missing?"

"I've hardly had a chance to look."

"So look," he said and turned his attention back to his clipboard.

Tricia threw Russ a glance, as if to ask if this was the way all law enforcement acted in Stoneham. He shrugged.

Tricia reentered her store, doing a quick walk-through. Save for the gaping hole in her window, everything seemed just as she'd left it a little over an hour before. The door to the stairs was still closed. The alarm would've sounded in the apartment, too. Poor Miss Marple was probably hiding under the bed, terrified.

Russ stood inside the doorway. "Want me to go upstairs with you, make sure everything's okay? I got Jim to promise he'd hang around at least another five minutes."

"If you wouldn't mind, thank you."

Tricia opened the door, threw the switch to bathe the stairwell with light, and bounded up. The door to the second-floor storeroom was locked, just as she'd left it. Still, she took out the key, opened it, and groped for the light switch and entered. Nothing looked out of place in the cavernous room full of stacked boxes—all of them containing books. She closed and locked the door.

Russ was behind her as she started up the stairs once again. The door to her loft apartment was unlocked and she quickly decided to amend her own personal security measures in the future. She'd left a light on for Miss Marple, but the cat was nowhere in sight.

"Miss Marple. Miss Marple!" she called. Sure enough, a pair of frightened green eyes appeared when Tricia lifted the bed's dust ruffle. She reached for the cat, scooping her into her arms. "Oh, you poor little thing," she cooed, as she struggled to her feet.

She found Russ standing in the middle of her kitchen. "Everything okay?"

"Yes, thank goodness." Miss Marple had already engaged her motor and nuzzled Tricia's chin, purring loudly. "She was just frightened."

Russ smiled. "I'll go downstairs and keep watch. Why don't you call the guys to cover the window?"

"Good idea. But first, I think someone deserves a treat." At the sound of the magic word, Miss Marple wriggled to get down and Tricia placed her on the floor. She spilled half a packet of kitty cookies into Miss Marple's bowl, knowing she'd only toss most of them later. But at that moment, she didn't care.

The board-up service the deputy recommended was available twenty-four/seven and promised Tricia someone would be there within the hour. Next up, a call to her security company. They weren't as helpful, saying a service rep *might* be by bright and early Monday morning. No more chances, Tricia decided. It was time to find another security company.

Miss Marple had had her fill of cookies and had settled on one of the breakfast bar's chairs, ready for a nap by the time Tricia headed back downstairs to the store.

Russ had closed the shop's door and the crowd had dispersed. He sat in the nook, reading an article in *CrimeSpree* magazine. He looked up as she approached. "Everything okay?"

She nodded.

Russ stood. "Seems like all I've asked you for the last hour is 'everything okay?'"

For the first time since she'd seen the cruiser's flashing lights, Tricia smiled. "The enclosure company will be here pretty soon. They said not to bother to sweep up the glass, they'd clean up everything. If the window's a standard size, they can have it replaced first thing Monday morning. They'll even take care of the insurance claim."

"Can't beat that for service." He handed her a paper that had been sitting on the nook's coffee table. "Here's the police report. And what about your security system?"

"That's another matter. I may have it back up on Monday, but I'm not going to bet on it."

"Should you stay here without it working?"

"I'll be all right. Besides, I can always hide under the bed with my cat."

"I'm serious, Tricia. Someone's trying to make you look responsible for Doris Gleason's death, and now this."

"There's no proof the two events are connected."

"That's not what you said to the deputy. Do you have a girlfriend or a relative you can stay with tonight?"

Tricia thought about Angelica, remembered she had a date with Bob, and immediately nixed that idea. "I'll be fine."

"I've got a guest room," Russ offered. "It's got a lock on the door."

"That's very kind, but—" She shook her head, thinking of the logistics of moving Miss Marple. Food and water bowls, toys, litter box . . .

The conversation lagged. "You don't have to stay, Russ. I'll be all right until the repair guys get here."

"No way," he said. "I want to prove to you that chivalry isn't dead in Stoneham."

Tricia almost laughed, considering the article he'd published on her only the day before. Still, she wasn't about to turn down an act of kindness. "At least let me offer you a cup of coffee while we wait."

"I'll take you up on it."

Russ retreated to the nook and his magazine while Tricia made coffee. Her gaze kept returning to the broken window, which a gale seemed to be blowing through. The rock, quite a hefty specimen, had crashed through *her* window—no one else's. Whoever had thrown it had had to have the strength to do it. Her chief suspect in Doris's murder was on a date with Angelica.

Who else wanted to frighten her?

Light from the street lamps outside was all that lit Tricia's bedroom. Sleep had not come and she'd been staring at the glowing red numerals on her bedside clock for almost two hours while Miss Marple, curled beside her on the comforter, snored quietly.

Tricia's thoughts followed a circular track: *Doris dead: someone wants to blame me. Rock through window: someone out to get me.*

She'd taken her security for granted in this quiet little village. Five years ago she'd led a much different life. Until her divorce, she'd never revealed her desire to open a mystery bookshop. She'd lived the life of a stockbroker's wife, had a gorgeous apartment overlooking Central Park West, spent many an evening at five-star restaurants and the theater, her days filled with . . . not much since the non-profit agency she'd worked for since college had down-sized staff. But she'd loved Christopher and the life they'd shared, even if he worked much too hard.

And then everything changed.

Christopher changed. Wanted a simpler life. A life that didn't include responsibilities . . . or a wife.

And yet . . . somehow they'd remained friends. And right now she wanted to hear the sound of a friendly voice.

On impulse, Tricia picked up the receiver on her bed-side phone, punched in the number she'd memorized but so far hadn't used.

The phone rang four times before a sleepy voice an-swered, "—llo?"

"Christopher?"

Long seconds of silence.

"Tricia?"

She sagged against her pillows. "It's me."

"What time is it?"

"After one. Oh, wait—that's eleven your time. You go to bed early these days."

"It's all that fresh air. There's nothing like it." She could hear the unspoken *should've done this years ago*. "What's wrong?"

"Can't a friend call a friend without something being wrong?"

"Trish," he admonished.

She sighed. "Someone threw a rock through my shop window tonight."

"What?"

"And my neighbor was murdered on Tuesday." She left out the part that she was the main suspect.

"You're not serious," he said, no longer sounding sleepy.

"It's all true."

"All those years in Manhattan without a problem, and you move to a small town in New England to find chaos."

"Could only happen to me, right?" she said, but the laugh that accompanied it was forced.

"I can't just come over and make it right for you."

"I know. I wouldn't expect you to. It's just . . ." She reached out, petted her cat, who began to purr. "Miss Marple misses you."

"I miss her, too."

She dared speak the words she'd been afraid to ask. "Are you with anybody?"

"Nobody could live up to you."

"Then why . . . ?" she asked, the hurt bubbling up once again. He didn't answer, hadn't had a real answer the day he'd announced his decision to leave. "I didn't want a divorce. We could've worked things out."

"No. I wasn't going to drag you down with me. You're too special for that, my girl."

But Tricia knew she would never be his girl again. "Are you happy?"

"Yeah. I am. It's a much different life. It's not something you'd enjoy. You need people. Stimulation. Tell me, were you happy before Tuesday, before all this crap happened?"

"Yes," she answered without hesitation. Admitting that did make her feel a bit better.

"When things calm down, you'll feel happy again."

"Angelica's visiting. She says she wants to move to Stoneham."

"Scratch that, then," he said, which made her laugh. That's why she'd called. Some part of her had known he'd make her laugh.

"It'll be okay, Trish. You're strong and you'll get through whatever's going on. You'll be fine."

"You promise?"

"Yes. Now close your eyes and dream about something wonderful. Like a cheese blintz."

Tricia couldn't help but smile. "I take it they're hard to find in the wilds of Colorado."

"You got it, sweetheart."

She laughed again. "Thank you for picking up the phone. I'm sorry I woke you."

"You know you can call me anytime."

It was time to hang up and actually doing it was proving harder than she'd anticipated. Saying what she had to say would be even more difficult. "Good-bye, Christopher."

"Good-bye, Trish."

Tricia carefully replaced the phone in its cradle, knowing she would never call him again.

THIRTEEN

Tricia inspected her makeup in the mirror over the bathroom sink. After three attempts to cover the dark circles beneath her eyes with concealer, she admitted defeat and set the little tube aside. Talking to Christopher hadn't settled her nerves, and Russ Smith's words of warning the evening before had stayed with her, keeping her from yet another decent night's sleep.

She'd come to no conclusions during her tossing and turning, grateful she could spare no time this morning to ponder the situation. Still, she took another moment to assess herself in the full-length mirror on the back of the door, wanting to look nice for Mike. She'd chosen the peach sweater set over beige slacks. With the days growing shorter, she'd soon put it away for darker fall colors. The idea of winter setting in and the possibility of spending it in the New Hampshire State Prison for Women did more than depress her.

I will not think about it, I will not think about it. And despite his chivalry after the rock incident, she cursed Russ for even hinting at the possibility she could end up in jail.

Out in the kitchen, Miss Marple rubbed her little gray body against the door leading to the stairs and the store below. "It's Sunday," Tricia told her, and took one last sip of her tepid coffee before dumping it in the sink. "You don't need to go to work until noon." But the cat would not be dissuaded.

Tricia grabbed her coat from the tree and snagged her purse and keys.

The phone rang. Who on Earth would be calling so early on a Sunday morning?

Miss Marple stood up, scratched the door, and cried piteously. Tricia unlocked and opened it for her. The phone rang again as the cat scampered down the stairs. Tricia snatched it on the third ring. "Hello?"

"Tricia, it's Angelica. What took you so long to answer?"

"I was almost out the door," she said, balancing the phone on her shoulder as she struggled into her jacket sleeves.

"I thought the store opened late today."

"It does. I'm going out to evaluate a private collection. Can this wait until later? I'm going to be late."

"Wait! I just heard about your store being vandalized. Are you okay?"

"Of course," she lied. "I'm perfectly fine. Why wouldn't I be?"

"There's a murderer running around Stoneham, and now someone's targeted you—maybe the same person."

"Don't be so melodramatic. It was only a window; it'll be replaced tomorrow. Besides, I wasn't even in the building at the time."

"Are you opening the store today?"

"Definitely. But as I said, I've got to head out right now or I'll be late."

"I think you should close the store and come house hunting with me today."

"You know I can't. There are at least two buses coming through this afternoon."

"Well, at least you close early, don't you?"

"At three."

"Fine. By then I'll have looked at two or three properties. If I find one I like, I'll want your opinion."

That was a first. Tricia couldn't remember her sister
ever consulting her on anything, be it a brand of designer
shoes or the ripeness of a banana. For some reason, it
pleased her. "Okay. Who's driving, you or me?"

"Me."

"All right. See you at three."

"Be careful," Angelica warned.

Tricia hung up the phone to find an annoyed Miss
Marple sitting at her heels. "You know perfectly well
there's a door at the bottom of the stairs and that it's closed
until I open it."

Miss Marple stood and swaggered back to the open
doorway. Tricia grabbed her purse once again and followed.

The Harris homestead was a lovely pseudo-Tudor nes-
tled in a quaint, upscale neighborhood with mature trees
and professional landscaping.

Tricia parked her car at the curb, noting Mike's sleek
black Jag sat under a massive maple, its highest leaves just
beginning to turn gold. The remnants of a now-untended
garden rimmed the front of the buff-colored, stucco-faced
house. A sense of recent abandonment clung to the property. Mike probably had his own home to take care of, and
the house was huge, much too big for one person—
especially someone with the beginnings of Alzheimer's
disease. Poor Mrs. Harris.

Tricia pressed the doorbell and heard a resounding
bing-bong from within. Moments later the heavy oak door
swung open. "Welcome," Mike greeted, ushering her into
an elegant foyer with its polished tile floor and matching
floral wing chairs flanking a marble-topped mahogany
table. To the left was a magnificent staircase, with ornately

carved banisters, that swept up to the second floor. Light streamed in through stained-glass panes of green and yellow diamonds, casting a warm glow on the carpeted steps.

"What a beautiful home," she said, wondering what other delights it might contain.

"Thanks. It was a nice place to grow up in. And as you can see, my parents took good care of it." He held out his hands. "Let me take your jacket. I've got a pot of coffee brewing in the kitchen. Can I get you a cup?"

"Yes, thanks," she said and shed her coat.

Mike took it from her and hung it in a closet off to the left at the base of the stairs. "How do you take it?"

"Milk or creamer only—no sugar."

"Coming right up. Most of the books are in the living room," he said, gesturing to his right. Go have a look—make yourself at home." He gave her an encouraging smile and took off down a dark hallway.

"Thanks," she called after him.

With Mike gone, an unnerving silence enveloped her. She took in a deep breath of stale air and wondered how long the house had been closed up.

Since she was there to see the books, Tricia figured she might as well get started and entered the living room through the opened French doors, where both chaos and order reigned. A stack of mismatched, taped cartons sat beside an empty curio cabinet just inside the doors, bald patches in the dust suggesting the shapes of the delicate objects that had once occupied it. Several seating arrangements compartmentalized the large room. Most of the furniture lay hidden beneath drop cloths, while other pieces, richly brocaded in shades of beige, were not. The carpet hadn't seen a vacuum cleaner in months. Rectangular patches on the walls hinted at where paintings, prints, or photographs had once hung.

Tricia picked her way across the room to the reading nook with its matching wide and inviting pillowed chairs and floor lamps, not unlike what she'd created for Haven't Got a Clue. The adjacent bookshelves stood on either side of a white painted mantel and drew her to them. It didn't take much imagination to conjure up an image of a sedate Mrs. Harris in her declining years, seated in one of the chairs before a roaring fire, book in hand, lost in its pages.

Now the room felt cold, empty. Without its mistress, the room—if not the home—had lost its soul.

Tricia shook away the image and retrieved her reading glasses from her purse, slipping them on to assess the titles. Mrs. Harris had eclectic taste in reading material, from mystery fiction to romances, biographies to travel books, as well as mainstream fiction and the classics, and she'd grouped them as such. Noticeable gaps on the shelves proved that the collection was not entirely intact.

She grabbed a mystery at random, *Deadly Honeymoon*, by Lawrence Block. It turned out to be a first edition with a mint condition dust cover. She'd sold a used, discarded library copy for eight dollars only a week before. This would bring much more. Checking the copyright dates on several other books was just as encouraging. Other titles by authors such as James Michener and Ann Morrow Lindbergh were also first editions. They'd be worth more signed, but were still valuable to die-hard collectors.

Mike reappeared with a tray containing two steaming mugs and a plate of Oreos, which he set on the dusty table in the nook. He handed her a mug. "So what do you think?"

"I'm no expert on most of what's here, but a lot appear to be first editions. That's always a plus."

"Could you give me a ballpark estimate on the whole lot?"

Tricia shook her head. "I shouldn't tell you this, but if you offer them to a dealer, you'll get substantially less than they're worth. Your best bet is to sell them on one of the online auction sites."

Mike frowned. "I figured as much."

"I see some of the books are already missing."

Mike's grip on his coffee mug tightened. "I gave them to friends of Mother's. At first I didn't realize they might be worth anything. I even considered boxing up the lot and taking them to Goodwill just for the tax write-off. Even then, I'd need an estimate on their worth—something I couldn't do."

"A lot of them may end up there anyway; for instance, the travel books and most of the paperbacks she has squirreled away. Unless of course she had some of the old pulp paperbacks from the forties and fifties. They're quite collectible if only for their lurid covers."

"Doesn't sound like Mother's cup of tea."

Tricia remembered her promise to Deirdre. "Did your mother have any cookbooks?"

"In the kitchen. Come on, I'll show you."

Tricia followed Mike down the dark hallway, past a formal dining room, and into a large airy kitchen, which hadn't seen a remodel since the 1970s. The harvest gold appliances and bicentennial patterned vinyl flooring, with 1776 stamped every few squares, seemed stuck in time. Then again, the oak table with stenciled Hitchcock chairs and the dark-stained woodwork were classic. Except for a layer of dust on just about everything, the room was tidy, the counters clutter free.

The hundred or more cookbooks resided in a glass-fronted double-doored cabinet above and between the sink and stove, no doubt to keep them grease free. Like in the living room, gaps on these shelves proved they had also stored more than were currently there. Would all the other cupboards be empty as well? And what did it matter? Mike had said he was liquidating the estate to pay for his mother's health care. A pity that was necessary.

Tricia opened one of the doors, selecting a book at random and thumbing through to the copyright page. "The Cookery is in need of new stock because of smoke damage after the fire."

"The Cookery? I thought it was closed. I saw it had been emptied out and someone was cleaning the place yesterday. I assumed it was the new tenant."

"Doris Gleason had a sister. She's taking over the

business and is looking for new stock. If you're going to dump these books anyway, you might consider offering them to Deirdre. Who knows, she might even vote for you in the election."

He laughed. "Thanks."

Tricia replaced the book, closing the cabinet. She turned to find Mike staring at her, or rather her bust. She pulled her long-sleeved sweater tighter about her, crossing her arms across her chest. "Goodness, our coffee's getting cold."

Mike seemed to shake himself. "Come on." He led the way back to the living room, and they resumed their places before the cold fireplace. Tricia picked up her mug, took a sip, and resigned herself to yet another cup of tepid coffee.

Mike grabbed a book at random from the closest shelf. A yellowed piece of paper jutted out of it, marking a place. He took out the paper and showed it to her: a recipe for Yankee bean soup torn from a magazine. "Still having problems with the propaganda leaflets?"

Tricia nodded, grateful for something else to talk about. "Yes. And you were right. The one I showed you was just the first in a series. They've stepped up to a direct advertising campaign. Ever hear of Full Moon Camp and Resort?"

"Can't say as I have," he said, crumpled the paper, and tossed it into the fireplace's maw. He replaced the book on the shelf.

"It gave a web address that said they were opening a new location next summer in southern New Hampshire, but it didn't specify where. I meant to call Bob Kelly about it, but with everything else that's been going on . . ."

Mike looked concerned. "Such as?"

"Didn't you hear about the rock through my window?"

"No. When did that happen?"

"About eight thirty last night."

"Huh. I was in my new office last night, unpacking. It must've happened after I left."

"What time was that?"

"Quarter after eight, maybe eight twenty."

Interesting.

Mike picked up his cup, swallowed a sip of cold coffee, and grimaced.

The conversation lagged.

"This really is a beautiful house," Tricia said finally.

"If you think this looks nice, you ought to see the bedrooms," he said à la Groucho Marx, and waggled his eyebrows for further effect. "I'd be glad to give you a personal tour."

Tricia's entire body tensed, but somehow she managed a weak smile. "Sorry, I can't stay too much longer."

"Your shop doesn't open for at least another two hours. That's plenty of time for us to get better acquainted," he said and moved a step closer

Tricia's already tense muscles went rigid. "I have a new employee I'm training today."

"Oh?"

"Mr. Everett."

"Oh, the old coot who's taken root in your store."

"He's a treasure," she said, feeling protective of the old gentleman. "He'll be a great asset at Haven't Got a Clue."

Mike turned away and set his mug back down on the tray. "You seem to be collecting men these days."

Tricia blinked. "Excuse me?"

"Last night when I walked to the municipal lot to get in my car, I saw you at the diner with Russ Smith," Mike said, a slight edge entering his voice. "That surprised me, especially after what he wrote about you. And what will people say about my girl being seen with another man?"

My girl? That's what Christopher always called her, and she'd liked the sound of the words—the emotions behind it. But coming from Mike, the words gave her a chill.

Tricia thought about the gaping hole in her shop window, the strength it had taken to heave the miniature boulder that had shattered it. Unease wormed through her as she realized how isolated the two of them were in the big vacant house. She swallowed down the lump that had suddenly appeared in her throat. "We've been out to lunch exactly one time, that hardly makes me 'your girl.'" She even managed a little laugh.

"Maybe I'd like to change that." Mike stepped closer, putting his hands around her and pulling her against him.

"Mike," she said, squirming in his embrace.

He didn't let go, his face hovering close to her own, his breath warm on her cheek.

"Mike," she said with more urgency.

He leaned in closer, brushing his lips across her neck.

Panicking, Tricia pulled her arms free and pushed against his chest. "Mike, please!"

He stumbled back, puzzled. "I'm sorry, Trish. I thought you were as attracted to me as I am to you."

"That's very flattering. It's just—" How do you tell someone he's just creeped you out?

"Ah," he said, a sympathetic lilt entering his voice. "Too soon after your divorce?"

"That's exactly it. And anyway, it's not like Russ and I are even friends. We only discussed Doris's murder, which quickly became tedious, believe me. And it wasn't a date. We each paid for our own dinners." She didn't mention Russ staying with her until the enclosure guys could show up. And why did she feel she owed him an explanation, anyway?

"Any new developments in the murder case?" Mike asked, with no real interest.

"Just that the stolen book's been found."

He raised an eyebrow. "That is news. Where was it?"

"In my store."

"That's not good."

"No, it isn't." Tricia picked up her purse. "Look, I really have to get back to the shop." She took a step back, but he reached out, capturing her arm in a strong grip.

"Are you sure you can't stay for another cup of coffee?"

Tricia forced a smile as she pried his fingers from her forearm. "Sorry. I really have to get going." She turned and practically ran from the room, then realized it would be bad manners to snatch her jacket from the closet and flee.

Yet she stood for long seconds in the empty foyer and Mike didn't appear.

As time ticked on and still he didn't appear, she figured the heck with manners and wrenched open the closet door. She'd expected to find it stuffed with coats, scarves, hats, and boots, but hers was the only jacket amongst the row of dark wooden hangers. She grabbed her jacket, slammed shut the door, and turned to find Mike, hands in his pants pockets, slouched against the wall, watching her.

"Um, thank you," she stammered, "for the coffee."

"I wish you didn't have to leave."

"Me, too," she said too cheerfully, the lie obvious. She inched closer to the front door.

"Thanks for the advice about the books," Mike said, his voice sounding oddly composed.

"You're more than welcome. Glad I could be of help." She had her hand on the door handle, turned it, and found it locked. Panicked, she pulled at it, fumbling for the lever.

A hand touched hers and she shrieked and jumped back.

"Calm down, calm down," Mike soothed and stepped forward.

Tricia backed away, afraid he might come after her. Instead, he flipped the dead bolt, pulled the door open. Fresh air and the sunny morning poured into the foyer once again. Tricia zipped past Mike and onto the step outside. The tightness in her chest relaxed a bit and she felt like an absolute idiot for her behavior. She turned back. Mike stood in the open doorway, looking concerned.

Tricia forced a smile. "See you in town." Her tone almost sounded normal.

Mike stared at her for long seconds, his face impassive, then nodded and closed the door.

Frozen in time, Tricia stared for long seconds at the barrier between the real world and the stifling air of the lifeless house before she turned and hurried down the steps, letting out a whoosh of air as she went.

It wasn't until she'd driven a block away that she felt anywhere near calm again.

Tricia welcomed the return to the familiar surroundings at Haven't Got a Clue. True to form, Mr. Everett had been waiting outside the locked door for her. As expected, he was full of questions and concerned about the boarded-up shop.

"We will open today, won't we?" he asked, anxiously, as she unlocked the door.

"Yes, although it does seem awfully dark in here. We'll have to turn on all the lights. Let me hang up our coats and we'll get started."

It soothed the last of Tricia's jagged nerves to walk Mr. Everett through the daily tasks, and it turned out he'd been observant during all the months he'd visited the store as a customer who never purchased anything. He probably knew everything about the daily routine except the combination to the little safe under the counter.

During the three hours the store was open they shelved four boxes of books, waited on fifteen customers, and sold seventeen novels. Not bad for what was usually her slowest day. They also found another twenty-two nudist leaflets. Who on Earth had been stashing them around the store, and why hadn't they caught the culprit?

Staying busy kept Tricia from thinking too much about her panic at being at the Harris home alone with Mike. Then again, too often lately she'd been employing a selective memory—especially when it came to what could be her future. And why had she ever agreed to go house hunting with Angelica?

True to her word, Angelica showed up at precisely 3 p.m., honking the car horn outside Haven't Got a Clue. Anticipating her sister's arrival, Tricia had closed a few minutes early, stuffed the day's receipts in the safe, waved good-bye to Mr. Everett, and was ready to go when the rental car pulled up out front.

"That stupid out-of-state car is still parked in front of your store," Angelica said in greeting, glaring at the offending vehicle.

Tricia buckled her seat belt as a horn blasted behind them.

Angelica hit the gas and the car lurched forward. "The shop looks dreadful. Couldn't you at least have that plywood painted to match the rest of the storefront?"

"It'll only be there another day."

"It's not likely to entice customers. You look dreadful, too, Trish. Those dark circles under your eyes are really unbecoming."

Tricia bit her tongue to keep from blurting a scathing retort.

Oblivious of her sister's pique, Angelica continued. "I have big news. I won!"

"Won what?" Tricia asked, glad for the change of subject.

"The parlay on Deborah Black's baby. He was born last night at eight thirty-seven p.m."

"How did you even know about it?"

"I told you, I visited all the stores in town. The owner of History Repeats Itself, Jim Roth, sold me the square. He's an absolute doll. Too bad he's married."

"Speaking of dolls, how was your big date with Bob last night?"

Angelica snorted. "Some date. He takes me to this little dump of a clam shack on the side of the highway and gives me an hour-long real estate pitch. Although I have to admit the food was pretty good."

A grudging admission if Tricia had ever heard one.

"Still, it reinforces my belief that what this little town needs is fine dining. And I might be just the person to make it happen."

Tricia was determined not to encourage her. "I had dinner at the diner last night and only three tables were occupied. They roll up Stoneham's sidewalks at seven."

"It might have to be a lunch-only establishment. Surely that little diner can't handle all the tourists at midday."

But Tricia didn't want to talk about restaurants. Her

window had been broken at about eight thirty. Where had Bob been at the time? "So what time did you invite Bob back to your hotel room?"

Angelica's hand's tightened on the wheel. "I did *not* invite him to my room."

"But surely he took you back to the inn. What time was that?"

"Terribly early. Somewhere around eight."

So, Bob could've thrown the rock. The question was, why?

"At least he invited me to the dining room for a nightcap," Angelica continued with disdain. "Otherwise I would've been in bed and asleep by nine o'clock."

"What time did he leave?" Tricia pressed.

"I don't know. Maybe nine fifteen."

Tricia's insides sagged. So much for Bob being responsible, though that still left him a viable suspect in Doris's murder. "The subject of where he went after he left us on Tuesday night didn't come up, did it?"

"It did. But it wasn't easy working it into the conversation," Angelica said, her attention focused on the road. "Bob doesn't like to talk negatively about Stoneham. And the first murder in sixty years is definitely negative."

"And?"

"He wouldn't say. Just that it was 'business.'"

"Typical of him." There had to be other avenues Tricia could explore, but right now she couldn't think of any so she concentrated on the matter at hand. "Did you find anything promising on your house hunt this morning?"

Angelica brightened. "Actually, Bob did steer me toward a darling little cottage that's for rent with an option to buy. The problem is the size. It's much too small."

"Is that where we're going now?"

"Yes. If nothing else, it's got potential."

Stoneham's small business district was already past, and trees and mileposts sped by.

"I'm trying to decide what to do with the money," Angelica said.

"Money?" Tricia asked, confused. "Oh yeah, the parlay. How much did you win, anyway?"

"Four hundred dollars."

"Four hundred dollars?" Tricia repeated, shocked.

"Not bad, huh? I think I'll send Deborah some flowers as a little thank-you."

Tricia sank back in her seat. "And you'll still have enough left for a Louis Vuitton key chain, too."

A number of businesses hugged the road that approached the highway. Tricia spotted the old smashed-up Cadillac Seville sitting beside a service station. "Stop the car!" she yelled, craning her neck as they whipped past.

Angelica slammed on the brakes, the car fishtailing onto the shoulder. "What's wrong? Did I hit something?"

"Back up, back up!"

Angelica jammed the gearshift into reverse and hit the accelerator.

"Whoa—stop, stop!" Tricia called, unhooking her seat belt and bolting from the car. She charged across the sea of asphalt surrounding the closed gas station, halting in front of the mangled mess that had once been Winnie Wentworth's most prized possession. The front end was now a tangle of metal, already rusting from all the rain they'd had since Winnie's death. The windshield's glass had been reduced to a spider's web of cracks. No sign of blood. With no seat belt, she might have been ejected out the driver's window. The outcome was the same: death.

Angelica was suddenly at her side. "This belonged to the woman who sold Doris the cookbook?"

Tricia nodded and leaned forward to try the rear passenger side door handle. It opened.

"Hey, wait a minute," Angelica said and pulled Tricia's hand away. "This is a crime scene."

"The sheriff said Winnie's death was an accident. There's no crime tape. Poking around inside the car isn't trespassing."

"Says you."

Tricia waved her sister off and climbed into the grimy,

damp interior. Various unpleasant odors assaulted her, and it was difficult to discern them: sweat, urine, and possibly mold? She rooted through the pile of gray clothes and blankets on the floor, coming up with a sheaf of yellowing newspaper clippings that had been stuffed under the driver's seat. She backed out of the car, shoving the papers toward Angelica, who stepped away in horror.

"I don't want to touch that. Think of all the germs!"

Tricia slammed the car door, shook her head in disgust, and set the fluttering papers on the right rear quarter panel. They were all the same: pages from the *Stoneham Weekly News* advertising section, listing tag sales, estate sales, and auctions, with a number of entries circled.

"There must be five or six weeks' worth here," Tricia said, flipping through the sheets.

"So what?"

"Maybe we can find the address where Winnie bought that cookbook."

Angelica frowned. "What good will that do?"

"It might lead us to whoever killed her."

"You just told me the sheriff said it was an accident."

"And if you believe her, let me interest you in some swampland in Florida. Oh, Ange, it's obvious Sheriff Adams doesn't care about actually solving Doris's murder. She seems to spend all her time trying to pin it on me!" She gathered up the scraps and started back for Angelica's car.

"You can't take that stuff along," Angelica said, struggling to keep up with her sister's brisk pace.

"Why not? The sheriff apparently didn't want it. It's just garbage now."

"Then throw it away."

Tricia stopped dead, turned, and faced her sister. "Not until I map out where Winnie found her treasures in her last few weeks."

FOURTEEN

Angelica started the car and pulled back onto the highway. "You *are* in a mood today."

Tricia clutched the papers on her lap. "I have reason to be." She let out a sigh and related her encounter with Mike Harris earlier that morning, feeling better for finally having unburdened her soul. "I'm even wondering if he could've thrown that rock through my store window last night."

"Hmm. Sounds more like you had a panic attack," Angelica commented, steering the rental car through the countryside with amazing familiarity. "My friend Carol used to get them whenever she had to face something unpleasant—like a visit with her in-laws. No wonder she could never stay married for more than six months at a time."

"It's never happened to me before."

"You're under stress," Angelica explained reasonably. "Who wouldn't be with the possibility of a murder charge hanging over her head?"

"I did *not* kill Doris Gleason, and I wish everyone would just stop saying that."

"My, we are very, *very* testy today. Mind you, right about now I could go for a tight embrace with a handsome man. And so far I've liked every man I've met here in Stoneham. They seem like the marrying kind."

"You'd be bored silly within a month and you know it," Tricia grumbled.

The idea of Angelica living nearby—and the possibility of Bob Kelly as a possible brother-in-law—was enough to make Tricia physically ill, especially since she still wanted to believe he had a hand in Doris's death. Too bad she didn't have a shred of evidence to prove it.

Time to ask the big question that had been so much on her mind. "Ange, isn't there any hope you and Drew can get back together?"

Angelica's mouth tightened, and she took her time before answering. "No."

"Do you mind if I ask what happened?"

"Oh, it's all so tedious," she said, with impatience.

"You obviously haven't found someone else. Has he?"

Again Angelica's hands tightened on the steering wheel. "If you must know, yes. And she's ten years older than me, with a face full of wrinkles! Some woman he works with. They talk about math and physics and bonsai, of all things. One thing led to another and . . . he asked me to move out so she could move in."

And that's why Angelica had lost weight and come to Stoneham—to lick her emotional wounds. And Tricia had dropped all those snide comments about Drew in front of Bob the night before. "I'm so sorry, Ange."

"It was his house, after all," she continued, her gaze riveted on the road. "Drew isn't a beast. I'll get a good settlement. He paid for the trip to Aspen, and for storing my things until I find a place to settle. He's really been very kind."

Except for tossing her aside like an old shoe. But then Christopher had been just as generous when he'd announced he'd wanted his freedom, too. Maybe the Miles girls were just doomed to be unlucky in love.

"It's taken me a few months," Angelica continued, resigned, "but now I'm ready to move on. I mean, what choice do I have?"

"There's no chance of counseling, or—?"

Angelica shook her head. "Apparently he's loved that woman for years, but always thought she was unattainable. Then her husband died last year, and Drew figured he wasn't getting any younger. Not that he was unhappy with me, he later told me. But one thing led to another and . . . well, the rest as they say is history."

Tricia let out a breath. At least Christopher hadn't left her for someone else. Freedom for him meant solitude, which he'd apparently found and savored.

"Ah, here we are." Angelica slowed the car and turned off the highway onto a long gravel drive lined with decades-old maples. A little white cottage stood in a clearing, looking like something out of *Snow White and the Seven Dwarfs*, with its forest green shuttered windows, gabled, slate roof, its foundation surrounded by alternating pink and red rosebushes still in bloom.

"Oh, Ange, it's darling," Trish said. "Can we go inside?"

"I wish. But the agent who showed it to me this morning said she couldn't come back today. I just wanted you to see it, to see what you think."

"I love it." And it was far enough away from the village that Angelica might not want to drive into town come winter when the roads were reputed to be icy and treacherous. Bad Tricia wanting to keep her sister at bay! And really, she wasn't sure she felt that way anymore. Well, at least some of the time, and that had to be progress. Didn't it?

"Do you want to walk around the yard?" Angelica asked, hope coloring her voice.

"Sure."

The sisters got out of the car and walked ten or so yards to stand before the cottage. "Isn't that slate roof just incredible?" Angelica asked.

A few tiles looked skewed; did that mean it leaked? Tricia sidled between a couple of rosebushes, shaded her eyes, and peered in through one of the leaded glass windows. The room inside was bare, but the walls, in neutral tones, looked freshly painted and the floors shone like they'd just been sanded and sealed.

"That's fir flooring, and look at the wonderful fieldstone fireplace. Imagine how cozy it would be on a cold winter's night," Angelica said wistfully.

Tricia stood back. "It's delightful. I had no idea a sweet little place like this was even available locally."

Angelica's smile was tentative. "I'm glad you like it. I thought you might be angry with me for wanting to live near you. It might not be forever, I just—I need you right now. Is that too terrible a thing for a sister to say?"

Touched, Tricia rested a hand on her sister's arm. "No, and I'm happy you feel that way. I just wish I could leave all the baggage from our childhood behind."

"I have none. But then why should I? I was the cherished child they never thought they'd have, and you were . . . well, you weren't expected. By that time Mother had moved on to other pursuits."

Angelica's words were nothing Tricia hadn't considered for herself too many times over the years, yet it did hurt to hear them. She withdrew her hand.

Angelica frowned. "I've spoiled the moment, haven't I?"

Nothing new, Tricia felt tempted to say, instead she turned and walked back to the car. Angelica took the hint and followed. Once inside, she started the engine, backed into the turnaround, and headed down the drive for the highway once again.

"Where to now?" Tricia asked, not caring what the answer was.

"I thought it might be fun to have dinner at the inn tonight. My treat. What do you say?"

Since the idea of cooking for herself was always a turnoff, and Miss Marple wouldn't be expecting her dinner for several hours anyway, Tricia nodded.

As she drove, Angelica gave a running commentary about the cottage's charms and its drawbacks, including the lack of closet space and how she thought she might like to add a patio and lap pool to the backyard and did Tricia know anything about pool maintenance?

"No."

Meanwhile, Tricia turned her attention back to Winnie's newspaper clippings. She must have circled forty or fifty addresses and Tricia wasn't sure she had a detailed map of the area to check them out. Stoneham had no map store, and she wasn't aware of any of the bookstores catering to local history, either. Maybe the chamber of commerce had done an advertising map. If she ran into Bob, she'd ask. Other than that she decided to just call Frannie at the C of C office on Monday.

Others must have had the same early-dinner idea as Angelica because the inn's parking lot was jammed, and though she circled the lot twice, there simply were no empty spaces. "Darn. Now I'm going to have to park behind the inn in the bungalow lot."

"So, there's a back entrance, isn't there?"

"Is there? I don't know."

Once behind the inn, Tricia pointed out the door that led to the building's secondary entrance, and Angelica parked the car next to the Dumpster, the only available spot in the back lot. They got out of the car and she pointed to the white Altima with the Connecticut plates that sat in front of the door. "Look, there's that stupid car that's been taking all the desirable parking places in the village. I've had enough. I'm going to ask Bess who owns it."

Angelica marched ahead, leaving Tricia struggling to keep up.

Bess was once again stationed at the inn's reception desk, but she was helping another guest and the sisters had to wait to gain her attention. Tricia wandered over to a wooden rack that held brochures detailing the local attractions, and much to her delight found a stack of chamber of commerce maps of Stoneham. She scooped one up. Dinner now seemed unimportant.

Angelica stepped up to the reception desk.

"I hope you're enjoying your stay, Mrs. Prescott," Bess greeted at last.

"Very much so. In fact, I'm so impressed with the whole place, I'm thinking of moving to Stoneham."

"That's wonderful. Now, how can I help you this evening?"

"There's a car in the back lot with Connecticut plates: 64B R59. Does it belong to a guest?"

Bess's smile faltered. "I'm not sure I should give out that information."

"But I'm about to become a townie," Angelica insisted.

"That's villager," Tricia corrected.

Bess frowned. "I guess it can't hurt," she said, although she didn't sound convinced. Angelica repeated the plate number. Bess tapped a few keys on her computer. "Let's see. Oh, here it is. The car belongs to Deirdre Gleason; she's in bungalow two."

Her words tore Tricia's attention away from the map.

"It can't be," Angelica asserted. "That car was here when I arrived on Tuesday, which was the day Doris Gleason died."

Bess checked the register. "Ms. Gleason checked in on the third."

"And Doris was murdered on the fifth," Tricia said.

"What difference does it make what day she checked in?" Bess asked.

"Until Saturday no one knew Doris even had a sister," Tricia said.

"I did," Bess said. "Deirdre Gleason told me so."

"When did she tell you?" Angelica pressed.

"I don't remember exactly."

"Why didn't you report it to the sheriff after Doris's death?" Angelica insisted.

"I didn't think about it. I mean why would I?" Bess said, sounding defensive.

Bess was right; she wouldn't have known the sheriff was looking for next of kin. Tricia turned her attention back to her map.

"Tonight's Ms. Gleason's last night with us. She's moving into her sister's home tomorrow," Bess said.

Angelica leaned against the counter, bending closer. "Really? Tell me, have you gotten to know Deirdre during her stay?"

Tricia unfolded another section of her map and rolled her eyes, only half listening to the conversation.

Bess shook her head. "Not really. She keeps to herself. Has all her meals in the bungalow."

"Has anything about her changed since her sister's death?" Angelica asked.

"Changed?" Bess echoed.

"Her appearance: clothes, glasses, makeup?"

Bess thought about it. "She got her hair cut real short."

"Did she really?" Angelica said slyly.

Tricia refolded her map and changed the subject. "Bess, do you know what tonight's special is?"

It took a moment for the question to register. "Um . . . seared scallops with tropical salsa."

Angelica glowered at Tricia. "Sounds yummy."

Snagging Angelica's arm, Tricia pulled her away from the reception desk. "Thanks, Bess."

"Trish!"

"Shhh," Tricia warned and steered Angelica toward the dining room. "What was all that about?" she whispered.

"I'm working on a theory. I'll tell you about it later."

The hostess arrived to seat them, and they followed her to a far corner of the crowded dining room. The table was not to Angelica's liking.

"This is outrageous," she grumbled, knocking her elbow against the paneled wall. We deserve a better table than this."

"And there aren't any others, so be quiet and read your menu." But Tricia wasn't looking at her own menu; instead, she squinted at the tiny print on the map's index.

"Aren't you even the least bit curious as to why Deirdre made it sound like she wasn't in town before her sister's death? And how come nobody in town even knew Doris had a sister?"

"Of course I'm interested," Tricia said, setting the map aside and diving into her purse for her reading glasses. "But right now I'm more interested in finding out where Winnie got that blasted cookbook."

It was Angelica's turn to shush Tricia.

"And the reason nobody in town knew Doris had a sister," Tricia whispered, "is because she's not a Stoneham native. Aside from a few people like Mr. Everett, not many of the townspeople frequent the bookstores. Bess probably didn't even know Doris existed until Deirdre came to visit."

"It still seems funny to me," Angelica griped, but focused her attention on the menu. "Especially since the sheriff told you the dead woman had no relatives."

Had the sheriff said so, or had Tricia only imagined she had? Now she wasn't sure.

She thought back. It had been Bob who'd said Doris had no heirs the day he'd cleared out the Cookery. He'd either been in denial or clueless.

"Speak of the devil," Angelica muttered, looking over Tricia's shoulder.

Tricia turned. Sheriff Adams was maneuvering her bulk past the Brookview's dining patrons, bumping into chairs and jostling tables and glasses as she made her way toward the sisters. "Now what?"

Sheriff Adams paused in front of Tricia's table, her thumbs hooked into her belt loops, a stance that would've done John Wayne proud. "Ms. Miles, I'd like to speak with you."

"Now? On a Sunday evening? In the middle of the Brookview's dining room? What about?"

The sheriff surveyed the dining room, as though making sure those at nearby tables could hear her. "Doris Gleason's murder. We can discuss it here, or we can do it in the lobby."

Tricia gauged the interest from her neighbors, who'd suddenly lowered their heads to study their soup courses or were now hiding behind menus. "I have nothing to hide. Ask away."

"I'm going to ask a judge to have your financial records subpoenaed. I contend that you stole that valuable book and killed Doris Gleason for financial gain."

"Interesting that you'd make such an accusation without proof and in front of so many witnesses," Angelica commented, still perusing her menu. "I'm sure you understand the legal ramifications of slander."

"I'm not talking to you," the sheriff growled.

"And you know something, Tricia, I don't think you should talk to the sheriff, either. I mean, not without a lawyer present. You want someone with legal experience who can document just how ridiculously this investigation is proceeding."

"Ange—" Tricia warned.

"I mean really," Angelica continued. "I'm sure you've got more money in your petty cash fund than the sheriff makes in a year. And since you couldn't give a Kadota fig about cooking or cookery books no matter how old and valuable they are, I don't see that continuing this conversation for an instant longer is going to be productive for either you or the sheriff. Especially when there are other people the law could be investigating."

"Like whom?" Sheriff Adams demanded.

"Bob Kelly, for one," Tricia said.

"We've already been over that territory."

"Then how about Deirdre Gleason," Angelica suggested. "She was in town days before her sister was murdered. Funny she didn't step forward to reveal her relationship with poor Doris until you went looking for her."

"She was out of town at the time of the murder," the sheriff said.

"And you have proof of that?"

"Deirdre Gleason was registered with the inn for three days before the murder. And although she paid for the room, she was out of town at the time of her sister's death. I'm satisfied with the information I've obtained to corroborate her story."

"And why aren't you satisfied with Tricia's answers? Because she's younger and prettier and much, much thinner than you?" Angelica asked pointedly.

Tricia slapped the table. "That's enough, Angie."

Angelica waved Tricia's protests aside, leveling her gaze at a pink-cheeked Wendy Adams. "Now unless you have specific allegations you want Tricia to address, please go away and let us have our dinner in peace. Perhaps you could do something useful, like finding out who broke Tricia's store window, or is even that beyond you?" She looked back down at her menu. "I think the herb-crusted sea bass sounds divine. How about you, Tricia?"

Tricia picked up her menu once again, struggling to keep her voice level. "I was thinking more along the lines of fowl. Perhaps the candied peacock?"

Sheriff Adams stood rooted to the spot, mouth open, eyes bulging, for a full ten seconds before she turned and stalked back across the dining room, jostling more tables as she went.

Tricia turned her menu so it hid her face from the onlookers. "That bit about me being thinner was a real low blow," she whispered. "But thanks for getting in the shot about my window."

"Well, she deserved it. There's no reason for her to keep hounding you. And do you really think she's looked into Deirdre's alibi?"

"I would think she'd have to. What makes you think Deirdre would've killed her sister?"

"Are you really sure it was Doris Gleason you saw lying dead on the floor of the Cookery? You saw her within an hour of her death; did you see her face? What was she wearing when you found her?"

Tricia thought back. "She had on the sweater she'd been wearing all day."

"Are you sure?"

She nodded and shuddered. "I can picture it—bloodstained—with the knife handle sticking out of it."

"What about her hair? Was it the same?"

"I . . . I don't know. It was all mussed—it covered her face, and at the time I was glad of it." She hadn't wanted to see the dead woman's lifeless eyes.

The waiter arrived to take their orders. Angelica took her time, consulting the wine list and asking for recommendations before settling on a sauterne that would go with both the appetizers and entrées. Tricia had plenty of time to think about their conversation.

The waiter departed and Angelica leaned close. "What are you thinking?"

"Suppose Deirdre did kill Doris, she might've high-tailed it back to her home in Connecticut to establish an alibi. And she also had plenty of time to plant that cookbook in my shop the day she came in and introduced herself to us. We were swamped and she wandered the store for a good ten minutes before I could stop long enough to talk to her."

"Yes, but you also said Bob could've planted it, or even Mike Harris. Make up your mind, Trish, just who is your prime suspect?"

"That's the problem. I'm as much in the dark as Sheriff Adams."

FIFTEEN

Miss Marple swished her tail, refusing to let Tricia pet her after Angelica dropped her off at Haven't Got a Clue. "Your dinner is only ten minutes late," she explained, but Miss Marple would have none of it.

Tricia gathered up the empty dish and water bowl, chose a can of seafood platter, and set the dish and freshwater down before the cat. Miss Marple sniffed, turned her nose up at the offering, and walked away. "You're just being contrary," Tricia accused, but Miss Marple continued across the kitchen before pausing to wash her front left paw.

With the track lights turned up to full over the kitchen's island, Tricia spread out her C of C map along with Winnie's newspaper clippings and several colored markers. She'd been itching to jump into the task since she'd found the papers in Winnie's car.

It didn't take a genius to figure out that Winnie had circled any sales that mentioned books, which wasn't at all unusual since she had apparently bought and then sold a lot

of them to the other booksellers in Stoneham. Too bad
Ginny had discouraged her from coming around.

Tricia took the first clipping and started charting the addresses in pink for the week prior to Winnie's death, blue
for the week she died. Miss Marple sashayed back into the
kitchen, rubbing her head on the backs of Tricia's calves.
"Don't try to get back in my good graces," Tricia muttered
and squinted at another listing, this from two weeks before
Winnie died. "Follow the signs on Canfield Road." That
was where Mike Harris's mother's house was located.

The ad didn't specify the house address, but Mike's
mother's home had a detached garage. Would he have been
so foolish as to sell the valuable old manuscript for pennies
at such a sale? Then again, the book had been in remark-
ably good condition. He might have considered it a repro-
duction and not given it a second thought.

Tricia eyed the phone. She could try to call Mike, but
what would she say? "Sorry I ran out of your house like a
raving idiot. Now did you sell a valuable book to an old
lady, kill another elderly woman for buying that book from
her, and then kill the first old lady to cover your tracks?"
That wouldn't go over well, but she would have to find a
way to casually run into him and tactfully ask some questions. And maybe hell would freeze over in the next couple
of days, too.

Miss Marple levitated onto the island. "Hey, you're not
supposed to be up here," Tricia scolded, but the cat merely
circled around, rubbed her head against Tricia's chin,
purring lustily.

Tricia scratched the cat's head, but kept her gaze on the
yellowing ad. "Follow the signs on Canfield Road," she repeated. Russ Smith should be able to check who'd placed
the ad. Surely there were no confidentiality issues between
a newspaper's ad page and the purchaser of said ad.
There'd be no one at the paper at this time on a Sunday
night. Another task for the morning, and something law enforcement ought to be doing.

Angelica taunting the sheriff hadn't been wise, and

while Tricia appreciated the sentiment behind it, she was still irked at her sister. Then again, why was the sheriff so intent on nailing her for Doris Gleason's death besides clearing up the matter before the pending election? And was that enough of a motive? One thing was certain, Sheriff Adams wasn't interested in finding another suspect. If her name was to be cleared, Tricia was going to have to do it herself.

Tricia leaned against the brick wall beside the door of the *Stoneham Weekly News*, clutching a cardboard tray with two cups of the Coffee Bean's best brew. The recorded message had said the paper's office hours were from eight until five, but Tricia had shown up at seven forty, anticipating Russ would arrive for work before office hours. And she'd been right.

"Been waiting long?" Russ asked, as he approached from around the corner. He pulled a set of keys from his jacket pocket, selecting one of them. He looked like a farmer in well-worn jeans with the collar of a blue plaid flannel shirt sticking out the neck of his denim jacket.

"About five minutes. Hope you're thirsty," Tricia said, proffering the cardboard tray.

"I am." He unlocked the door. "Come on in."

She followed him as he led her through the darkened office. He hit the main switch and the place was flooded with fluorescent light. Peeling off his jacket, he headed for a glass cubicle in the back of the room. The rest of the office was open landscaping, with two desks with computer terminals. Stacks of the most recent issue sat atop a long counter that separated the public part of the office with the work zone behind it.

Russ took his seat, powering up his computer. "To what do I owe the pleasure?"

Tricia set the tray down and handed him a cup, offering creamer and sugar. "Just a little thank-you for your help the other night."

"What're friends for?"

So now he considered himself a friend. All the better. Tricia took one of the standard office guest chairs in front of his desk. "As you know, the sheriff seems determined to prove I killed Doris Gleason, quite a feat as I didn't do it."

Russ made no comment, but dumped a tub of the half-and-half into his paper cup.

"I'm taking your advice and trying to find out who *did* kill Doris."

"And you want me to help." It wasn't a question.

Tricia leaned forward. "I'm convinced Winnie Wentworth bought Doris's stolen cookbook at a tag sale, and I think I've found the ad right here in the *Stoneham Weekly News*. I was hoping you could tell me who placed it."

Russ stirred his coffee, then leaned back in his chair. "Depends on how long ago it was placed. We purge our system on a monthly basis, otherwise it gets bogged down storing all that data."

"Why don't you just copy it onto a CD?"

"What for? It's not even old news. We don't really care who buys classified ad space. It's the display ads that bring in the money. And we keep bound copies of the paper for posterity—not that I think anyone would ever want to look at an old ad ever again."

"The ad I'm concerned with was printed in the August nineteenth issue."

Russ tapped at his computer keyboard, studied the screen, then shook his head. "Looks like Sherry has already purged the August ads."

Tricia gripped her cup, hoping her disappointment wasn't too obvious. "Well, thank you for looking."

Russ turned back to face her and picked up his cup once more. "Just who did you think placed the ad?"

"I don't think I should speculate, at least not to you, without some other kind of proof."

"How will you find it?"

"I don't know. But I'm not going to give up." Tricia took a sip of her coffee. Since Russ was supposed to be on top of everything that happened in Stoneham, she decided to tap him for more information.

"What's the scuttlebutt on a big box store coming to the area?"

He shrugged. "I hadn't heard about it."

"Is that so?" she said, incredulous.

Russ laughed. "I've got no reason to lie."

"You've at least heard about the nudist tracts someone's been leaving all over the village."

"Nudists?" Either he was clueless or the world's worst reporter.

"You need to get out of your office more often. According to the website listed on the leaflets, a nudist resort is supposed to open somewhere near here next summer."

He picked up a pen, jotted down a note. "Tell me more."

She gave him the name of the business. "Drop by any of the bookstores if you want copies of the tracts. We've all got them."

"I'll do just that."

Tricia stood and picked up her coffee. "The day's getting away from me." She turned to leave, paused, and turned back. "Just one thing: would you have told me who bought the ad if the information had still been available?"

Russ smiled. "Don't you know that a good reporter never reveals a source—be it of information or revenue?"

Tricia swallowed down her annoyance. "I'll remember that for future reference."

Piqued, Tricia discarded her nearly full cup of coffee in one of Stoneham's municipal trash cans and headed back for Haven't Got a Clue. The lights inside the Cookery were already on, and she could see that Deirdre had finished washing the walls and had even made some progress with her restocking efforts. Had Bob opened up the storage unit and let her reclaim the display pieces? Some of them even had books on them, perhaps from the stock stored on the second floor or from Doris's home storeroom.

Tricia hammered on the door and waited. Deirdre had to
be in the back room. She knocked again. Sure enough,
Deirdre lumbered out of the back. She looked uncannily
like her sister—but then wasn't that the way with identical
twins? She even seemed to have lost her glasses.

Deirdre opened the door, her smile of welcome almost
convincing. "Good morning, Tricia. You're out early."

"And you're already hard at work, I see."

"I've got a schedule to keep if I want to reopen the
Cookery next Monday. Come in." Deirdre stepped over to
one of the bookshelves. Several opened cartons sat on the
floor. She picked up a book and squinted at its cover.

"Did you lose your glasses?" Tricia asked.

"My what?" Deirdre asked, alarmed.

"Your glasses. You're not wearing them."

Deirdre patted her cheek in panic. "Good grief, you're
right. I must have taken them off when I first came in.
They're around here somewhere. Now what can I do for
you?" she said, changing the subject.

Tricia prayed for tact, knowing there really was no easy
way to begin what she had to say. "I'm sorry to say that
Sheriff Adams is convinced I killed your sister."

Looking doughy and toadlike without her glasses,
Deirdre merely blinked, apparently startled at Tricia's blunt-
ness.

"I did not kill Doris," Tricia asserted.

"I should hope not," Deirdre said.

"But I do have some questions for you."

Deirdre visibly stiffened. "Me?"

"Yes. Within hours of Doris's death, the whole village
was buzzing with the news. You were in town, registered at
the Brookview Inn. Why didn't you step forward and let
the sheriff know you were her next of kin?"

"I was *not* in Stoneham when Doris was killed. Yes, I'd
taken a room at the inn, but I'd gone home to take care of
some business and collect more clothing. I didn't arrive
back until days after her death."

"How many days?"

Deirdre's eyes narrowed. "What are you implying? That I had something to do with my own sister's death?"

Tricia hesitated. If she mentioned the insurance policy, Deirdre would wonder where she learned about it. Likewise if she mentioned anything else about Doris's daughter. "Of course not. I just thought it was funny you didn't come forward sooner."

"Well, I don't think it's funny at all. What if something happened to *your* sister and people accused you of doing her in? Would you think *that* was funny?"

"No, I—"

"And neither do I." She pointed toward the door. "I think you should leave."

"Deirdre, I—"

"Now, please," she said and grasped Tricia by the shoulders, shoving her across the room and out of the Cookery, slamming the door and locking it before stalking away.

"Deirdre! Deirdre!" Tricia shouted to no avail.

Suddenly Mr. Everett was standing beside her, looking through the Cookery's door as Deirdre disappeared from view. "She's in a bit of a snit, isn't she?"

"With cause." Tricia turned and walked the ten or so feet to the door to her own store, withdrew the keys from her purse, and opened the door. Mr. Everett trotted in behind her, hitting the main light switch. Miss Marple sat on the sales counter, ready for another hard day of sleeping on the stock or perhaps a patron's lap.

Juggling his umbrella, Mr. Everett shrugged out of his coat. "Would you like me to hang up your coat as well?"

"Yes, thank you. Looks like you're ready for rain."

"There's talk we'll get the tail end of Hurricane Sheila later today or perhaps tomorrow, depending on how fast it travels."

"Hurricane?" Tricia asked. Preoccupied, she hadn't turned on the TV or the radio in days.

"Would you like me to finish alphabetizing those biographies, Ms. Miles?"

"Please call me Tricia." Mr. Everett nodded, but she

knew he wouldn't. Any more than she could call him by his first name, which he'd written on his official application and she'd already forgotten. He'd always be Mr. Everett to her.

"Yes, go ahead. Oh, but maybe you wouldn't mind dusting the display up front. Should it be a sunny day, it's really going to be obvious it hasn't been touched in days. But be careful; there still may be some glass up there."

"I'll get the duster," he said and started for the utility closet.

Tricia opened the small safe from under the sales counter and sorted the bills for the drawer, settling them into their slots. She caught sight of the little scatter pin she'd bought from Winnie, which had resided in the tray since the day Winnie had died. On impulse, she scooped it up and pinned it on the left side of her turtleneck, wondering why she hadn't thought to take the little brooch upstairs to her jewelry box where it belonged.

She checked the tapes on the register and credit card machine, finding them more than half full, and though the store wouldn't open for more than an hour, she decided to raise the shade on the door and let in some natural light. Mike's office across the street was still darkened, and she wondered when or if he'd show up today. He'd said he still had some time left on the lease for his last office. Perhaps he started the day there and only came to the campaign office when work permitted.

Mr. Everett had donned one of the extra Haven't Got a Clue aprons and was happily dusting his way along the front window display. Tricia gave him a smile and turned back to stare out the window. If Mike had sold Winnie the Amelia Simmons cookbook, then found out how valuable it was, he might've decided to take back what had once been his property. He could've slipped across the street and done the deed in the thirty to forty minutes between Tricia speaking to Doris and then finding her dead. And then on Saturday morning Mike had also spent time wandering around Haven't Got a Clue when he could have planted the stolen book to avert suspicion. Not that anyone but Tricia suspected him. Or Bob. Or Deirdre.

She thought about her encounter with Mike at his mother's home the day before. What kind of woman had raised him? She looked over at her new employee. "Mr. Everett, what do you know about Mike Harris's mother?"

"Grace?" he asked, not looking up from his task. "She's a very nice woman. Used to be quite friendly with my late wife, Alice. It's a pity she had to go to St. Godelive's."

"I'm sorry?"

He paused in his work. "St. Godelive's. It's an assisted living center over in Benwell. I understand she came down with dementia. Such a pity." He shook his head in obvious disapproval.

Came down with dementia? Okay.

"It used to be only the indigent that ended up there, but it seems they've been trying to upgrade the place and are now taking patients who can pay for their services."

The indigent? Surely Grace Harris had arrived after they'd changed their policies. After all, Mike had said he'd been clearing out her home to pay for her medical expenses. She thought back to the birthday card that had fallen out of *American Cookery* two days before. "Just out of curiosity, what was Mike's father's name?"

"Jason."

And the other name on the birthday card found in Doris's cookbook was Letty. So the book hadn't been a gift from Mike's father to his mother. Scratch that notion.

Still, the possibility of Mike being a murderer nagged at her. Facts were facts. He visited the Cookery the day of Doris's death. If he'd sold the booklet to Winnie for pennies, and saw that she'd sold it to Doris and it was on display, he might have decided to take back the book—by force if necessary.

"Mr. Everett," she called, interrupting his dusting once more. "What do you think about Mike Harris running for selectman?"

His brows drew together in consternation. "I really

don't like to participate in idle gossip," he began. "Then again, I do believe I'm entitled to an opinion when it comes to the village's representation."

"So I take it you won't be voting for him."

"Certainly not!"

Tricia hadn't expected such vehemence from mild-mannered Mr. Everett.

"Do you mind telling me why?"

He exhaled a sharp breath. "His reputation as a youth was . . . soiled."

"In what way?"

"It seems to me he was always in trouble. Schoolyard fights, shoplifting, and when he got older, he was a terror on wheels. That's not someone I want to represent me, even in local government."

"I see. And you don't believe he's capable of redemption?"

"I suppose everyone is. However, there's also a saying I've come to believe in: a leopard doesn't change its spots." And with that, he turned back to his dusting.

Thoughts of Mike kept replaying through Tricia's mind like a CD on repeat. Although she really didn't know Mr. Everett all that well, she trusted his assessment of Mike's character. She was also sure Angelica would accuse her of taking out her anger at Mike by making him a possible suspect. Then again, Angelica was convinced Deirdre had killed Doris, taken the book to fake a robbery, and then tried to cover her crime with arson.

Confronting Deirdre was one thing; she had no fear of the older woman. Confronting Mike, with his strong hands and steel-like arms, would be another thing. And what if all her suppositions were wrong? What if Doris had been murdered by a complete stranger? But that didn't make sense, either. Doris had unlocked her door to let her killer in. Someone had planted the stolen cookbook in Tricia's store. Someone still in town.

Someone who didn't want to be arrested for murder.

SIXTEEN

As promised, the men from Enclosures Inc. arrived to replace the broken window at just past ten that morning. The whole operation took a lot longer than Tricia anticipated, and Miss Marple was extremely unhappy to be banished to the loft apartment during the repair. Her howls could be heard by everyone in the store, and Tricia found herself explaining to more than one person that no one was pulling the cat's tail. Still, the entire ordeal put a damper on business.

After the window was replaced and order once again reigned, Tricia again called her security company. They were still too busy to come out to fix her system, but she suspected her monthly bill would arrive on time with no mention of interrupted service. She documented the call and intended to start contacting other firms when she realized the day was once again getting away from her. And she had to at least try to smooth over the damage Angelica had done between her and Sheriff Adams before attending to other matters.

Tricia drove to the sheriff's office rehearsing her speech. When she got there, Wendy Adams listened, but from the look on her face, she wasn't likely to accept anything Tricia had to say.

"You're beginning to sound like a broken record, Ms. Miles," she said at last and leaned back in her office chair, folding her hands over her ample stomach. "Or maybe someone so desperate she can't wait to point the finger at anyone else to evade suspicion."

"Look, Sheriff, I'm sorry my sister was rude to you yesterday, but I have real concerns that you're not taking this investigation seriously."

"Oh, I'm very serious. And I'm going to prove that you killed Doris Gleason."

"Even if I'm not guilty? That'll be quite a trick."

"Ms. Miles, I've known Mike Harris nearly all his life—and mine. He's no more a killer than I am. Perhaps he had a few run-ins with the law as a teenager—speeding, I believe—but he hasn't had so much as a traffic ticket in recent memory." She picked up her phone, right index finger poised to push buttons on the keypad. "Now if you'll excuse me, I have *real* police work to attend to."

And what would that be? Tricia wondered. Issuing parking tickets? Even that seemed beyond the sheriff's capabilities, as she hadn't issued one ticket to Deirdre for monopolizing the parking space in front of Tricia's store. "Do you have any idea who broke my window, or is it considered too petty a crime to be worth the sheriff's department's time?"

Wendy Adams stabbed the air with her index finger, pointed to the door, her expression menacing.

Tricia turned and left the office, heading for her car. With Ginny and Mr. Everett taking care of Haven't Got a Clue, she had time to pursue her own investigation. Her next stop: a visit with Grace Harris. But first, she dropped in at her store to select a certain book off the shelf.

St. Godelive's Assisted Living Center squatted on a small rise, an older, bland brick building without the flash that seemed to come standard with newer homes for the infirmed. No retaining pond filled with cute ducks and geese, no water spout, and virtually nothing in the way of landscaping. In fact, all the place needed was a chain-link fence and razor wire to win a prison look-alike contest. The overcast sky only reinforced that notion.

Tricia parked her car and walked along the cracked sidewalk to the main entrance. Pulling open the plate-glass door, she stepped inside and sighed at the sea of institutional gray paint that greeted her. Everything seemed drained of color, from the tile floor to the glossy walls devoid of ornamentation, to the woman dressed in a gray tunic who manned the reception desk. Already feeling depressed, Tricia checked in and signed the guest book, was given a visitor's badge, and was directed to the third floor.

Stepping out of the elevator, Tricia was struck by the starkness around her—that and the nose-wrinkling scent of urine that all the air fresheners in the world wouldn't quite erase. The bland white corridor—wide enough to accommodate wheelchairs and gurneys—had no carpet, no doubt left bare for easy cleaning, with sturdy handrails fixed along the walls to aid those who no longer walked on steady legs.

A hefty woman in blue scrubs, whose name tag read "Martha," manned the nurses' station to her left. She greeted Tricia with a genuine smile. "Can I help you?"

"I'd like to visit Grace Harris."

"Are you a friend? She gets so few visitors. In fact, I think you're only the second or third person to visit her the whole time she's been with us."

Tricia frowned. "And how long is that?"

"Almost six months, which is a shame as she's improved so much in the past few weeks."

"Doesn't her son visit?" Tricia asked, surprised.

The nurse shrugged. "Occasionally. You'd be surprised how many people dump their relatives in places like this and never think to visit them again."

That wasn't the impression Mike had given her. "So you don't think he's a good son?"

The nurse shrugged. "It's not my place to judge." But it was clear she had. Martha rounded the counter. "This time of day Grace will probably be in the community room. Follow me, please."

Tricia noted that most of the patient room doors were open, with too many white-haired, slack-jawed elderly people staring vacant-eyed at TVs mounted high on the walls. They passed a few ambulatory residents shuffling through the hall, or slowly maneuvering themselves aimlessly back and forth in their wheelchairs, barely noticing the stranger in their midst.

Martha paused in the community room's doorway, pointing across the way. "There she is, over by the window. Let me know if you need anything else." Her smile was genuine.

"Thank you," Tricia said and turned to watch Grace as the nurse's footfalls faded.

She hesitated before entering the nearly empty room. Three old gents played cards at a square table off to the right, and a couple of older women sat together on a couch knitting or crocheting colorful afghans that cascaded across their laps. Except for the TV in the corner droning on and on, it was the only color in the otherwise drab room.

These residents seemed to be functioning on a higher level than those she'd already passed. However, Grace, a mere wisp of a woman dressed in a pink cotton housedress with slippered feet and looking like everybody's great-grandma, stared vacantly out the window at the cloudy sky. Her white hair had once been permed, judging by the flat two inches broken by a part in the middle. Pale pink little-girl bunny barrettes on either side of her face kept the hair from falling into her eyes.

Tricia padded closer to the woman and waited, hoping she wouldn't startle her. "Grace," she called softly.

Slowly the woman turned red-rimmed eyes on Tricia.

"Hello, my name is Tricia Miles. I live in Stoneham and own a bookstore there. I understand you like to read mysteries. I brought you one." She held out a copy of Lawrence Block's *Deadly Honeymoon*. "I understand you used to have a copy of this book."

Grace held out a wrinkled hand, took the book, which no longer had its dust cover, and studied the spine. "Used to have a copy?" she said, her voice sounding small, and looked up at Tricia, confused. "What happened to the one in my living room?"

She remembered! But then wasn't it true that with Alzheimer's disease old memories stayed intact while short-term memory faded? "Yes, that's right," Tricia agreed. "I thought you might like to read it again."

Grace turned her attention back to the book, flipping through its pages. "That was very thoughtful of you . . ." She looked up in confusion. "Who did you say you were?"

"Tricia Miles. I own one of the bookstores in Stoneham. It's called Haven't Got a Clue."

"Oh yes, the new mystery bookstore. I've been meaning to visit it. When did you open? Last week?"

"Five months ago."

Grace frowned. "That can't be right. I remember reading about it in the *Stoneham Weekly News*. The article distinctly said the store would open on April fourth."

Tricia swallowed down her surprise. "Yes, we did. But that was five months ago."

Grace's brows drew closer together, her face creasing in confusion once again. "Where did the time go?" She looked up at Tricia and her eyes opened wide in recognition, her mouth drooping. "Where did you get that pin? It's mine."

Tricia's hand flew to the gold scatter pin at her throat. "I bought it."

Grace shook her head. "Oh no. I would never have sold it. It belonged to my grandmother."

"Are you sure?" Tricia asked.

"Would you let me look at it?" Grace held out her veiny hand.

Tricia unfastened the pin and handed it to Grace, who held it close to her face, squinted at the curlicues and scrollwork, her right index finger tracing the pattern. "See here, it says Loretta. That was my grandmother's name."

She handed the pin back to Tricia, who also had to squint. She turned the pin around and around again, and finally did see that it wasn't just ornamentation, but a name: Loretta. She gave the pin back to Grace, who immediately fastened it to her housedress.

"Mrs. Harris, did you ever own a cookbook called *American Cookery*, by Amelia Simmons?"

"A book? I'm not sure."

Another sign of Alzheimer's?

"I did have a darling little pamphlet written by someone named Amelia that belonged to my mother. It may have even belonged to my grandmother—it was very old—but I don't think I ever made anything out of it. All that colonial food was so stodgy. Jason, my late husband, he was partial to ethnic food. He loved watching Julia Child on TV and often had me make her recipes."

Julia Child and ethnic food didn't seem to belong in the same sentence.

"Did friends call your grandmother Loretta, or did they have a pet name for her?"

Grace frowned. "Hmm. Seems to me they called her Letty."

"Was your grandfather Roddy?"

"Rodney," Grace corrected. "Why do you ask? Are you a long-lost relative?"

Tricia saw an unoccupied chair across the way and pulled it across the floor so that she could face Grace instead of towering over her. She sat. "I have some unhappy news for you. I believe the cookbook and that pin you're now wearing were sold. Probably many more items from your home have been sold, too."

"That can't be. My son Michael—" But her eyes widened

and her words trailed off. Slowly, her face began to crumple as tears filled her eyes. "Not again," she crooned, nearly folded in half, and began to rock. "Not again."

Tricia placed a hand on the old woman's arm. "I'm so sorry I had to tell you."

"If what you say is true, it isn't the first time he's stolen from me. I was a good mother. We gave him everything. Why would he keep doing this to me?"

"He said he needed the money so that you could stay here and be taken care of."

Grace turned sad eyes on Tricia. "But I have insurance. There should've been no need to sell my things—and especially without telling me."

"Does Mike have power of attorney?"

Grace shook her head. "No. There's no way I would ever give him that. My lawyer has instructions for my care when I can no longer make decisions; they specifically say that Michael is never to be permitted to represent my affairs."

"Are you aware that your son placed you here? He's been telling everyone you have Alzheimer's disease."

"I admit my memory hasn't been as good as it was, but lately I've felt so much more like my old self. I've been wondering how I ended up here and why no one comes to see me. I have many good friends . . ." Her voice trailed off again as her hand grasped the pin on her housedress, and her gaze slipped out through the window.

Tricia waited for a minute or two for the old woman to continue, but Grace seemed to have lost interest in the conversation.

"Mrs. Harris? Mrs. Harris?"

"How is it you came to buy this pin?" Grace said at last.

"I bought it from a woman named Winnie Wentworth. I believe she got it at a tag sale at your home. She sold it to me last week. She was killed in a car accident the very same day."

"Killed? Oh my. An accident?"

"I'm not sure."

A tear rolled down Grace's cheek, and her gnarled hand still clasped the pin on her chest. "I love this pin. It meant so much to my grandmother. She gave it to me when I was a bride. I have her wedding band hidden with some of my other jewelry. It would break my heart to know it, too, was gone."

Feeling the need to ease the old woman's pain, Tricia found herself patting Grace's back. "Do you remember the last time you saw your son?"

Grace stared straight ahead again, her gaze unfocusing. "At my home. We argued over . . ." She shook her head. "We argued."

Probably over money, or Mike's pilfering. And shortly afterward, Grace had ended up in St. Godelive's.

"I've asked about leaving here," Grace said, "but they won't give me a straight answer, and I must get to my home to stop Michael from stealing from me. I don't know you, but—" She glanced up at Tricia with worried bloodshot eyes. "Would you help me?"

Despite the need to clear her own name, Tricia had no hesitation in answering. "Of course. What do you want me to do?"

"Please make sure the rest of my jewelry is safe. I had two beautiful jewelry boxes in my bedroom, but I've also hidden some of my most valuable items just to keep them out of Michael's reach. Gifts from my husband, and some that belonged to my mother and grandmother. Then there's Jason's coin collection. It's worth tens of thousands. Michael helped himself to some of it after his father died."

"Where should I look?"

"There's a small trapdoor on the floor at the head of the bed in the master bedroom. I don't think Michael knows about it."

"How will I get into the house?"

"You'll find a spare key inside the garage. It hangs on the back wall on a nail under a little framed picture of flowers . . . if he hasn't sold that, too," she added bitterly.

"I'll try to get there either tonight or tomorrow, and I'll come back and tell you what I've found."

Grace clasped Tricia's hand. "I'm trusting you—a stranger. Please help me."

Tricia swallowed down a lump in her throat and nodded. "I will."

SEVENTEEN

Tricia stood at St. Godelive's third-floor nurses' station, trying to make sense of what she'd just learned. "And you say Grace's memory just seems to have returned—like magic?"

"More like a miracle," Martha said, and grinned. "I've worked with the elderly for over twenty years, and you don't see it happen often, but when it does, it truly is a gift from God."

Miracle my foot, Tricia thought cynically. Something had to have changed for Grace, but Tricia wasn't about to speculate in front of someone working for St. Godelive. Could she trust any of them? Mike would had to have had help in keeping Grace senseless. But who? A staff member? Maybe her own physician? No one else came to visit Grace, so that seemed most likely.

"I'd like to come visit Grace again. You don't see any problem with that, do you?"

"Not at all. In fact, stimulation is the best thing for her at this point in her recovery."

Tricia gave the nurse a smile. "Thank you."

* * *

Dressed in a neon pink Hawaiian shirt, Frannie Mae
Armstrong stood on the porch outside the chamber of commerce's offices, watering the fuchsias as Tricia drove past.
She slowed and honked the horn. Frannie bent down,
squinted, recognized her, and waved.

Tricia parked her car in the village's municipal lot and
hiked the half a block to the C of C office. With no sign of
Frannie outside, she entered the log cabin to find the
secretary-receptionist attending to her indoor plants. "Hi,
Frannie," she called.

"Well, how-do, Tricia. What brings you back to the
chamber?"

"I've been admiring your flowers on the porch," she
lied. "They're beautiful."

"I feed 'em liquid plant food. Works like a charm. But
they won't last much longer. First frost and—" She made a
slashing motion against her throat. "Then again, the porch
roof might protect them for another week or two, unless
the remnants of Hurricane Sheila washes them away in the
next twenty-four hours. It's always a crapshoot with those
babies." She retreated to the counter and set down her watering can. "I saw your window had been broken when I
drove by yesterday. Did the sheriff figure out who did it?"

"Not yet."

Frannie clicked her tongue. "It's just terrible what's
been going on here in Stoneham this past week. I would've
never believed it. Maybe in Honolulu, but not here."

"Honolulu?" Tricia asked. Talk about a non sequitur.

Frannie smiled broadly. "Where I plan to retire. It's a
big city compared to Stoneham. Mighty expensive, too.
But my heart's set on it." She pulled at the lapel on her shirt
and winked. "I've already got my wardrobe."

Tricia could do little more than gape at the woman.

"Now," Frannie said, all business. "What can I do for
you today?"

Tricia struggled to change mental gears. "I'm still trying

to figure out where Bob Kelly could have been last Tuesday night after he left the Brookview Inn. Any chance you can tell me?" she asked brightly.

Frannie's lips tightened. "He had a business meeting."

"With a representative from a big box company?"

"I can't tell you that," Frannie said. "I can't tell you any more."

"Oh, come on," Tricia chided. "It's no secret. Everyone in the village is talking about it."

"Who?"

Tricia shrugged. "Everybody."

"Now, Miss Tricia, you wouldn't want me to blab my boss's business, risk my job, just to satisfy your curiosity, now would you? Surely you'd expect that kind of loyalty from your own employees."

Tricia blinked. "Well, yes, of course. It's just that—" She realized that no matter what she said, she already looked a fool. "I'm sorry, Frannie. I didn't mean to put you in a compromising position."

"Well, of course you didn't," Frannie said in all sincerity. "I can understand where y'all are coming from. Things don't look good for you right now." She lowered her voice confidentially. "We all read the story in Friday's *Stoneham Weekly News*."

Tricia's cheeks burned, but she kept her lips clamped shut.

"It's been said you think Bob might have killed Doris Gleason. Now, I don't know about you, but I prefer to believe in the good in people. My daddy always said hearsay and gossip is just not nice. And I know in your heart of hearts that you don't believe Bob would hurt anybody. He's a good man, and I know you're a good woman. I just know these things."

"Thank you," Tricia managed, feeling even smaller.

An awkward silence fell between them.

The phone rang and Frannie picked it up. "Stoneham Chamber of Commerce. Frannie speaking. How can I help you?"

Tricia inched away from the counter, reaching behind her to find the door handle.

"Hold on just a sec," Frannie told the caller. "Now you have a good afternoon, Miss Tricia."

Tricia forced a smile. "Thank you," she said and hurriedly left the office.

An impatient Ginny stood at the door when Tricia returned to Haven't Got a Clue. "Thank goodness you're here. I've nearly been jumping out of my skin for the last hour waiting for you."

"What's happened?" Tricia asked, concerned. "Why didn't you call me on my cell phone?"

"You've got it turned off," she said with disdain. "Again!"

Tricia waved her off and headed for the sales counter to stow her purse. "So what's the big news?"

"We caught her!" Ginny said with triumph.

"Caught who?"

"The mad leaflet dropper!"

Tricia's head whipped round so fast she was in danger of whiplash. "Who is it?"

"You mean today? Just some tourist."

Tricia waved her hands beside her ears, as though brushing away a pesky fly. "Run that by me again. A tourist?"

Ginny's smile was smug. "It's a racket." She signaled for Mr. Everett to join them. "I got her to tell me her part, but it was Mr. Everett who tracked down the whole story, and I think he should be the one to tell you."

"You give me too much credit," the older gentleman said as he approached. "Ms. Miles, the customer told me which bus she came in on, and I went in search of it to talk to the driver. It seems he's seen this happen several times over the last week or so. A man in a business suit approaches one of the tour members, someone who doesn't appear to be with friends. He offers that person money if they'll hide the leaflets in books or other merchandise when they visit the booksellers in Stoneham. He pays them in cash—as much as fifty dollars."

Tricia crossed her arms over her chest. "Where did the tour originate?"

"In Boston."

She exhaled a long breath through her nose. "It was probably a representative from the Free Spirit chain of nudist camps and resorts. It's helpful information, but unfortunately it doesn't help us stop the problem."

"Perhaps we could ask for the sheriff's help," Mr. Everett suggested. "These people are in a sense littering. Perhaps if a deputy met each bus and warned them—"

"It's a good idea—if it can be worked out. But I'm afraid I have no pull with the sheriff's office," Tricia said, her unpleasant visit with Wendy Adams still too fresh in her mind.

"Why don't you ask Mike Harris to deal with it?" Ginny proposed. "He's running for selectman."

Tricia fought to keep a grimace from pulling at her mouth. "Mike and I . . . aren't exactly on friendly terms today." And she wanted to keep it that way.

"I see," said Mr. Everett. "Then perhaps we could enlist one of the other booksellers to approach the sheriff. I'd be glad to speak with Jim Roth over at History Repeats Itself."

"No, that would be my responsibility, but thank you just the same, Mr. Everett."

He nodded. "Very well," he said and turned back for the bookshelves.

"Did all your errands go all right?" Ginny asked.

Much as she liked her employee, Tricia didn't feel comfortable sharing with Ginny everything that was happening. Instead she forced a smile. "Just great."

Ginny nodded. "We're slow right now if you want to go see Jim."

"Yes, perhaps I'd better," Tricia said, although after her encounters with the sheriff and Frannie, all she really wanted to do was pull the shades and hide.

* * *

"I put an offer in on the cottage," Angelica said offhand-edly. It was almost eight o'clock, and she stood at the stove in Tricia's loft with her back to her sister, stirring a pot of Irish lamb stew.

Tricia paused, about to lay a fork down on the place mat. "Oh?" Was she supposed to sound happy? Maybe she should be. The two of them had actually been getting along for most of the past week, but that couldn't last. At least it never had before.

"Did you bid high or low?"

"Low. I mean, it does need a lot of work. It's much too small for my needs, and it's really much too far out of town."

Tricia struggled to keep her voice level. "It doesn't sound like you really want it."

"Oh, but I do. It's just . . . I don't know. I guess I really didn't think you'd approve."

"It's not a question of my approval," she asserted once again. "You've decided to live in the area. You're the one who has to actually stay there . . . if you get it."

Angelica turned back to her pot. "I could just 'flip' it— you know, fix it up a little and sell it off quickly. Or turn it into a shop. Or maybe a restaurant. If it weren't for the lo-cation, it would make a sweet little tearoom." Angelica peeked at her sister over her shoulder.

"Are you really thinking of opening a restaurant?"

Angelica turned back to her stew. "I don't know. I just know that my life hasn't worked out so far and it's time for a major change."

No doubt about it, moving to the outskirts of a small vil-lage like Stoneham was going to be a tremendous change for life-of-the-party, shopaholic Angelica. And yet, if Tri-cia was honest with herself, Angelica hadn't annoyed her half as much as in years past. Tricia was even beginning to anticipate their nightly meals together, knowing it would end sooner rather than later.

Angelica seemed to be waiting for some kind of comment.

"I think it's great," Tricia said at last. "And, if nothing else, I think you'll have a lot of fun fixing it up and decorating it."

Angelica's smile was small, but pleased. She changed the subject. "And what did you do today?"

One thing she wasn't about to disclose was her talk with Frannie. Never had she been shamed so thoroughly and sweetly.

"I made a trip to Benwell, spoke to Mike Harris's mother at the assisted living center."

"The poor woman with Alzheimer's?" Angelica asked.

"I don't think she has dementia of any kind. She even remembered the date my store opened."

"Then what's she doing in an old folks' home?"

"Good question. And as I suspected, it looks like her son has been selling off her assets without permission."

"The rat. Why are half the men I meet rats?" Angelica asked.

"Grace is concerned about her jewelry and her late husband's coin collection. Apparently Mike has stolen from her before."

"Then I don't blame her for being upset."

"She wants me to check out her house and make sure those items are still there."

"And you want to do that tonight?" Angelica asked, her eyes gleaming with delight.

"I thought about it. You busy?"

Angelica planted her hand on her left hip. "Would I be here with my sister if I had a man to cook for?"

"You tell me."

Angelica didn't answer, but bent down to peek through the oven's glass door at the Irish soda bread she had baking.

Tricia wandered over to the kitchen island, rested her elbows on the surface, with her head in her hands. "It bothers me that Grace was committed to St. Godelive's for dementia, six months ago, but suddenly her symptoms have disappeared. What if she never had dementia? Could Mike have faked the symptoms that put her away?"

"Very easily," Angelica said. "Remember Ted, my third husband? His doctor prescribed some new heart medicine for him that interacted with another drug he was already taking. Suddenly the man I loved was gone. It was a nightmare until I figured out what was wrong—with the help of our local pharmacist, of course. Took more than a month for Ted to get back on an even keel. Of course we broke up six months later when he fell in love with said pharmacist. He felt she'd saved his life." She rolled her eyes.

Poor Angelica. Dumped by at least two of her husbands. And that wasn't fair. She was a woman of worth. What was wrong with these jerks?

Tricia changed the subject. "I also saw Sheriff Adams today. That woman is more stubborn than a terrier. She's determined to prove me guilty of Doris Gleason's murder."

"All the more reason to check out Grace's house. The soda bread will be ready in a few minutes. Take out the butter and let's chow down and hit the road."

Tricia smiled, pleased. "Okay, but only if you insist."

All this intrigue had Angelica thinking like the heroine in a suspense novel, and she insisted on parking her rental car several blocks away from the Harris homestead. Despite the threat of rainy weather, the clouds remained high, blocking out the moon. They left their umbrellas in the car and prayed the rain would hold off, as Tricia didn't want to leave any wet, muddy telltale footprints in and around the house.

Dressed all in black and armed with the large orange flashlight, Tricia felt like a cat burglar and was grateful for the canopy of trees blocking most of the light from the street lamps. She and Angelica turned up Grace's driveway and seamlessly blended into the darkness.

Mike hadn't bothered to leave on any outside lights, and

none of them appeared to have motion sensors, leaving the yard spooky and uninviting. However, trying to lift the garage door proved it was either locked or was fitted with a door-opening system and effectively locked. They circled the garage and found a door, but it, too, was locked.

"Break the glass," Angelica urged. "You *do* have permission to be here."

"I'm sure the sheriff would disagree with you on that. Besides, Mike would see it the next time he came by."

"Isn't there a window on the side? Break it."

Easier said than done. The window was old, three-over-three panes; she'd have to break the whole bottom level in order to have enough room to struggle through, and then there were the mullions. She'd have to somehow dismantle them, too, and they'd brought no tools. The flashlight proved to be as effective as a hammer, and Tricia was grateful the next-door neighbors' windows were closed, with a good fifteen or more feet away from the sound of breaking glass and splintering wood.

"How am I going to get in without getting cut on all that glass?" she hissed.

"You'll have to go feet first. I'll help you."

Tricia was thankful there was no one nearby with a video recorder to chronicle the deed as she and Angelica hauled a heavy trash can to the window.

"What's in here, lead?" Angelica complained.

Tricia removed the lid and shone the light inside. Paper, stuff that should have been shredded. Old bills, receipts, and . . . "Photographs?" An old album of black-and-white photos and lots of torn color shots of people Tricia didn't know. As she flipped through the pictures she recognized many of Grace.

"Why would Mike throw away all these pictures?" Angelica asked.

"Maybe he doesn't have a love of family. From what I understand, it's just him and his mother left."

"All the more reason to hold on to your memories of the past."

The thought didn't comfort Tricia, who rescued as many pictures as she could see, piling them by the side of the garage. "I'll save these for Grace. Maybe take a few of them to her tomorrow. Hopefully we'll find a bag inside to make it easier to carry them back to the car."

With half its contents removed, the trash can was considerably lighter and easier to maneuver. But worming through the window was a lot harder than Tricia would've thought. Climbing onto the can, she poked her feet through the window and Angelica huffed and puffed to raise her derriere up high enough to push her torso through and into the garage. Next Angelica held on to her hands as Tricia bent back like a limbo dancer and lowered herself into the garage, her sneakered feet crunching broken glass as she landed. Once inside, Angelica handed her the flashlight. "Be careful."

The bobbing light failed to give adequate illumination, and Tricia's hips bumped and banged against a number of tables haphazardly heaped with kitchen items, old clothes, and glassware, no doubt items that hadn't sold at Mike's tag sale. Tricia sidled her way to the back of the garage. Old dusty rakes, snow shovels, and other garden tools hung on the wall and she waved the beam back and forth, searching for the little flowered print Grace had assured her would be there.

"What's taking so long?" Angelica demanded in a harsh whisper.

Tricia ignored her, and restarted her search, this time painting the light up and down, noticing an old spiderwebbed set of golf clubs, aged, stained bushel baskets, and finally—a little, faded print of pansies. She pulled the framed picture from its nail and just as Grace had said, found an extra set of house keys.

"Eureka!" She replaced the picture, unlocked the door, and turned off the flashlight before stepping back outside and closing the door once more. "Angelica? Where are you?" she whispered into the inky blackness. A tap on the shoulder nearly sent Tricia into cardiac arrest. "Don't do that!"

"Well, you did call me. I take it you have the key?" Angelica asked.

"Keys," she said, and held them up. "Come on, let's get inside before someone sees us."

They walked to the back of the house and Angelica held the flashlight while Tricia tried the first key, which didn't fit. What if Mike had changed the locks? She tried the next one. Still no luck. "There's only one left." She slid the brass key into the hole and this time it turned.

"Thank goodness," Angelica breathed.

Tricia turned the handle, pushed the door open, and stepped inside, with Angelica close enough to step on her heels. "Give me the flashlight and close the door," she whispered. Angelica complied and Tricia searched for a light switch, flipping it as soon as she heard the door latch.

Bright white light nearly blinded them and it took a moment for Tricia to realize they'd entered the big house through the butler's pantry. Dark-stained oak shelves and cabinets lined the ten-foot walls clear up to the ceiling, with a little ladder on a track making the highest regions accessible. The shelves, however, were completely empty. No crystal, no dishes. No cans of peaches or coffee. Just an accumulation of dust. And in that small, enclosed space, Tricia was suddenly aware of Angelica's perfume.

"What is that you're wearing?"

Angelica pulled at her jacket. "This little thing?"

"No, your perfume. Do you bathe in the stuff?"

"I won't even dignify that question with an answer. Now, do you think the neighbors will think something funny is going on if we turn on the lights?" Angelica asked.

"Maybe we'd better close the blinds, just to be on the safe side." And Tricia did.

"Where does that doorway lead?"

"The kitchen."

"Why are we whispering?" Angelica asked.

Tricia cleared her throat. "Didn't we go through this at Doris's house?"

"It's you who keeps whispering," Angelica pointed out.

Tricia gritted her teeth. "Come on."

They entered the kitchen, and Tricia flicked on a flashlight.

"Whoa! Time warp," Angelica declared, taking in the color of the dated appliances and décor.

The kitchen looked exactly as it had when Tricia had been there only the day before with Mike—with a couple of small additions. A mortar and pestle sat on the counter, along with a canister of gourmet cocoa.

"This looks suspicious," Angelica said.

"Yeah. What do you think the odds are that if we looked through the drawers—or maybe the garbage—we'd find some empty medicine vials?"

"I'm game to look," Angelica said and pulled open a drawer with the sleeve of her jacket drawn over her fingers. "Look, Trish, plastic gloves. I assume you didn't bring any this time. Maybe we'd better use these. We wouldn't want to leave any incriminating evidence behind."

Having read a score of *CSI*-based books, Tricia knew they probably already had. Still, she placated her sister and donned the pair of gloves Angelica handed her. Angelica pulled open another drawer.

"The nurse on Grace's floor mentioned she had made a sudden improvement. I'll bet Mike sent her there with a supply of her favorite cocoa and they ran out in the last couple of weeks. Looks like Mike's concocting a new batch."

"Sounds plausible," Angelica said and shut her fourth drawer. "No sign of any little amber bottles."

"We'll check the rest of the kitchen and the garbage on the way out. We'd better get moving in case Mike shows up."

"It's almost nine thirty. If he was going to steal more of his mother's possessions, wouldn't he do it earlier in the day?"

"Who can fathom the criminal mind?" Tricia took off down the darkened hall, the flashlight beam guiding her way. She paused in the foyer at the base of the grand stairway leading to the upstairs.

"Can't we turn on any lights?"

"Not unless we can be sure they can't be seen from the street."

"What do we tell the paramedics if one of us falls and breaks her neck?"

"Oops?" Tricia aimed the light up the long, dark stairway, wishing she'd taken Mike up on his offer of a house tour. Then again, she might've unwillingly ended up in one of the beds.

They crept up the stairs, with Angelica so close behind Tricia that she could feel her sister's breath on her neck. A stair creaked, Angelica squeaked, and a shot of adrenaline coursed through Tricia.

"If any vampires jump out at us I'm going to lose it completely," Angelica rasped.

They made it to the top of the stairs without any attacking bloodsuckers descending and Tricia ran the flashlight's beam across the floor and into an open doorway. Angelica grabbed her sleeve as she started forward, following her step for step.

The prim and proper formal sitting room had Victorian furniture and décor, from the clunky marble-topped tables, embroidered pillows on the horsehair couches, to the frosted glass sconces on the walls. They found another parlor across the hall, but this was furnished for more masculine tastes, no doubt the domain of the late Jason Harris.

A computer sat on the desk, with neat stacks of papers at its side. Tricia trained the light over one of the pages. "Exhibit one," she said, the light focused on the eBay logo on the top of the sheet. It was a listing for the online auction site, complete with a picture of a Hummel figurine. "I'll bet this is one of the things from Grace's now-empty curio cabinet downstairs. He's been listing her stuff. This is only dated yesterday. And I'll bet I gave him the idea," she said, angry with herself.

"Don't be ridiculous. Look at that stack," Angelica pointed out. "Nobody could accomplish all that in only a day. See, there are photos for everything, too. Doesn't the background look like the kitchen counter and backsplash?"

She was right.

Tricia folded the paper, stowing it in her pocket. "I'll show this to Grace to confirm it's one of her figurines. Maybe there's a way she can recover it, or at least prove that Mike's been stealing from her."

"We'd better get moving," Angelica advised.

"The bedrooms must be in the back," Tricia whispered and turned away for the doorway, still unable to squelch the feeling they were violating the house with their presence.

The two small bedrooms on the right side of the hall were connected by an old-fashioned bathroom. The first, painted in tones of blue, would've suited a boy, and had probably been Mike's. The other, a tiny guest room with a small empty closet, had only a bed, an empty dresser, and a straight-backed wooden chair.

They crossed to the other side of the hall and Tricia played the flashlight's beam across an unmade king-sized bed. "Aha, the master bedroom."

"Now can we turn on a light?" Angelica asked.

Tricia threw a switch and the lights blazed. Unlike the other rooms that were more or less intact, the once-pretty master suite had been ransacked. What Tricia had taken as a rumpled bed proved to be destroyed—the sheets torn and the pillows shredded. The gold-edged French provincial dresser's drawers had all been dumped, with piles of woman's clothes littering the floor. She didn't see the jewelry boxes Grace had told her about.

"Looks like the result of a lot of anger," Angelica said.

"I hope this means he didn't find Grace's hiding place."

"And you know where it is?"

Tricia nodded. "Help me move the mattress and box springs."

"Do I look like a stevedore?" But Angelica did help Tricia pull the mattress up to stand against the wall, and they hauled up one of the twin box springs against it, too. Grace hadn't mentioned the trapdoor would be under a large area rug. They ended up moving the other box spring, dragging away the heavy headboard and side rails in order to pull up the rug. The trapdoor was exactly as Grace had described it, although much larger than Tricia had anticipated, measuring one by two feet. Tricia knelt in front of the recessed brass ring, pulled it up, and yanked open the door. The hiding space was even bigger than the door to it, and filled with an assortment of little black velvet-covered boxes.

Angelica grabbed one and popped it open. "Trish, look."

It was empty.

It took ten minutes of searching to find that they were all empty.

Tricia's eyes grew moist. She hadn't thought the loss of Grace's treasures would affect her so much. But anguish soon turned to pique. "That stinking rat."

Angelica sniffed. "Maybe you were right. A man who could steal from his own mother probably *is* capable of throwing a rock through a storefront window. Do you think he's already sold everything?" Angelica asked, her voice soft.

"You saw all those eBay sheets." Tricia picked up the first of the boxes and replaced it in the hiding place. "Have you seen his expensive little car? I'm not saying an insurance agent couldn't afford it, but it seems pretty coincidental that he bought it after his mother was put in the home—and her assets started disappearing." She glanced around at the devastation. "This had to just happen."

"How do you know?"

"Just yesterday morning Mike offered me a tour of the upstairs. He wouldn't have if the room was in this shape."

"Unless he was hoping to suddenly discover a robbery with a handy witness in tow."

Tricia frowned. "He did seem eager for me to come up here." Maybe Angelica was right and it wasn't her feminine wiles that had precipitated the invitation.

She shook her head. No, the slimeball had made his intentions well known.

"How did he ever find Grace's hidey hole?" Angelica

wondered. "I mean, this isn't exactly the easiest place to find."

"He's been throwing out receipts. There were lots of them in the trash. He could've found one from whoever built this hiding space."

"It's possible," Angelica agreed, but she sounded skeptical. She helped Tricia replace the rest of the boxes before they restored the room to the way they'd found it. Hopefully Mike wouldn't notice if the sheets, pillows, or bedspread weren't in the exact same positions.

Tricia turned the flashlight on and switched off the overhead light. They waited for their eyes to adjust to the darkness before she led the way back down the long staircase, with Angelica at her heels once more.

They'd reached the bottom of the stairs and just started down the hall toward the back of the house when Tricia stopped dead, flicking off the flashlight.

Angelica ran right into her. She opened her mouth but Tricia pivoted and clamped a hand across it. "Shhh!"

Voices.

In the kitchen.

Mike, and he was with another person . . . a woman, whose voice Tricia recognized.

EIGHTEEN

With her right hand still clamped across Angelica's mouth, Tricia shuffled across the Persian runner and into the dining room, dragging her sister along with her. She plastered herself against the wall of the darkened room, closed her eyes, and listened—concentrating.

Yes, it *was* Deirdre Gleason's voice.

"I can't make out what they're saying," Angelica complained.

Tricia's hand tightened around her sister's arm, silencing her. She closed her eyes again, concentrating on the muffled voices, but caught only snatches of words:

"Books . . . case price . . . wholesale . . ."

"Total—cash only . . ."

Obviously they discussed some kind of financial deal. No doubt after their talk the day before, Mike had contracted Deirdre, eager to dump more of his mother's possessions. And a cash deal left no paper trail.

Although risking detection, Tricia crept forward and peeked through the crack in the door, hoping to hear better.

A solemn-faced Deirdre stood beside the counter, a book in hand, looking very much like a professor in mid-lecture. Could she have picked up that much knowledge about cookbooks in such a short time? Then again, Tricia didn't know how much the sisters had discussed the business before Doris's passing. Or perhaps it was her accountant's background that made Deirdre such a hard negotiator.

Finally, a deal was struck and Mike disappeared into the butler's pantry while Deirdre started taking down the cookbooks from the kitchen cabinet.

Tricia grabbed Angelica's arm and hauled her back into the hallway where they crept along, backs pressed to the wall. "We've got to hide."

"Where?"

"There's a closet in the foyer."

"Ooohhh . . . please don't make me hide in a closet," Angelica whined. "I'm claustrophobic."

"We get caught and you'll feel a lot more claustrophobic sitting in a jail cell."

With exaggerated care, Tricia opened the closet door, but the hinges were well lubricated and nothing squeaked except Angelica as Tricia pulled her inside and closed the door.

Tricia was glad she'd donned her good old dependable Timex and not the diamond-studded watch her ex-husband had given her on their tenth anniversary. She pressed the little button and the watch's face lit up: 9:53.

"How long do you think it'll take before they leave?" Angelica whimpered.

"I don't know. I just hope Mike didn't go looking for boxes in the garage. He's sure to see the broken window if he does."

"That doesn't mean he'll come looking for us in here."

"I can't remember if I put the pansy picture back on the wall."

Angelica let out another strangled whine. "I hate this, I hate this. I want to go home. Please let me go home. This

isn't fun anymore. In fact, it never was fun. I don't like being a criminal. How did I ever let you talk me into helping
you?"

"You volunteered!"

"Keep that light on, will you? I can't stand being in
here."

"It'll wear down the battery. Besides, if you can't see
you're in a closet, you can't be claustrophobic."

"Do you have to keep reminding me!"

"Shhh!"

Footsteps creaked along the hardwood floor, paused.
Tricia thought about Angelica's perfume. Could Mike have
caught the scent?

Panic started to grow within her as the seconds ticked
by and she heard nothing else. Then, the footsteps moved
away, probably heading for the living room. Could Mike be
searching for them or had he just gone looking for another
empty cardboard box?

Angelica began making small squeaking noises again
and Tricia pressed a hand over her mouth once more. But
the sounds of anguish were also beginning to tear at her
soul and she found herself putting her other arm around
her sister's shoulder in hopes of comforting her. Hot tears
rolled over Tricia's fingers and Angelica began to tremble.
"Not too much longer. You're doing great," she lied.

To prove her wrong, Angelica's knees went rubbery and
she started to slide. Tricia struggled to hold her upright, but
ended up on the closet floor beside her. Angelica drew her
knees to her chest, crossed her arms over them, and rested
her head on her hands, her stifled sobs bringing stinging
tears to Tricia's eyes. Never had she inflicted such suffer-
ing on another human being, and yet she didn't open the
door, didn't dare risk their being found.

The footsteps came closer again, then headed down the
hall and faded.

Long minutes passed.

The air in the closet seemed to grow staler. Finally Tricia

could stand it no longer and reached for the handle, opening the door a crack. Fresh air rushed in, and Angelica hiccupped.

"Shhh!" But this time Tricia's aim was to soothe, not rebuke.

Time crawled. Except for their breathing, no sounds broke the absolute silence.

Eventually Tricia poked her head around the door, listening.

Nothing.

More minutes passed.

Finally Tricia pulled herself up, muscles stiff from their confinement.

Angelica didn't move.

Tricia slipped out of her loafers, crept down the hall, saw no light coming from beneath the door that led to the kitchen. She padded into the dining room, peeked around at the crack around the door to the kitchen. It was dark, silent, and once again empty.

With more speed than agility, she headed back down the hall.

"It's okay, they're gone. You can come on out," she called, but still Angelica didn't move.

Tricia stepped back into her shoes, bent down, and fumbled for the flashlight, which was still on the closet floor. She switched it on and trained the light on her sister's inert form. "Ange. Ange!" She shook her sister's shoulder.

Angelica lifted her head, blinked red-rimmed eyes. "I think I fell asleep," she said, her voice tiny.

Tricia helped her to stand, threw her arms around Angelica. "I owe you big-time, big sister."

"Can we go now? I think I need a really strong drink."

"You're not the only one. Come on."

Linking arms, Tricia steadied Angelica as they made their way back to the kitchen. She pointed the flashlight at the cabinet, which was now devoid of books. "Looks like Deirdre took the lot."

"She can have them."

Tricia ran the flashlight's beam across the kitchen counter. "Hey, look." The mortar and pestle hadn't been put away, but the cocoa container was gone.

Angelica upended the bottle of chardonnay, watching as a single drop fell into her empty stemmed glass. "Got anything else to drink?"

"I think you've had enough," Tricia said, dipping another slice of baguette into herb-laced olive oil. She closed her eyes, leaned back, and let the bread lay on her tongue, savoring the spices of Tuscany.

On the way back from Grace's house, they'd diverted to Milford and a Shaw's grocery store where, despite being an emotional wreck, Angelica had been only too willing to toss together a grocery basket of comfort foods featuring bread, artesian cheeses, fresh fruit, and a couple of bottles of wine. Returning to Haven't Got a Clue, the sisters settled on the sumptuous sectional in Tricia's living room, with mellow jazz on the CD player, a purring cat, and a desire to totally pig out.

Tricia cut herself another slab of St. Agur, a French blue cheese so buttery and mild it made her think of running away from home to forever milk contented cows in lush mountain meadows. She savored the flavor again, closing her eyes and reveling in it—only to open them again to see Angelica's vacant gaze had wandered out the darkened windows that overlooked Main Street beyond.

"Don't think about it," Tricia said.

Angelica shook herself, cleared her throat. "Think about what?"

Tricia didn't have to say. "I'm so sorry, Ange. I had no idea you had a problem with—" The words hung like a wet blanket at a birthday party.

"How could you? I mean, it's not like we were ever close." Angelica's eyes grew moist. "Until maybe . . . now?"

"What happened with us? Why didn't we ever talk? Why couldn't we ever be close?"

Angelica sighed. "I was five when you were born. That's a lifetime to a little girl. I was the star, the loved one. The sun rose and set on me, and then you came along—an intruder, something to tear Mother's and Daddy's love from me."

"But I didn't."

"Of course you didn't. I told you, I *was* the star. And you were this little mousy thing only too happy to stand in my shadow."

Tricia bit her tongue, struggling to hold on to the warm feelings she'd experienced toward her sister, afraid it had all been for nothing.

"Too bad Mother and Daddy didn't just smack my bottom and tell me to get over it. Think of the years we've wasted." She held up her glass, with only a drop or two of wine at its bottom.

"Where did your claustrophobia come from?"

Angelica sighed. "I was locked in a closet when you'd just started to walk."

Tricia's stomach roiled. "I couldn't have locked you in there."

"Of course you didn't. You were just a baby, fussy and sick that day. I was annoyed you were getting all the attention. So I . . . kind of . . . pinched you, made you cry, only I didn't know Grandmother was watching. She threatened to send me to an orphan home. To escape her wrath I fled to Mother's bedroom closet and shut the door—only I couldn't get it open again. They didn't find me for hours and hours, and by then I was a basket case, sure they'd forgotten me and that I'd never be loved again. I've hated small, closed-in spaces ever since. Didn't you ever wonder why I never fly anywhere?"

"I did . . ." But not very hard, Tricia admitted to herself. "How can you drive?"

"When I'm behind the wheel, I'm in control. In other situations . . . let's say I just don't do as well." She let out a breath. "There, now it's in the open. I'm sorry if I embarrassed you."

"I'm sorry to have made you go through it all again tonight."

Angelica's lower lip sagged. "Thank you. Let's try not to have a repeat performance." She sniffed and sank back into the sofa cushions. "And can we please change the subject? Like what's going on with Mike Harris and Deirdre Gleason?"

Tricia, too, was glad to leave the night's events behind them. "I still say that Mike had the motive and opportunity to kill Doris."

"Or do you only believe that now because he's proved himself to be a lying, cheating son?"

Tricia shook her head, wouldn't back down.

"Okay, give me his motive," Angelica said mechanically, lounging against a stack of pillows.

"Stealing that rare cookbook."

"Give me the opportunity."

"Stoneham's sidewalks roll up at six p.m on a Tuesday. The street was empty, the shops all closed. He could've crossed the street from his campaign headquarters, stabbed her, and fled on foot with the book. It was small enough to hide under his shirt. And he's a known entity with a reason to be on Main Street at that time of night. No one would even think twice about seeing him."

"Yada, yada, yada," Angelica muttered, leaning forward and slathering another piece of baguette with creamy cheese.

Tricia folded her arms across her chest in defiance. "Okay, give me Deirdre's motivation for killing her sister."

"Money. It always comes down to money, same as you figure for Mike. She inherits her sister's business, life insurance policy—"

"Doris's business was on the downslide. She complained to me that if Bob raised her rent, she'd have to close down."

"And isn't it amazing that he's backed off that demand—"

"Only for a year, and only because he fears being sued."

"Every sibling in the world has, at one time or another, wanted to kill his or her sisters and brothers. It's been that way since the days of Cain and Abel."

Tricia opened her mouth to deny it, but closed it again.

"I pinched you when you were a baby. If I'd been a really rotten kid, who knows what I would've done. Of course, after that one incident I rose above such base instincts." She gouged another lump of cheese from the rapidly disappearing slab.

Only the threat of being sent to an orphanage had curtailed young Angelica's homicidal tendencies. And while Tricia had often found her sister as irritating as a thorn imbedded in her skin, she'd never actually harbored feelings of fratricide. Not seriously at least.

"The problem is," Angelica said offhandedly, "nobody but the two of us is even worried about who killed Doris Gleason, or who might be cheating Grace Harris. And there's really nothing we can do about either situation."

"I'm not so sure. We just haven't got enough information."

"And where are we going to find it?"

"I'm going back to St. Godelive's tomorrow to make sure Grace isn't given any more of Mike's cocoa, and I'm going to see what it'll take to get her out of that place."

"Haven't you forgotten something?"

"What?"

"The sheriff is trying to pin Doris's death on you. You may not have much more time before she decides to come after you. I think you should call an attorney."

"I've got a business to run—"

"Which you can't do from jail," Angelica pointed out.

"Then why don't you find me a lawyer? You haven't got anything else to do."

"In this little burg?"

"It might be better than bringing in some hotshot from Boston. A local guy—"

"Or gal—"

"—might know how to manipulate Sheriff Adams," Tricia continued.

"Or deliver you straight into her hands," Angelica warned.

Tricia raised her wineglass to her lips but paused before drinking. "I'll take that risk."

NINETEEN

Tricia wasn't exactly sure how Angelica ended up in her bed while she and Miss Marple were relegated to the couch, but she vowed it wouldn't happen again. She'd run four miles on the treadmill, showered, and breakfasted before Angelica even opened an eye.

"Coffee," Angelica wailed, as she shuffled into the kitchen. Her hair stood out at odd angles and Tricia's white terry bathrobe was at least two sizes too small for her. She settled on a stool at the island and allowed Tricia to place a steaming mug in front of her. "Please, don't ever let me polish off an entire bottle of wine again."

"I've got to get the store ready for the day. Hang out here as long as you want. I left the phone book over on the counter."

Squinting, Angelica peered over the rim of her cup. "Phone book?"

"You said you'd find me a lawyer today."

"Oh yeah." She closed her eyes and took a tentative sip. "I didn't sleep real well last night. Had a lot of time to think. You've got too much going on, what with chasing around and looking for killers, so I've decided the least I can do is help out at Haven't Got a Clue."

Sudden panic gripped Tricia. If Angelica made herself comfortable in the store, she'd never get rid of her. "No need. I've just hired Mr. Everett. Between him and Ginny, and me, we're covered."

"But Mr. Everett has spent a lot of time watching Deirdre, and you've got to go see Grace Harris. And Ginny has to have a lunch break at some point. No, I insist. And I intend to help you as long as I'm here in Stoneham."

Tricia didn't bother to argue. Instead, she turned and marched down the stairs to her shop. As expected, Mr. Everett was waiting at the front door, with his umbrella in hand. She let him in and he immediately went to the coffee station, pulled out a new filter, and measured coffee for the Bunn-o-Matic.

"You're ready for rain again, I see," Tricia said and moved to the counter to watch him, marveling at how easily he'd slipped into Haven't Got a Clue's daily routine.

"Doppler radar shows what's left of Hurricane Sheila sweeping through western New York. We'll see it by the afternoon, I'm afraid."

Tricia nodded. Thinking about the day ahead, she asked, "Mr. Everett, would you mind keeping an eye on Deirdre again today?"

His brow puckered. "It's not as interesting as working here, but if that's what you need me to do, I'm happy just to feel useful."

Time to dig a little deeper. "Has she . . . mentioned her sister much?"

Mr. Everett hit the coffeemaker's start button. "She doesn't really talk to me, except to order me about. I must say I expected her to be a little kinder than Doris. Then again, they are twins."

Were twins, Tricia automatically corrected to herself. "I assume you haven't told her that you're on my payroll."

"Not exactly. I told her that you were concerned about her safety and had asked me to help out."

That being the case, it wasn't likely she'd say anything of any use in front of Mr. Everett. Still, having a mole in enemy territory could be beneficial.

"What time does Deirdre usually show up at the Cookery?"

He consulted his watch. "Right about now."

As if on cue, the white car with Connecticut plates pulled into the parking space in the empty slot between Haven't Got a Clue and the Cookery.

"Why don't you take Deirdre a cup of coffee? And maybe you can find out where she's getting her new stock."

Mr. Everett smiled. "Shall I pretend I'm master spy George Smiley?"

"Why not? It may even make your day go faster."

"I will admit that I'm looking forward to Ms. Gleason reopening her store so that I may come back here and do some real work. Those biographies could still use reorganizing."

"I'm sure it'll only be for another couple of days. And I really appreciate you helping Deirdre out like this. I'm fairly certain she won't voice her gratitude to us directly."

Ginny arrived as Mr. Everett departed. "Grab my coat when you hang up yours, please."

Ginny did as she was asked. "Going somewhere first thing in the morning?"

Tricia finished counting the bills for the cash drawer. "I've got an errand to run that just won't wait."

"No problem. I can handle just about anything that crops up."

Tricia closed the register, remembering something she'd meant to ask Ginny before this. "You worked for Doris Gleason at one time. Did she always have that ugly jet-black hair?"

Ginny laughed. "No. She only started dying it in the past year."

"Do you remember when she started?"

Ginny let out a breath, frowning. "It must've been just before I came to work for you. I thought she looked downright stupid."

"What about that pageboy hairdo?"

"She used to have long white hair pinned up in a bun. I had to bite my lip to keep from laughing the day she showed up with it cut short and dyed coal black."

"Tricia!" came the sound of Angelica's voice from the stairwell to the loft apartment.

Tricia snatched her jacket and struggled into the sleeves. "My sister thinks she might like to help out around the store. But I want to make it clear that *you* are in charge. And whatever you do, don't let her bully you. In fact, if she insists on helping, start her out stocking shelves. Hauling around heavy boxes ought to discourage her from volunteering in the future."

Ginny's grin was positively evil. "This could be an awful lot of fun."

Tricia grabbed the photo album she'd rescued from Grace's trash can, stuffed it into a plastic bag, snagged her purse, and hurried for the door. "Make it so—and thanks."

"Tricia!" Angelica called again.

The door closed on Tricia's back with the jingling of little bells. She headed down the sidewalk at a brisk pace, but made sure to look through the Cookery's plate-glass window, where she could see Deirdre already bullying Mr. Everett. A big first-week bonus was definitely in store for the patient little man.

Tricia parked her car, huddled in her jacket, and headed up the long concrete walk toward St. Godelive's main entrance. Just since the day before, a riot of yellow and magenta chrysanthemums had been planted around the entryway, giving the somber brick entrance a badly needed splash of color on this gray day. She walked through the entrance and was surprised that the foyer's drab, institutional gray paint had been replaced by a sunny yellow. New original art, beautifully framed, adorned the walls. A small plaque gave the names of the residents who had made the paintings.

"What happened?" Tricia inquired at the reception desk, taking in the entryway with the wave of her hand.

The receptionist grinned. "New management. The official takeover was almost two weeks ago. So far the changes have been invisible—mainly new client procedures, that sort of thing. I'm hoping we see a lot more physical changes to the building and grounds. It'll make life a lot more comfortable and cheerful for our residents and staff."

"And your visitors, too. I'm here to see Mrs. Grace Harris."

The woman pushed the guest book and pen in front of Tricia with one hand and a visitor's badge with the other.

The elevator doors opened to the same depressing sight Tricia had witnessed on the previous day. It would no doubt take weeks—maybe longer—before the whole building saw a cosmetic makeover. Could the new patient procedures be responsible for Grace's return to her senses?

Tricia made a point to stop at the nurses' station. Martha was once again on duty.

"Hi, Martha. I'm here to see Mrs. Harris again."

"Welcome back. She's either in her room or the community room where you found her yesterday. Would you like me to take you there?"

"No need. I was thinking it might be nice to bring Grace a gift. Maybe some fruit, or candy, or—"

Martha shook her head. "I'm afraid we can't allow that."

"Is that one of your new rules?"

She nodded. "Well-meaning family and friends were bringing in outside food and desserts that played havoc with our clients' medical problems. For instance, there are a number of medications that interact with grapefruit. And a box of chocolates given to a diabetic can mean hospitalization."

"I understand Grace's son often brought her special gourmet cocoa. Do you still have it?"

Martha shook her head. "When St. Godelive's was sold, the staff was given strict instructions to dispose of any contraband that could compromise a client's well-being. That means everything not provided by the parent company was immediately trashed."

And days later Grace's personality emerged from a drugged state.

"Well, I can certainly understand your banning such things. Perhaps I could bring her some flowers or a plant instead?"

"I'm sure she'd love that. And it would sure brighten up her room."

Tricia leaned in closer, lowered her voice. "What would it take for Mrs. Harris to leave St. Godelive's?"

"She'd have to have somewhere to go where someone could watch over her. Although she's made splendid progress, she might even be able to live alone once more, but that would be up to her doctors and her family."

And perhaps the help of a good attorney.

"What do the doctors think caused Grace's remarkable recovery?"

"We're not allowed to talk about our clients' conditions."

"But surely her son was notified when she started to get better."

"Of course. But I can't—"

"—talk about it," Tricia finished for her. "I understand. Thank you." She gave Martha a sweet smile before starting down the hallway.

Once again she found Grace in the community room, in the same chair, staring out the same window, her expression blank. She still clasped the book Tricia had given her the day before, and for a moment Tricia's heart sank. Had Grace's recovery been only temporary? In a scant eighteen hours had she descended back into the maelstrom of fog that had held her captive for months?

"Grace?"

The light blue eyes flashed with recognition as Grace looked up. "Tricia! You came back. Did you bring me another book? Look, I've already finished *Deadly Honeymoon*." She held up the book, opening it to the last page.

"Did you enjoy it?"

"Just as much as the first time I read it. I'd love to reread all of Block's Bernie Rhodenbarr books again. Do you have any of them?"

"I'm sure I do. And I'd be glad to give them to you."

"Oh no. I can pay." She patted the chair next to her, inviting Tricia to sit. "I could barely sleep last night. So many thoughts circled through my head. First of all, were you able to go to my house?"

Tricia moistened her dry lips before answering. "Yes."

As Grace studied Tricia's face, her expression began to sag. "It's gone, isn't it? All my jewelry. All Jason's coins. Everything."

"I'm afraid so," Tricia said, sadly.

Grace's hand flew to the little gold scatter pin Tricia had given her the day before. "Then this is all I have left from my grandmother." Her bottom lip trembled. "Jason would've been so disappointed in Michael. I can barely think his name without getting angry."

"You need to use that anger to get you out of here."

But Grace wasn't listening. "That boy has been the major disappointment of my life. We tried giving him pets when he was small, but he'd only torment them. A week didn't go by that we weren't called by the principal's office during his school years. In desperation, we sent him to boarding school for his last two years of high school. That seemed to straighten him out for a while. He flunked out of three colleges before he finally managed to graduate. He stayed away for a number of years after that. After Jason died, Michael came back to Stoneham, but it didn't take long before I'd found him helping himself to his father's possessions."

"The coin collection?"

Grace nodded. "And more."

Tricia opened her purse, took out the folded piece of paper she'd appropriated from the computer desk in Grace's house. "Do you recognize this figurine?"

Grace studied the ink-jet photo. "Jason gave me one just

like this for my birthday one year. He gave me one every year since the late 1970s. I've got quite a collection." She studied the page, seemed to understand its significance. "They're all gone, too, aren't they?"

"If that's what you kept in your curio cabinet in the living room, then I'm afraid so."

"I only kept a few in there, along with some Waterford crystal," she shook her head, her eyes glistening. "All my beautiful things . . ."

"I'm afraid I have another unhappy piece of news." Tricia explained about the drug-laced cocoa and the fact that St. Godelive's being sold was what had saved her sanity. "Unfortunately, the chocolate Mike provided has been discarded, that means we can't prove what he's done to you, but at least he can't bring in any more."

"You've got to contact my lawyer, Harold Livingston. His office is in Milford." She shook her head impatiently. "I don't understand why he hasn't come looking for me. Not only is he my lawyer, but we've been friends for over thirty years . . . at least I always thought so."

"I'll give him a call as soon as I get back to my store." And maybe Mr. Livingston could help Tricia protect her own interests, too. "I brought you something." Tricia withdrew the photo album from the plastic bag and handed it to Grace.

"Where did you get this?"

"I found it and a lot of other photos in the trash at your house."

"Oh dear, no," Grace said, and tears began to flow once more.

"It's okay. I rescued all I could find. I've got them safe at my store, and I'd be glad to hold on to them until you're out of here."

Grace turned moist eyes on Tricia. "You've been very kind to me, dear. Why?"

So she could clear her own name and get Sheriff Adams off her back?

Definitely.

Because Grace strongly reminded her of her own grand-mother?

Maybe.

Because it was the right thing to do?

No contest.

TWENTY

Hand clutching the office door handle, Tricia paused to wonder if what she was about to do was the right course of action. She'd debated with herself during the twenty-minute trip from St. Godelive's to the county sheriff's office, and the entire hour Sheriff Adams had let her sit in the reception area's uncomfortable plastic chairs waiting for an audience. It was now showtime.

Wendy Adams sat back in her worn gray office chair behind a scarred Formica desk, hand clamped to a phone attached to the side of her head. She waved Tricia to the same straight-backed wooden chair before her that Tricia had taken the day before. Comfort for visitors was definitely not a high priority for Sheriff Adams—and was no doubt a calculated decision.

With ankles and knees clamped together, hands folded primly on her purse, Tricia waited for another five or six minutes for the sheriff to complete her phone conversation, which consisted of a number of grunts and "uh-huhs" until Tricia was sure there was no one on the other end of the

line and the sheriff was merely trying—and succeeding—
to annoy her.

Tricia spent those final moments rehearsing her speech.
She would not raise her voice. She would not lose her temper.

She hoped.

Finally Sheriff Adams hung up. She sat up, shuffled
through some pages on the blotter before her, and without
looking up spoke. "Now what was it you wanted to talk to
me about?"

"Grace Harris."

The sheriff opened a drawer, rooted through the contents, and came up with a pen, which she tested on a scrap
of paper before signing a document before her. "And who's
Grace Harris? You going to accuse her of killing Doris
Gleason, too?" She laughed mirthlessly.

"Grace Harris is Mike Harris's mother—you know, the
guy running for selectman in Stoneham. Your lifelong
friend? Grace is currently a resident at St. Godelive's Assisted Living Center in Benwell."

The sheriff looked unimpressed. "What's that got to do
with anything?"

"It's rather a complicated story. But it turns out Grace
was the original owner of the Amelia Simmons cookbook
that was stolen from the Cookery the night Doris Gleason
was murdered."

Contempt twisted Sheriff Adams's features. "And how
did you come up with that?"

Don't get upset. Don't get angry, Tricia chided herself.
No matter what, you will remain calm.

"The story begins with a spoiled son who decided not to
wait until his remaining parent died before helping himself
to what he felt was his inheritance."

She recounted the whole chain of events in chronological order: how Winnie Wentworth had purchased the rare
booklet in what was probably a box lot of paperbacks and
other ephemera. That Winnie had sold the booklet to
Doris Gleason, who was probably murdered in an attempt

to recover the book. How days later Winnie sold Tricia the little gold scatter pin and died before she could recount where she'd obtained it and the booklet. How Tricia had examined Grace's book collection at Mike Harris's behest. How her own curiosity compelled her to visit Grace at St. Godelive's, where she found the woman recovering from what had at first appeared to be dementia, but was in all likelihood a drug interaction. If not for the home's new rules and regulations, how Grace would've been sentenced to live out her days in a foggy netherworld, while her son sold off her assets and treated himself to a lavish lifestyle, while bankrolling his campaign for Stoneham selectman.

During the entire recitation, the sheriff's expression remained impassive. When Tricia finally finished, Wendy Adams stood, hunched over, planted her balled fists, gorilla style, on her desktop, and drilled Tricia with her cold gaze.

"Since day one of this investigation, you have done your best to misdirect my efforts with wild accusations to divert attention from your own guilt," she said, her voice low and menacing. "I will not stand for this any longer. Mike Harris is a longtime resident of this village. If you continue to slander his good name, I will see to it that you face a lawsuit that will strip you of every asset you possess before I arrest you and see you rot in jail for the murder of Doris Gleason."

Stunned, Tricia could only stare at the woman in front of her. Mike's good name? Not according to Mr. Everett. And what possible reason could Sheriff Adams have for hating her so? Then in a flash it occurred to her: Mike Harris had shown interest in Tricia. Had asked her to lunch. Had invited her to his mother's home. Could Wendy Adams possibly have a crush on Mike? Or worse, could she be in bed with him—both literally and figuratively? Mike told Tricia he considered her his girlfriend. As a man skilled in manipulation, he could've said the same thing to Wendy Adams and she, being plain, overweight, and never married, chose to believe him. She wouldn't be the first intelligent woman to fall for flattery and the chance at romance with someone unworthy of her.

Struggling to remain calm, Tricia tried again, this time with Angelica's scenario. "There's also Deirdre Gleason's arriving in town prior to her sister's death. Why didn't she step forward? Why did she wait for you to contact her about Doris's murder before she——?"

For such a bulky woman, Sheriff Adams stepped around her desk with amazing speed, stopping only a foot in front of Tricia, towering over her. "I've had just about enough. If you're smart, you'll get out of here before I call in a deputy and have him arrest you on the spot."

"And the charge?" Tricia asked.

"Obstructing justice."

Tricia swallowed, somehow managing to hold on to her composure, and stood. "Thank you for your time, Sheriff Adams. I'm so glad you approach your job with such an open mind. I would hate to think you let personal feelings influence the way you serve the people of this county."

Wendy Adams straightened, leveled her blistering stare at Tricia, but made no further comment.

All eyes were upon her as, head held high, Tricia exited the sheriff's office and walked through the reception room and out to the parking lot. At some level, she hadn't really believed the sheriff would follow through with her threat of arrest. She did now. Angelica was right. She needed a lawyer, and fast. What was Grace's attorney's name? Sounded like some old explorer. Stanley? No, Livingston—— Harold Livingston.

The sky to the southwest was darkening as Tricia headed back to her car. Her hands were shaking as she withdrew her cell phone from her purse and found that once again she hadn't bothered to switch it on. It promptly announced that she'd missed two calls—both from Haven't Got a Clue. She dialed the number. It rang three times before a cheerful voice said, "Haven't Got a Clue, this is Angelica, how can I help you?"

It took a few moments for Tricia to find her voice. "Aren't you tired of playing store by now?"

"Trish, is that you? You sound funny."

Funny was not the word. "Ginny is in charge. You are not to try to take over," she said firmly.

"Oh, she made that abundantly clear," Angelica said, woodenly. "And she's been working me like a slave—shelving books, vacuuming. My back may never be the same. How did things go with Grace?"

Tricia had to take a calming breath before she could answer. "She wants me to talk to her attorney. It's a firm in Milford. Can you look up the number for me? The guy's name is Harold Livingston."

"Of Livingston, Baker, and Smith? Office on Route 101 A, right off 'the Oval'?"

"Uh, I guess. Why?"

"Because that's the firm I called to help you out." She paused. "What's an 'Oval'?"

"It's a rotary."

"A what?"

"A roundabout." Silence. "A traffic circle?" she tried.

"Oh. Well, anyway, you have an appointment with Mr. Livingston at two p.m."

"Looks like I need him. The sheriff just told me she definitely has plans to arrest me and hopes I rot in jail."

"Well, of course she'd say that. She's facing reelection. Even if the charge doesn't stand, she's got to have someone to pin the crime on. Why should she care if it costs you thousands in legal fees, plus your reputation? I already told you who murdered Doris—it was Deirdre."

"Try convincing the sheriff of that."

"I will. Yikes, look at the time. You'd better get going if you hope to make that two o'clock appointment."

Tricia glanced at her watch. "But I haven't even had lunch yet."

"I'll make you a big dinner. Here's the number," and she rattled it off.

Tricia jotted it down, then heard the tinkle of the bell over the shop door.

"A bus just unloaded another bunch from a cruise ship. I'm going to really push that stack of Dorothy L. Sayers books Ginny made me shelve. Gotta fly," Angelica said and the connection was broken.

Tricia lowered the phone and frowned at it. Angelica seemed to be enjoying playing store clerk a little too much. She called the attorney's office, received the address and directions, and headed for Milford.

The law firm of Livingston, Baker, and Smith was located in a charming Victorian house, a painted lady done in shades of blue, and it was obvious the building had been lovingly restored and maintained. Raindrops were just starting to fall as Tricia parked between a Lexus and a Lincoln Navigator along the south side of the building. She grabbed her umbrella from the backseat but didn't bother to open it, and walked around to the front and up the wooden stairs for the main entrance, with its stained-glass double doors.

The foyer's marbled floor looked freshly waxed. The grand, curved oak stairway directly in front led to apartments on the upper level, disappearing somewhere above the twelve-foot ceiling. The law office was to her right and through another tall oak door. A Persian rug and comfortable tapestry-upholstered chairs ringed what was once a formal parlor, its gray marble fireplace sporting a bushy fern in its maw. A painting of a distinguished older gentleman in a navy suit graced the back wall. Before it stood a counter; behind it, a receptionist looked up from her workspace. "May I help you?"

Tricia approached the desk, noticed the brass nameplate below the portrait read "Harold Livingston."

"My name is Tricia Miles. I have a two o'clock appointment with Mr. Livingston."

The receptionist, a thin, fiftysomething woman in a gray suit, stood, reminding Tricia of a blue heron. "He's waiting for you. Please come this way."

Tricia followed the woman down a brightly lit corridor. Evidently the rest of the first floor had been gutted to accommodate the partners' offices, however, they must have been rebuilt with architectural salvage, the result looking more like an old bank, with oak-and-frosted-glass doors, the occupants' names painted in gold leaf.

The receptionist knocked and opened the door at the far left. "Your two o'clock is here, Mr. Livingston." She turned back to Tricia. "You can go right in."

Tricia stopped at the room's threshold to stare at the man seated at the polished mahogany desk. Instead of a stately gray-haired gent, she found a dark-haired thirtysomething man, the sleeves of his white dress shirt rolled up, looking like he should be on a Hollywood movie set, not in a New England law firm.

"There must be some mistake. I understood I was to see Mr. Harold Livingston."

The younger man stood. "My late uncle. I'm Roger Livingston." He offered her his hand and she stepped forward to take it. Firm, but not crushing. One point in his favor. "Please sit." He indicated one of the client chairs before his desk.

"When did your uncle . . . pass?"

"Just over six months ago." Which would explain why he had never gone looking for Grace. Had Mike known this? Had he been biding his time, waiting for Grace to be especially vulnerable before implementing his plan to pillage his mother's estate?

"I understand you have quite a problem. I've only handled a couple of criminal cases, but I interned at a firm in Boston that took on a lot of pro bono work, defending at-risk youths."

"I'm afraid Sheriff Adams is determined to arrest me for murder, despite the fact there's no evidence or motive for me to have committed the crime. But I was also hoping to talk to your uncle about a client of his, Mrs. Grace Harris."

"Attorney-client privilege would've prevented that," he explained.

"Mrs. Harris is in desperate need of legal protection. If you've taken over your uncle's practice, I'd appreciate it if you could review her file. She told me your uncle had drawn up papers—including power of attorney—that specified who did and who did not have the right to take care of her affairs should she become incapacitated."

"As I said, I'm not at liberty to talk about Mrs. Harris's affairs."

"Would you at least speak to her? She was committed to an assisted living facility under suspicious circumstances. Her son seems to have been selling off her assets and she wants it stopped."

Roger took out a pen, jotted down a few notes. "Where is she now?"

"At St. Godelive's Assisted Living Center in Benwell."

He nodded. "I know the place."

"Will you go see her, today if possible? I'd be glad to pay you up front for your time."

"Are you a friend of Mrs. Harris's?"

"I met her yesterday, but I suspect her problems may be linked to my own legal troubles."

Roger Livingston set down his pen and leaned back in his chair. "I think you'd better tell me everything."

TWENTY-ONE

The drizzle had escalated into a driving rain as Tricia drove back to Stoneham and Haven't Got a Clue. Although it had cost her five thousand in a retainer's fee just to cover her size-eight butt, she felt better about the entire situation. Unless she'd manufactured evidence, the sheriff had no probable cause for an arrest. And Tricia had firm instructions not to even speak to the sheriff again. "Talk to my lawyer, talk to my lawyer," would now become her mantra. Thankfully, Roger Livingston remembered Grace Harris and promised he'd look into her situation as well.

Tricia parked in the village's municipal lot, grabbed her umbrella, and hurried down the empty sidewalk. The rain seemed to have chased away the tourists, and from the look of the weather, the gray skies had settled in for the rest of the day. She glanced at her watch and found it was already 3:40.

Passing by the Cookery, she saw Mr. Everett looking dour as he stood holding the ladder for Deirdre, who placed books on a shelf. From the look on the older woman's face, she wasn't giving him a compliment. Okay, that was enough. As of today, she would free Mr. Everett from his mission and allow him access to his beloved biographies and his rearranging.

She hurried past and backed into Haven't Got a Clue to close her umbrella before entering. At times like these she wished 221B Baker Street had had an awning over the front door so her shop could be likewise outfitted. Ginny looked up from her post at the sales counter; beside her, Miss Marple sat with paws tucked under her, haughty and dignified. "'Bout time, too," Ginny said in greeting and immediately shifted her gaze toward the nook. Eyes closed, and resembling a sack of potatoes, Angelica had stretched out on one of the upholstered chairs, her feet resting on the big square coffee table.

"Ange, we don't sit while the store's open. It's not good for business," Tricia admonished.

Angelica opened one eye, glared at her sister. "You people are slave drivers. You don't even give your help decent lunch breaks. I barely had time to whip up a grilled cheese sandwich, let alone eat it, before Simon Legree here was screaming for me to get back to work."

"I needed help with the customers," Ginny said, her attention dipping back down to the magazine on the counter.

Tricia set her wet umbrella down beside the radiator to dry, then marched straight over to Angelica, grabbing her by the arm and pulling her to her feet.

"There're no customers, why can't I sit?" she wailed.

"It looks bad to potential customers who look through the windows." As if to emphasize her words, the door opened, the bell over it tinkling, but it was only Mr. Everett.

"Ms. Miles, I quit!" he said resentfully, crossed his arms over his chest, and stood firm.

"Why?"

"I simply refuse to be bullied by that . . . that . . . horrible woman next door. I regret I must tender my resignation if I'm not permitted to do the work for which I was hired—"

"It's okay, Mr. Everett," she placated, hands outstretched. "Twice today I saw your expression as she barked at you, and I agree you've gone above and beyond the call of duty."

"That woman verbally abused me. I didn't tolerate that kind of disrespect when I owned my own business, and I can't abide seeing it in others."

"You owned your own business?" Ginny asked.

The older man puffed out his chest. "Yes. At one time I owned and managed Stoneham's only grocery store. We were forced to close when the big chain stores came into Milford."

Tricia stepped forward, touched the elderly man's arm. "Starting right now, you can help us here in the store again."

"What about me?" Angelica demanded.

Tricia turned on her sister. "I can't afford three employees."

Angelica's sour gaze swept across the room to land on Ginny, as though daring Tricia to fire her.

"We can barely squeeze the customers in now," Ginny said, worry creeping into her voice.

"Was that a crack about my weight?" Angelica growled.

"Ladies, please!" Mr. Everett implored, hands held out before him in supplication. "I've heard enough harsh words for one day. Can't we all just get along?"

Tricia lost it, bursting into laughter.

"Now, if you'll excuse me, I'll just get busy with those biographies," Mr. Everett said and turned for the back closet where he retrieved his Haven't Got a Clue apron, donned it, and set off to work.

A tinny, electronic version of Gloria Gaynor's "I Will Survive" broke the quiet. "Oh, my cell phone!" Angelica said and patted at her waist, finding the offending instrument. "Hello?"

The shop's old-fashioned telephone rang as well. Ginny picked it up. "Haven't Got a Clue, this is Ginny. How can I help you?"

"Really?" Angelica squealed and practically jumped. "Yee-ha!"

"You're kidding," Ginny said, crestfallen.

"What's the rest of it?" Angelica asked, her eyes wide.

"Can't we counter?" Ginny asked, her words caught in a sob.

Tricia's head swiveled back and forth as she tried to follow the two conversations.

"And the tentative closing date?" Angelica asked with glee.

"Are you sure?" Ginny asked. Her shoulders had gone boneless.

"Thanks so much for calling, Bob," Angelica said, bouncing on the balls of her feet.

"Thank you for letting me know," Ginny said, her voice so low it threatened to hit the floor.

Both women hung up.

"I lost my house!" Ginny wailed, closing her eyes in angst.

"I got my house!" Angelica crowed, and pumped her right arm up and down in triumph.

Suddenly the air inside Haven't Got a Clue seemed to crackle as the two women's heads whipped around to face each other.

"You!" Ginny accused.

"Uh-oh," Tricia said under her breath.

"Me?" Angelica asked.

Ginny's eyes had narrowed to mere slits. "What house were you bidding on?"

Angelica eyed her with suspicion. "A little white cottage on the highway."

"Slate roof? Pink and red roses out front?"

Angelica nodded.

Ginny's face crumpled, her eyes filling with tears. She smacked her clenched fists against her forehead.

Tricia wasn't sure what to do. Congratulate her sister or commiserate with her employee?

"Well," Angelica started. "Well . . . I bid low. I really did. You must've bid really, really low."

"It was all Brian and I could afford," Ginny cried, tears spilling down her cheeks.

Tricia stepped forward, captured Ginny in a motherly hug. "I'm so sorry, Ginny."

Angelica's mouth dropped open, her eyes blazing.

"We're getting married next year," Ginny managed between sobs. "We figured it would take us that long to fix the place up. We had it all planned out, right down to the nu—nu—nursery."

"All's fair in love and real estate," Angelica said, defiantly crossing her arms over her chest. "And how was I supposed to know you were even interested in that house?"

"You weren't," Tricia said, looking over at her sister while gently patting Ginny's back. "Come on. Have a cookie. You'll feel better." She led Ginny over to the coffee station, but the cookie plate was empty. Instead, she poured Ginny a cup of coffee.

"How was I to know she was interested in that house?" Angelica groused.

A customer entered the store, and Angelica sprang into action. "Welcome to Haven't Got a Clue. Can I help you find something?" She hurried over to the woman.

"*She* hasn't got a clue where anything is," Ginny growled, then gulped her coffee, setting the cup down with a dull thunk. "I'd better help the customer before your sister helps us right out of business." She wiped her eyes on the back of her hand, straightened, and stepped forward, heading for the customer. "Did you say Ngaio Marsh? Right over here."

Scowling, Angelica backed off and stepped up to the coffee station. "I really didn't know Ginny wanted that house," she hissed.

"She'll get over it. Have a cup of coffee." Tricia poured

the last of the pot into one of the store's cups and gave it to Angelica.

Angelica swirled the dregs, then glanced over the assortment of creamers, choosing hazelnut. "How did it go at the lawyer's office?"

"Better than I thought. And he's going to try to help Grace, too."

"That's great. I wonder if he does real estate closings."

Ginny cleared her throat, glared at Angelica. "Have you finished unpacking that case of Dashiell Hammetts yet, Ange?"

"Don't call me Ange. And no, I haven't."

Tricia wasn't about to get caught up in a Ginny/Angie catfight and headed to the back of the store where Mr. Everett was already happily rearranging the biographies. "Mr. Everett, you mentioned Deirdre was grumpy. Just what was bothering her today?"

The older man straightened, holding on to a biography of Anthony Boucher by Jeffrey Marks. "That woman is just as disagreeable as her sister ever was. In fact, if I didn't know she was dead, I would swear I'd spent time with Doris, not Deirdre Gleason."

"Did you know Doris well?" Tricia asked.

"Not well, but I'd observed her enough times. I was a grocer. I knew how to cook a few basic dishes, and when my wife died I attended a number of the Cookery's demonstrations to learn more. Macaroni and cheese from a box palls after a few meals," he confided.

"Would you say the sisters' personalities were interchangeable?" Angelica asked from behind Tricia, who hadn't heard her sister approach.

"Ms. Deirdre puts on airs when she thinks she's got an audience, but in private she's just as irascible as her late sibling."

Angelica gave her sister a jab. "Didn't I tell you? I'd bet my Anolon cookware the woman next door is really Doris, not Deirdre."

"Don't be absurd. We've been over this before."

"And I'm still right. I'll bet when they were kids those identical twins switched personalities whenever it suited them. And if that's so, why wouldn't they do that later in life?"

"Nobody in their right mind agrees to change identities, especially if they're about to be killed."

"Well, of course Deirdre wouldn't agree to the idea—not if she was the victim. But if Doris did take her identity, she'd have it all. The insurance payout would cover her debts and she'd also have access to whatever assets Deirdre, a successful businesswoman, had owned, which would save her failing shop and also help support her daughter. And why should she feel guilt? Her sister had a fatal illness, she would've died anyway. Doris may have justified the act believing she'd saved Deirdre from the horror of a painful death."

The idea made sense, but Tricia didn't want to embrace it. Not only did it negate her own theory that Mike Harris killed Doris, but there was no way on Earth she wanted Angelica to be proven right—again.

"Maybe I should go next door and talk to Deirdre. I know a fair bit about cooking. If she does, too, it would only help prove my point."

"Do what you want," Tricia said and waved a hand in dismissal. "Talking about all this isn't getting the work around here done."

Mr. Everett bent over his task once more as Angelica rolled her eyes theatrically. "Says she who's been away from the store all day."

"There won't *be* a store if I can't get Sheriff Adams off my back," Tricia countered.

"Well, even if you do go to jail, *I'm* still here to pick up the pieces. And isn't that what family is for?"

Tricia found her fingers involuntarily clenching—her body's way of saving her from another murder rap by preventing her from choking the life out of her only sibling. Meanwhile, Angelica stood before her, waiting for some kind of an answer.

Tricia turned away. "I'm starving, I haven't had a thing to eat since breakfast. Where's the bakery bag? There must be a few cookies left."

"Sorry," Angelica apologized. "I ate the last one just before you came back."

Suddenly fratricide seemed like a wonderful solution to all life's problems.

TWENTY-TWO

Tricia tried not to keep an eye on the clock, but after Angelica had been gone for almost an hour she began to worry. What if Angelica said or did something to tip Deirdre off about her suspicions? What if Deirdre threatened Angelica? The what-ifs in her mind began to escalate and she was glad to wait on the few customers who'd braved the elements to patronize Haven't Got a Clue.

The rain had not let up and the street lamps had already blinked on. Tricia let a still-distraught Ginny leave early, and she and Mr. Everett were discussing the merits of doing more author signings and the possibility of staring a reading group when Angelica finally returned.

"Well?" Tricia asked.

Angelica pushed up her sweater sleeves and shrugged. "That woman would make a pretty fair poker player."

"What was her attitude?" Mr. Everett asked. "Polite or had she reverted to type?"

Tricia blinked, surprised. That made twice in one day Mr. Everett had shown irritation.

"She was polite, but she has absolutely no clue how to sell a room," Angelica said and made an attempt to fluff up her rain-dampened hair. "Then again, her house was no better."

Mr. Everett frowned, puzzled by the remark.

"That's because she's selling books—not a room," Tricia grated, hoping Mr. Everett wouldn't ask Angelica how she knew about Doris's home.

"Yes, but if you want to be successful," Angelica continued, oblivious of her gaffe, "you've got to have atmosphere, which you've achieved here with your hunter green accents, sumptuous paneling, the copper tiled ceiling, the oak shelves—you've even got great carpet. This room makes you want to sit down with a good book, a glass of sherry, and a cigar."

Mr. Everett blinked at this last.

"Well, not me personally—I don't smoke—but you know what I mean. Whoever that woman is next door—she's clueless when it comes to selling."

"And what would you do to entice a customer to buy old cookbooks?" Mr. Everett asked.

She turned to face him. "I'd offer more than just books. Exotic gadgets—even just as décor. I'd have samples of dipping sauces, tapanades, mustards, relishes, jams, jellies, and chutneys. I'd feature different cuisines, from Indian to Irish to Asian fusion."

"Doris used to have cooking demonstrations. And don't forget, the lure of Stoneham is rare and antiquarian books," Tricia told her.

"So why can't you offer the new with the old? Tricia, people love to eat. For a big segment of the population, food is more important than sex. Why else would there be an obesity crisis in this country? When life hands you lemons, you make a meringue pie or a luscious curd."

Had Angelica found solace in food? Then again, she'd recently lost a lot of weight. Maybe she'd made the effort to appear more attractive to the husband who no longer wanted her.

"My point is," Angelica continued, "her shtick is food. She ought to play it up."

"Did you tell her that?"

Angelica frowned. "Not exactly. I did tell her I was thinking of opening a restaurant, and we had a nice discussion about food prep."

"Did she seem to know a lot about cooking?" Tricia asked.

"She asked a lot of questions. The kind someone might ask if they weren't sure what they were getting into."

"Where does this leave your theory about her?"

"I don't know," Angelica admitted. "She may have been testing me, or maybe just giving me a snow job."

"I didn't know you wanted to open a restaurant, Mrs. Prescott," said Mr. Everett. "I'm an old hand when it comes to fresh produce. I'd enjoy having a dialogue on it with you some time, if you wouldn't mind."

"I'd love to. How about tomorrow? We can unpack books and talk asparagus and Swiss chard."

"I'll look forward to it," he said.

Thunder rumbled overhead. Tricia looked around the empty shop. "Thanks to what's left of Hurricane Sheila, I don't think we're going to have any more customers tonight. Why don't we call it a day? You can head on home, Mr. Everett."

"If the weather were better, I would insist on staying on until our normal closing time, but I think I will take you up on your generous offer. I will be here bright and early tomorrow, however." He took off his apron and went to the back of the store to retrieve his jacket and umbrella. "Until the morning, ladies."

"Good night," the sisters chorused, as the door shut on his back.

"I'd better head upstairs and get that chicken in the oven if we're ever going to eat tonight," Angelica said.

"What chicken?"

"I went out during a lull and got the fixings. If I'd

known I'd have something to celebrate, I would've gotten steaks. We can have that tomorrow."

"Isn't roast chicken kind of pedestrian for you?" Tricia asked.

"Comfort food is comfort food." Angelica glanced around the shop. "Miss Marple, are you coming?"

The cat, curled up on one of the nook's comfy chairs, opened one eye, glared at Angelica, and closed it again.

"So much for trying to make friends with *you*." All business, she headed toward the stairs at the back of the shop. "Okay, I'm off."

"I've got things to do," Tricia called. "Be up in a few minutes."

Tricia locked the door and pulled the shades down on the big plate-glass window that overlooked the sidewalk on Main Street, thankful to have a few minutes to herself to decompress. Roger Livingston had made her feel better about her own legal situation, but poor Grace Harris was still alone, still trapped at St. Godelive's.

Tricia crossed to the sales counter. With Angelica gone, Miss Marple decided to be more sociable and hopped down from the chair, trotting over to jump up on the counter and then over to the shelf behind the register next to the still-nonfunctioning security camera.

Tricia planted her hands on her hips. "How many times have I asked you not to get up there?"

Miss Marple said, "Yeow!"

Tricia lifted the cat from the shelf, placing her on the floor. Not one to take direction well, Miss Marple jumped up on the sales counter and again said, "Yeow!"

"Don't even think about getting back up there," Tricia cautioned and turned back for the camera. How could one eight-pound cat continually knock a wall-mounted camera out of alignment? Tricia usually had it pointing at the register—in case someone tried to rob them—but she often thought it made more sense to train it on the back of the shop where shoplifters tended to steal the most merchandise. Now it pointed out toward the street, in the direction of the Cookery, exactly as it had on the night of Doris Gleason's murder.

Tricia peeked around the side of the shade, glancing across the street to Mike Harris's darkened storefront campaign headquarters. She hadn't pulled the shades down on the night of the murder. If Mike had killed Doris, he would've had to cross the street to enter the Cookery during the interval Tricia had left the village to pick up Angelica at the Brookview Inn and her return some thirty minutes later.

She glanced over her shoulder at the camera still mounted on the wall. Had it been in operation at the time? If so, what would she find if she studied the tape?

Footsteps pounded at the far end of the shop, and Angelica appeared at the open doorway to the loft apartment. "Are you ever coming up? I want you to give me a hand making stuffed grape leaves. My version is just divine."

"In a minute," Tricia said, annoyed.

Angelica padded across the shop in her stocking feet. "What's got you so hyped up?"

"What do you mean?"

"The look on your face. It almost says 'eureka!' "

"I'm just wondering . . . Miss Marple messed with my security system the night Doris was murdered. I don't think I reset the system before I left to pick you up at the inn. What if it recorded Mike Harris crossing the street from his new offices and showed him going to the Cookery?"

Angelica frowned. "It might show him crossing the street and heading north, but you couldn't prove he went next door."

"No, but it might be something my new lawyer could use to help prove me innocent should Sheriff Adams make good her threat to arrest me."

"Well, I'm all for that. I've got the chicken in on low if you want to play your tape. Do we need to take it upstairs?"

"I only have a DVD player in the loft, but we could play it back on the shop's monitor."

"Go for it."

Always interested in technology of any kind, Miss Marple moved to the edge of the counter to study the operation. Tricia hadn't touched the cassette since the morning before Doris had been murdered, and the whirr of it rewinding in the player fascinated the cat.

Tricia noticed Angelica's bare feet. "Where are your shoes?"

"They got wet. Maybe I'll bring a pair of slippers over tomorrow."

"Don't get too comfortable. You'll soon have your own house here in Stoneham."

The tape came to a halt with a clunk and Tricia was about to press the play button when someone banged sharply on the shop door. "Ignore it," Angelica advised. "The store's closed."

The banging came again, this time accompanied by a voice Tricia recognized: Mike Harris. "Open up. I know you're in there, Tricia. The lights are still on," he bellowed. Miss Marple jumped down from her perch and hightailed it across the shop and up the stairs to the apartment. Tricia bit her lip, looked back at the door.

"Don't you dare open that door," Angelica ordered. "He sounds ticked."

The banging continued. Then got much louder.

"I think he's kicking it in," Tricia said, alarmed. "What if he gets inside?"

"Call the sheriff's department," Angelica said.

"Are you kidding? They'd probably lock *me* up, not him!"

The wood around the door began to splinter.

"Don't you have any friends in this town you can call?" Angelica asked anxiously.

"Mr. Everett and Ginny."

Angelica grabbed the shop's phone and started dialing. "Why couldn't you have a modern phone?"

"Use your cell," Tricia implored.

"I left it upstairs. Ah, it's ringing. Come on, Bob, answer!"

The door crashed open and Mike burst into the shop, soaking wet, chest heaving, his face twisted in anger. "Where the hell do you get off accusing me of murder?" he demanded.

"Answer the phone," Angelica implored.

"Hang up!" Mike ordered.

A defiant Angelica held on to the receiver.

"I said hang up!"

"Bob, it's Angelica! Get over to Haven't Got a Clue right now. There's a madman—"

Before she could finish her sentence, Mike had charged across the carpet, yanked the phone from her hand, and pulled the cord from the wall. Both she and Tricia darted behind the sales counter, putting it between them and the crazy man before them.

"Why did you visit my mother at the home and fill her head with nonsense?"

"What are you talking about?" Tricia bluffed.

"I just got a call from Sheriff Adams. She said you'd visited Mom, accused me of trying to poison her and steal from her. That's a bold-faced lie!"

"Is it?" Tricia said. "The home changed their practices, stopped serving her the gourmet chocolate laced with who knows what that you brought her. It only took a couple of days for her mind to clear. She filed papers to keep you away from her assets. Winnie Wentworth may be dead, but you left enough evidence to nail you for selling off items from your mother's home without her permission."

His eyes had narrowed at the mention of Winnie. "You have no proof."

"An admission of guilt if I ever heard one," Angelica quipped.

"Ange, shush!" Tricia ordered.

"Come on, Trish, you were all hyped just now to see if he was on that tape."

"Ange," Tricia warned.

"What tape?" Mike demanded.

"From the security camera. It was focused out on the

street the night Doris Gleason was murdered," Angelica said.

"Give it to me," Mike commanded.

"In your dreams," Angelica said with a sneer.

"Ange," Tricia said through clenched teeth. "You're going to get us killed."

"I said give it to me!" Mike lifted the heavy phone with both hands and smashed it through the top of the sales counter, sending chunks and shards of glass spraying across the carpet.

Both women jumped back and screamed.

Deirdre suddenly stood in the open door, her big red handbag dangling from her left forearm. "What's going on?" she demanded.

"Call the sheriff! Call the sheriff!" Angelica squealed.

Instead, Deirdre stepped inside the shop, pushed the door so that it was ajar—but it wouldn't shut properly with the doorjamb broken and hanging.

"I said what's going on?" Deirdre repeated.

"They've got something I want," Mike said, then turned. "Now give it to me."

The sisters stole a look at each other. Angelica barely nodded, but it was enough for Tricia to reach down to retrieve the tape from the video recorder. She handed it to Mike and backed up, hitting the wall, nearly cracking her head on the shelf that housed the useless video camera.

Mike dropped the tape to the carpeted floor, stomped on it with his booted right foot until the case cracked. Again and again his foot came down until the plastic gave way and he was left pummeling the ribbon of magnetic videotape.

Breathing hard, he looked up, his eyes wild. "Give me a bag."

Tricia blinked, unsure what he meant.

"I said give me a bag!"

Angelica pulled one of the green plastic Haven't Got a Clue shopping bags out from under the counter and threw it at him.

Mike picked up the largest pieces of tape, shoving them in the bag. "We're safe now, Doris."

"Shut up," Deirdre/Doris growled, moving closer, her expression menacing. "We're not safe. You and your stupid temper. Can't you see you've ruined it all?"

Mike's mouth twitched, but he didn't say anything, just kept picking up the plastic fragments.

Angelica stepped back, bumping into Tricia. "I told you she killed Deirdre," she hissed.

Tricia reached out, pinched Angelica to silence her.

"These two are now a liability. We'll have to get rid of them." Doris opened her purse and brought out a couple of the wickedly sharp kitchen knives that matched those from the Cookery's demonstration area. "Take this," she said, shoving the handle of a boning knife toward Mike. "Ladies, come out from behind the counter. Slowly. No funny business."

Funny business was the last thing on Tricia's mind. She gave Angelica a shove in the small of her back. Angelica stayed rooted.

"Look," Angelica said, her voice relatively level. "I've got a nice roast chicken in the oven. I'm making a wonderful appetizer, too. Can't we all have a glass of wine and talk this over?"

Doris's lips were a thin line. Her cheeks had gone pink, her grasp on the knife handle tightened.

Tricia gave her sister another slight shove. "Ange." Finally, Angelica took a step forward.

"What are we going to do?" Mike asked.

Doris ignored him. "Out in front, ladies, hands where I can see them."

Tricia and Angelica stepped around to the front of the cash desk, Tricia's shoes crunching on glass. Angelica yelped, stepping away from the sparkling shards, leaving a patch of blood on the carpet.

"You." Doris nodded toward Tricia. "Where's your car?"

"In the municipal lot."

She turned to Angelica. "You?"

"My car's there, too."

"So's mine," Mike groused. "Terrific, now how do we get out of here?"

"Deirdre's car is parked just outside." Doris fished inside her purse and came up with a set of keys. She tossed them at Tricia, who caught them. "You'll drive."

"Where?"

Doris nodded toward the street. "Just get in the car."

"Oooohh," Angelica crooned in anguish, and shifted from foot to foot, the patch of blood growing larger on the rug.

Mike grabbed Tricia's arm, pushed her ahead of him, pressing the knife against her hip. "If I'm not mistaken, the femoral artery is near the tip of this knife. You wouldn't want it severed and ruin your beautiful carpet, not to mention your day."

Doris stepped forward, brandishing her shorter vegetable knife. "Don't think I can't do a lot of damage with this," she told Angelica. "I can filet a five-pound salmon in under a minute. Just think what I could do to your internal organs in only seconds. Liver anyone?" she said and laughed.

No one else did.

She shoved Angelica forward, toward the door.

The wind had picked up and the rain came down like stinging pellets as Tricia led the way to the pavement outside her shop, with Mike practically attached to her. They paused and he looked up and down the dark, empty street. No one stood on the sidewalk. No hope of rescue.

Mike pushed Tricia toward the driver's door. "Get in. Don't try anything—unless you want Doris to slice your sister."

Tricia yanked the door handle. It was like a bad movie, including Doris's and Mike's corny dialogue. *I'll wake up from this nightmare, I'll wake up soon.* But it wasn't a dream.

Already soaked through, she got in, slammed the door,

and on automatic pilot, buckled her seat belt. Glancing over her shoulder she saw Doris with one hand on Angelica's shoulder, the knife-wielding one hidden in shadow.

Mike got in the passenger side, brandishing the wicked knife clenched in his left hand at mid-chest—the perfect position for slashing. "You really blew it, Trish. We could've been great together."

"Is that what you told Wendy Adams?"

"We've talked," he admitted, his expression a leer. "And more."

The right rear passenger door opened. Angelica ducked her head, got in, scrambled across the seat with Doris crawling in after her. The door banged shut.

For a long moment no one said anything.

"Start the car," Doris ordered. "And don't try anything funny. You saw what happened to Deirdre. She thought I didn't have the guts to kill. They say it's easier the second time."

"What about Winnie?" Tricia asked.

"Not my handiwork," Doris said and glanced at Mike.

Tricia swallowed, her gaze focused on Doris's reflection in the rearview mirror. "Then it doesn't matter if you kill us here or someplace else."

"Think I'm joking?" Doris lunged to her left and Angelica cried out.

"She cut me, Trish! She cut me!"

Stomach churning, Tricia's neck cracked as she whirled to look, but the heel of Mike's hand caught her shoulder with a painful punch. "Ange?" Tricia shouted.

"I'm okay, I'm okay!" Angelica cried, but the fear in her voice said she was anything but.

Tricia's eyes darted to the rearview mirror. She could just make out Angelica's bloody left hand clutching the slash in her light-colored sweater.

"I'll cut her again, only with more precision, if you don't start the car. Do it now!"

Tricia tore her gaze from the mirror, fumbled to put the key into the ignition, turned it until the engine caught.

"If you don't want to see your sister's throat cut, I suggest you put the car in gear and head north to Route 101," Doris ordered.

Tricia glanced askance at Mike, hoping her pleading gaze would be met with some shred of compassion, but there was none. And why would he show that emotion for her when he'd shown Winnie no mercy and treated his own mother so callously?

Tricia turned her gaze back to the empty rain-soaked street. All the other shops had closed; the only beacon of light was the Bookshelf Diner. Even if she blasted the horn, no one was likely to hear or even pay attention to the car as it passed. Their one ace in the hole was Bob Kelly. Had Angelica reached him or his voice mail, or had she simply been bluffing?

Come on, Bob.

Then again, Mr. Everett knew of their suspicions. If they turned up missing, he could point the law in Mike's and Doris's direction. That is, if Sheriff Adams would even listen to him. And if he spoke, would he become the next murder victim?

Stalling, Tricia fumbled with the buttons and switches on the dash until she found and turned on the headlights. Next, she checked the mirrors before pulling out of the parking space and driving slowly down Main Street, heading out of the village. Within a minute the glow of friendly street lamps was behind them, the inky darkness broken only by the car's headlights.

"Turn here and go straight until you reach Route 101," Doris directed.

"Then where?"

"You'll head for Interstate 93."

"Where are we going?" Angelica asked, uncomprehending.

Tricia could guess. The interstate cut through the White Mountain National Forest, the perfect place to dump a couple of bodies where they wouldn't be found for months—if ever.

No one spoke for a long minute.

Angelica cleared her throat. "Does anyone have a hand-kerchief or something? All this blood is ruining my sweater. Not that I could ever find anyone in this town who can repair cashmere, even if they could get the stains out."

Tricia exhaled a shaky breath. Was Angelica's claustro-phobia acting up, or was she simply in shock? Either she didn't realize what was going to happen to them, or she was in deep denial.

Time was running out. If they got as far as the interstate, they were as good as dead.

"My foot's still bleeding, you know," Angelica went on. "I think there might be a piece of glass in it."

Mike smashed his fist against the dashboard. "Will you shut up!"

Tricia clenched the steering wheel. Route 101 was only a couple of miles ahead. If she was going to save them, it had to be in the next few minutes—and she could only think of one option: crashing the car.

She'd read too many mysteries to think of disobeying Mike's or Doris's direct orders—Angelica's bleeding shoul-der was proof of that. Still, she couldn't remember any fic-tional scenario from a book that would keep herself and Angelica alive.

The most famous car crash she could recall was that of Princess Diana in a tunnel in Paris. The one passenger wearing a seat belt had lived—the others didn't. Only Tri-cia wore a seat belt. If she crashed the car, would Angelica survive? How fast did she need to go to incapacitate her captors without permanently maiming her sister?

The headlights flashed on a mile marker.

The dashboard clock's green numerals changed.

Not much time left.

"What happened, Doris? Did Mike witness Deirdre's murder and hit you up for money?"

"None of your business," she snapped.

"He didn't have to see the murder," Angelica said. "I'll bet he planned it."

Collusion! Suddenly, it all made sense. "You sold Doris the million-dollar insurance policy, and when she told you her sister was dying and she'd have to change the beneficiary—"

"All very neat, really," Doris said. "It solved all our problems."

"Not Mike's. His mother has regained her memory."

"I'm having her moved from St. Godelive's in the morning. She'll go right back to loving her nightly mug of cocoa tomorrow night."

Not with Roger Livingston looking after her affairs, but Tricia wasn't going to voice that fact.

"Why did you throw the rock through my window?" Tricia asked Mike.

He laughed. "Just to keep things interesting."

"Did you really think I was going out with Russ Smith?"

"It crossed my mind."

"Oh please," Angelica groused.

Keep them talking, something inside Trish implored. "There's still something I don't get."

"And what's that?" Doris asked.

"Why did you set the Cookery on fire and disable the smoke alarms when you had every intension of keeping it open with 'Deirdre' as the owner? You could've destroyed everything. Or did you have the contents heavily insured as well?"

"The place wouldn't have burned. That carpet is flame-retardant. I know, I paid a small fortune for it."

"Stop all this yapping and turn on the defroster. Can't you see the windshield's steaming up?" Mike carped, and rubbed at the glass with his free hand.

Tricia glanced down, couldn't find the control. Instead, she fumbled for the window button on the door's arm, pressing it. The window started to open.

"I said turn on the defroster!"

"I don't know where it is!" She held the button until the window was completely open. The rain poured in and she eased her foot from the accelerator.

Mike leaned closer, searching the dashboard. "Doris, where the hell is it?"

"I don't know. This is Deirdre's car. Keep pushing buttons until you find it."

With Mike preoccupied, Tricia knew her window of opportunity was short. Headlights cut through the gloom on the road up ahead. If she could sideswipe the vehicle, or merely scare them into thinking she would, they were sure to call the sheriff. If she didn't kill them all first.

"Now or never," she breathed and jammed her foot down on the accelerator.

Mike fell back against his seat, the knife flying from his grasp, disappearing onto the darkened floor.

Tricia aimed straight for the oncoming car.

"What are you, crazy?" Angelica screamed from behind.

Tricia risked a glance in the rearview mirror, but Angelica wasn't talking to her; she wrestled with Doris in the backseat—trying to disarm her.

Mike's hands fumbled around Tricia's legs, yanking her foot from the accelerator, grappling for the missing knife.

The wail of the approaching car's horn cut through the rain pounding on the roof and Angelica's screams. Tricia steered to the right, barely missing the oncoming car.

Mike grabbed the steering wheel, jerking it left, and Tricia jammed her foot on the brake, sending Mike flying. The car hydroplaned on the slick, wet road, sliding sideways.

Tricia wrestled with the wheel, but the car had a mind of its own, hit the guardrail, and went airborne, sailing into the black, rainy night, flipping before it landed in the swollen waters of Stoneham Creek.

TWENTY-THREE

Stunned, for a moment Tricia didn't realize the car had come to a halt. It was only what was left of the deflated air bag hanging out of the steering wheel and in her face, and the rising chilly water swirling around the crown of her head that brought her back to full consciousness. Blinking did no good, she couldn't see a thing, but finally it sank in that she hung suspended by the seat belt, about to drown from the water that gushed through the car's open window. The sound of rushing water filled her ears as she fumbled for the catch.

The belt released and Tricia plunged into the freezing water. Arms flailing, she pawed for the aperture, found it, and pulled herself through into open air, then fell into the raging torrent. The current immediately slammed her against the car. Winded, she groped for and clung to the undercarriage above the water. Shoes gone, her stocking feet slipped on mossy rocks, and she struggled to find a foothold on the driver's window frame.

Upside down, the car was hung up on the rocks in the creek bed, listing at a forty-five-degree angle. Raking aside the hair flattened around her face, Tricia realized light shone down from above and behind her—the glow of a mercury vapor lamp on the bridge over Stoneham Creek.

"Help! Please help me!" Tricia looked around, realized the weak voice came from inside the car.

Angelica!

Sliding down the side of the car, Tricia sank back into the arcticlike stream, fumbled for the door handle, pulling with all her strength, but the rushing water was too powerful—she couldn't yank it open.

"Help—oh, please help," came the voice, sounding fainter.

Grasping the window frame, Tricia took in a lungful of air, sank down, and pulled her upper body into the black interior. In only a minute or so the car had filled with water; just a pocket of air remained along what had once been the car's floor. Fumbling fingers captured Tricia's hand and she pulled with all her strength, trying to keep her head above water. "Be careful," she gasped. "Come on. I've got you!"

The hands clamped around her forearms in a death grip.

Muscles straining in the numbing-cold water, Tricia pulled and tugged and eventually a dark, bulky figure emerged from the car, coughing and sputtering.

"Thank you, oh, thank you," Doris Gleason cried, clutching at the car to find a handhold.

"Where's my sister?" Tricia demanded, steadying the woman.

"I don't know—I don't know," Doris wailed, inching away from her and toward the car's front tire.

Panicked, Tricia pulled herself back into the driver's compartment. The cockpit's air bubble was half the size. Tricia took a gulping breath and plunged into the black water, fumbling behind the driver's seat, searching, searching for her sister. Angelica was claustrophobic—she'd be terrified! But suddenly the midsized car's backseat area seemed to have expanded.

The back of her hand scraped something sharp and Tricia grabbed, capturing the chunky stone of Angelica's diamond ring. She pulled the hand and the body attached to it toward the driver's compartment with all her might, but Angelica was a dead weight, too large to drag under the driver's seat.

Fighting panic, Tricia groped for a lever, to make the seat recline.

Where in God's name was it?

Finally, her fingers clasped a plastic handle. She pushed it, yanked it.

Nothing happened.

Come on!

She had to let go of her sister, wrenched the lever with one hand while she beat on the saturated seat with the other.

With lungs ready to burst, she was forced to seek out the air pocket, took several painful gulps, and plunged down again.

More seconds flashed by as she struggled with the lever. At last it moved, and so did the seat, but only by inches. It would have to be enough.

Angelica had slipped back into the black abyss. Maddening eons passed as Tricia's frozen hands once again probed the icy darkness.

Her fingers were nothing more than pins and needles from the cold when something brushed against her. She snatched at it—Angelica's sweater. Hanging on, she maneuvered her legs out the driver's window.

Tricia pulled and tugged and jerked until she dragged a lifeless Angelica around the seat and out through the window. She slipped on weedy rocks, plunging into the water, gashing her knees on the rocks. Skyrockets of pain shot through her, but she managed to grab her sister as she tumbled into the torrent. Angelica's foot caught on the window frame and she hung suspended, with most of her body underwater. Tricia captured Angelica's arms, yanking her free, and the force of the water smashed them against the side of the car.

Nearing exhaustion, Tricia struggled to keep her own

and her sister's head above water. Mike was still in the car—probably near death, and yet Tricia wasn't sure she had the strength to keep Angelica from drowning, let alone look for another victim.

"Get away! Get away! You'll push me in," Doris screamed.

If she'd had the energy, Tricia would've gladly slapped Doris, the cause of all their problems. Instead, she looked down at her sister. It took a long few moments for reality to register in her brain.

Angelica wasn't breathing.

"Ange. Ange!" Tricia screamed, panicked. She didn't know CPR, had never bothered to take a class.

Why hadn't she ever taken a class?

"Breathe! Breathe!" Tricia commanded, slapping Angelica's cheek, but Angelica's head lolled to one side.

Not knowing what else to do, Tricia shoved her sister's body against the car, pressing hard against her back.

Again. Harder.

Again! Harder still!

"Come on, Ange! Breathe!"

Once, twice, three more times she slammed Angelica into the side the car until she heard a cough, and a gasp, then choking sounds as Angelica vomited.

"Stop, stop! You're hurting me," she cried weakly.

Tricia threw an arm around her sister to hold her up and rested her head against Angelica's shoulder, allowing the pent-up tears to flow.

"Need help?" came a voice from the bridge, one that sounded vaguely familiar.

"She tried to kill me!" Doris cried. "Get me out of here. She tried to kill *us*!"

Tricia craned her neck to look. From the safety of the bridge above them, Russ Smith tossed Doris a rope. "Tie it around yourself. I'll pull you over to the bank."

"Call nine-one-one. There's still someone trapped in the car!" Tricia called.

"Already called." Something flashed repeatedly. Tricia

glanced over her shoulder to see Russ lower a little digital camera. "This is going to make a great front-page story for the next edition of the *Stoneham Weekly News*," he said with zeal.

"Who cares about that? Get me out of here!" Doris demanded, again, already tying the rope around her chest.

"I want to go home," Angelica sobbed.

Tricia's cheek rested against her sister's shoulder once more and she closed her eyes, ready to collapse. "Me, too."

TWENTY-FOUR

Tricia bowed with theatrical aplomb, holding the polished silver tray in front of her guest. "Care for a smoked-salmon-and-caviar bite? They're absolutely delicious."

Juggling a martini in one hand and a china plate already heaped with hot hors d'oeuvres in the other, Russ Smith shook his head and laughed. "I already feel like the fatted calf. I'll need to go on a diet after this feast."

"Nothing is too good for the man who saved my life." Ensconced in the plushest chair in Haven't Got a Clue's reading nook, her leg resting on the south edge of the nook's large square coffee table, Angelica toasted Russ with her own glass. Her ankle, encased in a pink fiberglass cast, had been broken in three places, but she'd been getting around in a wheelchair for the last few days. Despite her near-death experience, she looked fabulous in a little black cocktail dress, one black pump, a string of pearls around her neck, and nails polished to match her cast. In comparison, Tricia felt positively frumpy in her usual work clothes.

She handed the tray to Ginny, who took a crab puff and placed it on the table, which had been cleared of its usual stacks of books and magazines. "Excuse me," Tricia said, "but I believe I'm the one who pulled you out of that car and kept you from drowning."

"Yes, but I would've died of hypothermia if this darling man hadn't used his cell phone to call nine-one-one. Never complain about paying your taxes, Trish, darling—not when the county employs such cute paramedics."

Tricia wasn't likely to complain at all. Her own cuts and bruises were nothing compared to Angelica's assorted injuries. Crutches weren't likely to be in her future until her two cracked ribs healed—an injury caused by Tricia's clumsy but successful attempt at resuscitation. Makeup had done a reasonable job of covering up Angelica's blackened eyes, but it was the defensive knife wounds on her arms she'd received fighting off Doris that had finally convinced the law that they'd been the kidnap victims—and not the perpetrators. By comparison, Tricia's aches and pains were of little consequence.

Miss Marple sashayed around the nook, her little gray nose twitching at the aroma of salmon and caviar. "Shoo, shoo!" Angelica admonished, and the cat reluctantly retreated to a spot several feet away, her gaze never leaving the food on the table.

"How did you show up in the nick of time?" Ginny asked Russ.

He tipped his glass toward Tricia. "I was on my way back from Milford when your boss aimed her car directly at me."

"It wasn't my car—it's was Deirdre's—or Doris's. Well, it wasn't mine," she defended.

"At the last second, it swerved. I saw the car go out of control and doubled back to see if I could help. The rest, as they say, is history." He popped another canapé into his mouth, chewed, and swallowed. "These are the best finger foods I've ever eaten."

"All my recipes," Angelica bragged. "I had the executive

chef at the Brookview Inn whip them up for us." She picked up a canapé from her own plate. "They're almost as good as I make them."

Tricia clenched her teeth. She'd been doing a lot of that lately, as well as biting her tongue. Angelica had been insufferable since she'd been fished, more dead than alive, from Stoneham Creek exactly one week before. Yet, grateful her sister still lived, Tricia had indulged Angelica's every whim, including this little party at Haven't Got a Clue.

"Could I please have a glass of wine?" she asked Mr. Everett, who stood behind the makeshift bar that had been set up on the newly repaired sales counter. He uncorked a bottle of chardonnay, poured, and handed her the glass. She took a deep gulp.

After Angelica had been released from the hospital, Tricia had temporarily moved into the Brookview Inn to take care of her sister. From her palatial bed piled high with lace-edged pillows, Angelica had taken care of all the party details, from ordering the food and liquor to coordinating the guest list, although so far only Russ had arrived. By the amount of appetizers heaped on platters and crowding the nook's table, Tricia expected an army.

Someone knocked on the shop door, the CLOSED sign apparently keeping them from entering. Tricia leapt up to find her new attorney standing outside. "Come in, Roger."

"I've brought a friend," he said and held out a hand to his companion.

Grace Harris had undergone a dramatic change since the last time Tricia had seen her. White hair trimmed and perfectly coiffed, the elderly woman looked slim and elegant in a long-sleeved pink silk shirtwaist dress, accompanied by a single strand of pearls. Several gold bracelets graced her wrists, and the little gold scatter pin Tricia had given her decorated the lace collar at her throat. One of her first stops after leaving St. Godelive's must've been a jewelry shop. Grace allowed Roger Livingston to hold the door for her as she entered the shop.

"Dear Tricia—my savior," she said and rushed forward to pull Tricia into a warm embrace.

Tricia stepped back. "Come inside and meet everyone, won't you?"

Grace took in the others. "I believe I already know two of them. Hello, Russ." The newsman nodded a greeting as she walked past him to join Mr. Everett, who took her hands in his.

"It's been far too long, Grace."

"Oh, William, you don't know how good it is to see an old friend."

Mr. Everett's eyes were shining. "I did visit you several times when you were in St. Godelive's. I'm sorry to say you didn't know me."

Grace smiled. "I know you now. And I thank you."

Tricia introduced Grace to Angelica and Ginny before ushering her into the chair next to her sister. Mr. Everett, an excellent bartender, soon placed a glass of sherry in Grace's freshly manicured hand.

Grace swept the shop with her gaze. "My, my. I'm so sorry I missed your grand opening, Tricia. You've done a wonderful job reinventing this old building."

Tricia smiled, pleased at the compliment, and settled on the broad arm of Grace's upholstered chair. She took a more reasonable sip from her glass, realizing the inevitable couldn't be avoided.

"I'm so sorry about Mike," Tricia said. She'd spent the last week wrestling with guilt over his death. She hadn't had the strength to enter the partially submerged car a third time to attempt his rescue.

Grace sipped her sherry, her expression thoughtful. "I'm sorry to say I lost Michael a long, long time ago, dear."

"You're torturing yourself unnecessarily, Tricia," Russ said, all business. "The medical examiner ruled Mike Harris's death an accident. He hit the windshield and died on impact. You weren't to blame."

Was that really true? When push came to shove, Tricia

hadn't been able to crash the car. More than anything she wanted to believe that fate—and Mike grabbing the steering wheel—had caused the car to careen out of control. She hadn't meant for him or Doris to die; she just wanted to save herself and Angelica.

"Did we miss the service?" Angelica asked, looking to Tricia for guidance.

"Under the circumstances, I thought it best not to have a public memorial," Grace said, her voice subdued. "He was cremated and I scattered his ashes in my backyard yesterday morning. He loved to play there as a small boy. I prefer to remember him that way."

Her admission cast a bit of a pall on the party. No one seemed to know where to look. It was Mr. Everett who broke the ice. "Does the district attorney feel he's got a good case against Ms. Gleason?" he asked Roger Livingston.

"Fingerprints proved that the woman killed at the Cookery was indeed Deirdre Gleason. Her doctors in Connecticut confirmed she suffered from pancreatic cancer and had only a few months—possibly weeks—to live."

Russ picked up the story. "The cops theorized Doris saw her sister's illness as the answer to all her problems. With a successful financial background, Deirdre had invested wisely. Her portfolio was worth at least two million dollars. However, her will stated that the bulk of her estate was to go to a number of charitable organizations. She'd only designated a paltry ten thousand to be paid to her only surviving sibling. I can imagine that didn't sit well with Doris, whose business was on the rocks and she was faced with a new lease she couldn't afford. Killing Deirdre and taking her place had to seem like the answer to all Doris's problems."

"And don't forget," Angelica added, "Doris as Deirdre also stood to inherit at Doris's so-called death, too."

Ginny shook her head. "This is all so convoluted it's making me dizzy."

Russ hadn't brought up Mike Harris's part in Deirdre's

death. Out of respect for Grace, Tricia didn't mention it, either. And his excusing her part in Mike's death sounded all well and good, yet the memory of seeing his limp body being pulled from the hulk of Deirdre Gleason's car would haunt Tricia for a long time to come.

Grace patted Tricia's hand. "It's all right, dear. Please don't dwell on what happened. Michael won't hurt anyone ever again, and now no one will ever hurt him, either."

Tricia wondered if she could be so charitable if put in Grace's shoes.

"I'd still like to see Sheriff Adams apologize for hounding you, Tricia," Roger said.

"That'll never happen. Mike was a charmer, and I'm afraid he charmed Wendy Adams. She saw me as a threat to whatever relationship she thought she had with him. And despite the coroner's report, she blames me for Mike's death."

"I'm afraid my son used his charisma to get himself out of many scrapes over the years," Grace said.

Tricia thought back to that awful night. Wendy Adams had stood on the little bridge over Stoneham Creek as the local firefighters had hauled Mike's body out of Deirdre's car. She'd inspected his cold, dead face and then walked up to Tricia, who stood on the roadside shoeless and shivering under a scratchy blanket. Fighting tears, the sheriff had stared at Tricia for long seconds, and Tricia had been sure the woman was going to slap her. Then, abruptly, Wendy Adams had turned away. Shoulders slumped, she'd gotten back in her police cruiser and driven off into that bleak, rainy night.

They hadn't spoken since. A deputy had been dispatched to Haven't Got a Clue to take Tricia's statement, but Tricia had no doubt that Wendy Adams now considered her an enemy—the person who had robbed her of a future of love and companionship.

Still, Tricia felt only pity that the sheriff had been so easily duped, so manipulated by a handsome man with a glib tongue.

The shop door opened, the little bell above it tinkling merrily, and a smiling Bob Kelly stepped inside. "Am I too late for the festivities?"

Angelica's face lit up and she held out her hands. Bob surged forward, clasped both of them, and bent down to draw them to his lips for a kiss.

"You look beautiful as ever," he gushed.

"You're a liar, but after the week I've had, I can use the compliment," Angelica said, a blush coloring her cheeks.

Tricia rose and turned away from the sight, ready to gag.

Angelica patted the arm of her chair and Bob dutifully perched beside her, still holding her hand. Mr. Everett offered him a drink and Bob accepted a Scotch and soda.

Russ set his plate aside and straightened in his chair. "You've been avoiding my calls for a week now, Bob. What's the story on the big box store coming to Stoneham?"

Bob took a sip of his drink. "I hadn't planned on announcing it until later this week, but since the *Stoneham Weekly News* won't be out for another five days, I suppose I can break my silence."

The room seemed to crackle with electricity as everyone leaned forward to listen.

Bob sipped his Scotch, milking the anticipation.

"Come on, Bob, spill it," Tricia said. "What big company is coming to town?"

"None."

"None?" Russ repeated, incredulous.

"The rumors were just that—rumors. But come summer there will be a new business venture opening on a one-hundred-acre site just north of town."

"Some kind of light industry?" Tricia guessed, remembering her lunch conversation with Mike.

He shook his head. "New Hampshire's newest spa and resort."

"Ah, another venture like the Brookview Inn?" Angelica speculated. "Yes, Stoneham is in need of more fine dining."

"No, lovely lady, not an inn."

Spa and resort? "Don't tell me," Tricia began, "a Free Spirit Full Moon Nudist Camp and Resort?"

"The very same," Bob said and tipped his glass back.

"Nudists?" Grace said, appalled.

"It's only the second nudist resort in New Hampshire," Bob explained. "They're very family oriented. Should bring in a lot of tourist dollars."

"Didn't I tell you, Tricia," Ginny piped up. "Nudists get bored and like to read, too."

"How on Earth did you convince the Board of Selectmen to go for it?" Russ asked.

"Tax dollars," he explained simply. "That land isn't worth much the way it is, but once they start developing it with their lodge, spa, snack bar, Olympic-sized pool, and other amenities, we'll see a nice surge in the tax base. It's also far enough out of town that none of our residents should be offended."

"But nudists!" Grace protested.

"I hope this means we've seen the last of the nudist tracts in our stores," Tricia added.

Bob cleared his throat, looking embarrassed. "Yes, well, Free Spirit wanted to get the word out to the last of our summer tourists. I've spoken to them to them about it and they've promised it won't happen again."

"Hallelujah!" Tricia said.

"Can I quote you on this?" Russ asked.

Bob nodded. "I'll have a press release ready for you by Wednesday. And I have more news to share," he said, hoisting his glass as though for a toast. "The Cookery's assets have been sold. You'll soon have a new neighbor, Tricia."

Tricia wasn't sure she was ready to hear what else he had to say.

"Do tell," Ginny said, rolled her eyes, and picked up another crab puff, popping it into her mouth.

"I'd be glad to." But instead of launching into his story, Bob inspected the morsels on the plates and trays before him. He chose the biggest stuffed mushroom on a tray and took a bite, closing his eyes and throwing back his head theatrically. "This has got to be the most delicious thing I've ever eaten in my entire life."

Quelling the urge to throw up grew more difficult. "Come on, Bob, you're obviously dying to tell us," Tricia said.

He chose a piece of the prosciutto-wrapped asparagus from one of the platters and downed it in one gulp. "Heaven. Just heaven."

Tricia tapped her foot impatiently.

Bob took a fortifying sip of his drink before setting down his glass. "It seems Deirdre Gleason's assets have been frozen. Doris needed money to hire a good defense attorney so she's sold the Cookery, lock, stock, and barrel. And I have already rented out the building."

"To whom?"

Bob pulled a set of keys from his pocket and handed them to Angelica, who smiled coyly. "Me."

Tricia's stomach tightened. "But I thought you wanted to open a restaurant."

"All that time lying around got me to thinking about the long hours and the low profit margin associated with owning a restaurant. And—and I thought it would be such a kick to have my own little business right next to yours. Aren't you just thrilled, Tricia?"

Thrilled wasn't the word.

"That little demonstration area Doris devised is absolutely perfect. I can cook all day while my employees run the store. I'll have a steady income and get to do what I love. It's as simple as that."

"But you don't know the business. Where will you get your stock? Have you ever hired or trained an employee? Do you have any idea about the paperwork involved juggling inventory, vendor invoices, and taxes?"

"Trish—" Angelica cut her off. "That's the beauty of having my shop right next door to you. You already have all the knowledge I need and I can tap into your brain anytime I want. What could be better? Now you must tell me who did your loft conversion. Of course, I'm leaning toward French country for my decorating scheme, but I was thinking it would be neat to knock a hole through the bricks and put in a door linking my apartment with yours."

"No way!" Tricia declared, worried she'd never again have a private moment to herself.

"What's going to happen to the house you bought?" Ginny asked, her eyes flashing with interest.

Angelica turned to Bob.

"By canceling the deal, you've forfeited your deposit, I'm afraid. But the house is back on the market. It sat for a long time. I'm sure if you upped your offer by a few thousand, you'd get it, Ginny."

"It would be a stretch, but I think we could do that," Ginny said, her hope restored.

"One more reason to celebrate," Angelica said. "This calls for champagne."

"We don't have any," Tricia said, feeling like a party pooper.

"Yes, we do," said Mr. Everett. And he brought out a chrome champagne bucket on a stand from behind the sales counter.

"If you'll look under that tray on the shelf over there, Ginny, I think you'll find the crystal flutes. Isn't it amazing what you can rent in a wonderful little village like Stoneham?" Angelica said and beamed.

For a small-town grocer turned bibliophile, Mr. Everett would have made a pretty fair sommelier. He popped the cork with style, and Ginny captured the geyser of sparking wine in a couple of glasses, passing them to Angelica and Bob, and then to the rest of the gathering, including herself and Mr. Everett.

"Who'll make the toast?" Roger asked.

Tricia stepped forward, feeling anything but cheerful. "I suppose it had better be me." She turned her gaze to her sister, exhaled a long breath, forced a smile, and raised her glass. "To Angelica, and her new venture."

"Here, here," chorused the rest of them and sipped.

"I should like to make a toast as well," Angelica said. "To Tricia, who makes all things possible."

Tricia waved an impatient hand. "Like what?"

"Like what? You've given Ginny and Mr. Everett here jobs—that's good for the local economy. Through your efforts Grace has been freed from her imprisonment at that assisted living center, and your shop brings happiness to all those tourists with nothing to read."

Tricia shrugged. "I guess."

"And because of you I've got a new life. New friends." She eyed the gathering and gave Bob a modest smile. "A new job, and will soon have a new home." Angelica raised her glass, tipping it in her sister's direction.

Tricia raised her glass as well and managed a smile. "Not bad for the village jinx, huh?"

ANGELICA'S RECIPES

Spaghetti Sauce

1–2 tablespoons olive oil
1 large onion, chopped
3 cloves garlic, chopped (I often toss in a lot more)
1 pound country spareribs
1 pound Italian sausage links (I use hot)
1 can crushed tomatoes (28-ounce size)
2 cans tomato puree (28-ounce size)
1 can tomato paste (6-ounce size)
3 bay leaves
1 teaspoon salt
1½ teaspoons sugar

In a large pot, heat oil, brown onion and garlic, sear ribs, and brown sausage.

Empty contents of all the cans (tomatoes, puree, and paste). Add bay leaves, salt, and sugar.

Simmer 3 to 4 hours, longer if you like a thicker sauce. Stir occasionally.

Serve over your favorite pasta with grated Parmesan or Romano cheese, and with crusty bread.

Lobster Bisque

> 1 lobster (1½ pounds)
> 2 stalks celery
> 1 cup butter (½ pound)
> 2 shallots, minced
> 1 small onion, chopped
> 2 cups half-and-half (or whole milk)
> 1 teaspoon paprika
> salt, white pepper
> ½ cup sherry
> 1 cube chicken bouillon
> 1 cup flour

Place lobster and celery in a heavy saucepan and cover with cold water. Bring to a boil; boil for 10 to 15 minutes or until lobster is red and cooked.

Remove lobster, set aside to cool. Strain broth and set aside.

In a large saucepan, melt butter. Sauté shallots and onion until soft and translucent. Add half-and-half plus some of the lobster broth (reserving 3 cups for later). Heat thoroughly, then add seasoning, sherry, and bouillon cube. In a bowl, mix together the flour and 3 cups of lobster broth. Add flour mixture to the saucepan. Heat until thickened.

Remove meat from lobster and add to the bisque. Allow the bisque to simmer (do not boil) for 15 minutes, stirring occasionally.

STROMBOLI

Angelica is a stickler for making things from scratch. Unfortunately, not all of us have the time. Therefore, this recipe uses a shortcut of two loaves of frozen bread dough. But if you'd like to follow in Angelica's footsteps, by all means use your favorite from-scratch bread recipe. Feel free to play with the ingredients and add others to this wonderful bread that makes a meal when accompanied by most soups.

> 2 loaves (1 pound each) frozen bread dough, thawed
> 1/2 pound sliced ham
> 1/4 pound sliced pepperoni
> 1/4 small onion, chopped
> 1/4 cup chopped green pepper
> 1 jar (14 ounces) pizza sauce, divided
> 1/4 pound sliced hard salami
> 1/4 pound sliced mozzarella cheese
> 1/4 pound sliced Swiss cheese
> 1 teaspoon dried basil
> 1 teaspoon dried oregano
> 1/4 teaspoon garlic powder
> 1/4 teaspoon pepper
> 2 tablespoons butter, melted

Let dough rise in a warm place until doubled. Punch down. Roll loaves together into one 15-inch-by-12-inch rectangle.

Layer ham and pepperoni on half of the dough (lengthwise). Sprinkle with the onion and green pepper. Top with ¼ cup of pizza sauce. Layer the salami, mozzarella, and Swiss cheese over sauce. Sprinkle with basil, oregano, garlic powder, and pepper. Spread another ¼ cup of the pizza sauce on top.

Fold plain half of the dough over the filling and seal the edges well. Place on a foil-lined, lightly greased baking pan.

Bake at 375 degrees for 30 to 35 minutes. Brush with melted butter. Heat the remaining pizza sauce and serve with the sliced Stromboli. Serves 4 to 6.

CRAB PUFFS

> 1 cup crabmeat (canned will also work)
> ½ cup shredded sharp cheddar cheese
> 2 tablespoons chopped chives
> 1 teaspoon Worcestershire sauce
> 1 teaspoon lemon juice
> 1 teaspoon dry mustard
> 1 tablespoon dill weed
> ½ cup (1 stick) butter
> 1 cup beer (can also substitute chicken broth or clam juice)
> ½ teaspoon salt
> ½ teaspoon lemon pepper
> 1 cup all-purpose flour
> 4 large eggs

Preheat oven to 400°F. Line baking sheets with parchment paper or aluminum foil.

In a bowl, combine crabmeat, cheese, chives, Worcestershire sauce, lemon juice, mustard, and dill weed. Set aside.

In a large saucepan, melt butter, add beer, salt, and lemon pepper. Bring to a boil. Add flour, remove from heat, and stir briskly with a wooden spoon. Return to heat. Continue to beat until a dough ball forms. Remove from heat.

Add eggs to dough, one at a time, beating vigorously after each addition until well combined.

Fold crab mixture into dough.

Drop by spoonfuls onto baking sheet.

Bake crab puffs 25 to 30 minutes until crispy and golden brown. Best served warm.

Makes 35 to 40 crab puffs.

BEAST STROGANOFF

3 cups sour cream
1½ tablespoons prepared Dijon-style mustard
3 tablespoons tomato paste—sun-dried in a tube
  gives the strongest flavor
3 tablespoons Worcestershire sauce
2 teaspoons sweet paprika
¾ teaspoon salt
black pepper, freshly ground, to taste
1 pound medium-sized mushrooms
10 tablespoons butter (1¼ sticks)
2 medium onions, sliced thin

> 3 pounds beef, veal, or venison, sliced thin on the
> diagonal (you can used leftover meat if you have
> it)

In a medium-sized saucepan, combine the sour cream, mustard, tomato paste, Worcestershire sauce, paprika, salt, and pepper and simmer slowly for 20 minutes, then remove from heat, cover, and keep aside while you cook the rest of the ingredients.

After washing mushrooms, slice thin and sauté in 3 tablespoons of butter until tender. Put in a separate container.

Cook the sliced onions in 2 tablespoons of butter until they are transparent and lightly browned, about 10 minutes. Put them in a bowl with the mushrooms.

Cook the meat over high heat in the remaining butter (if using leftover meat, just until warm; if raw meat, 3 or 4 minutes until lightly browned).

Put sauce over medium heat, bring to a simmer, and add the mushrooms and onions; let simmer for another 5 minutes.

Add meat and simmer until meat is heated through, about 2 minutes.

Serve over wide noodles and enjoy!

Angelica's Irish Soda Bread

> 4 cups all-purpose flour
> ¼ cup sugar
> 1 teaspoon baking soda

2 teaspoons baking powder
1 teaspoon salt
2 large eggs
1½ cups buttermilk
¼ cup corn or canola oil
2 teaspoons caraway seeds
1 cup golden raisins
1 tablespoon milk

Preheat oven to 350 degrees. Foil-line a baking sheet, lightly grease.

In a large bowl, stir the flour, sugar, baking soda, baking powder, and salt together. In a separate bowl, beat the eggs, buttermilk, and oil together. Make a well in the center of the flour mixture and pour in the buttermilk mixture. Add the caraway seeds and raisins. Stir until a soft dough forms.

With floured hands, shape the dough into a large ball on a lightly floured board or waxed paper. With a sharp knife, make an X across the top of the dough. Place the dough on the prepared baking sheet. Brush the top with milk. Bake in the center of the oven until golden brown (30 to 40 minutes).

Serve warm with butter.

IRISH LAMB STEW

3 pounds stewing lamb
6 large all-purpose potatoes
4 yellow onions
2 tablespoons finely chopped parsley
1 teaspoon thyme

1 teaspoon salt
Freshly ground black pepper
1½ cups chicken broth
1½ tablespoons butter, softened
1 tablespoon flour

Preheat oven to 350 degrees.

Cut the lamb into slices or cubes. Peel the potatoes and onions and cut them into thin slices or chunks.

Mix the parsley and thyme together. Butter a casserole.

Arrange a layer of ⅓ of the potatoes on the bottom of the casserole. Cover with a layer of lamb, then a layer of onions. Season with the herbs, salt, and pepper. Repeat to form 3 layers, seasoning between each layer and ending with the onions. Add the broth (add enough broth so that the contents of the casserole are nearly covered but not submerged).

Cover the casserole and cook in a 350-degree oven for 1½ hours until the lamb is tender.

Combine the butter and flour in a small bowl and add the paste to the casserole (distributing it evenly). Continue cooking 5 minutes until the juices are thickened.

Makes 6 servings.

STUFFED MUSHROOMS

24 large mushrooms
2 tablespoons butter

1 large onion, finely chopped
4 ounces pepperoni, finely chopped
1/2 cup green pepper, finely chopped
2 small cloves garlic, minced
1 cup firmly crushed cracker crumbs
6 tablespoons Parmesan cheese
2 tablespoons minced parsley
2/3 cup chicken broth

Wash and dry mushrooms. Remove stems, chop finely.

Melt butter in skillet; add onion, pepperoni, green pepper, garlic, and chopped mushroom stems. Cook until tender.

Add crumbs, cheese, and parsley. Mix well. Stir in chicken broth.

Spoon stuffing into mushroom caps.

Bake uncovered at 325 degrees for 25 minutes.

Serve hot.

ALSO FROM NATIONAL BESTSELLING AUTHOR

Lorna Barrett

Bookmarked for Death

To celebrate her bookstore's anniversary, Tricia Miles hosts a book signing for bestselling author Zoë Carter. But the event takes a terrible turn when the author is found dead in the washroom. Before long, both police and reporters are demanding the real story. So far, the author's assistant/niece is the only suspect. And with a sheriff who provides more obstacles than answers, Tricia will have to take matters into her own hands—and read between the lines to solve this mystery...

penguin.com